SEAL
THE DEAL

Holly,
Love my SEALs!
Sharon Hamilton

SHARON HAMILTON

AUTHOR'S NOTE

I always dedicate my SEAL Brotherhood books to the brave men and women who defend our shores and keep us safe. Without their sacrifice, and that of their families—because a warrior's fight always includes his or her family—I wouldn't have the freedom and opportunity to make a living writing these stories. They sometimes pay the ultimate price so we can debate, argue, go have coffee with friends, raise our children and see them have children of their own.

One of my favorite homages to warriors resides on many memorials, including one I saw honoring the fallen of WWII on an island in the Pacific:

"When you go home Tell them of us,
and say For your tomorrow,
We gave our today."

These are my stories created out of my own imagination. Anything that is inaccurately portrayed is either my mistake, or done intentionally to disguise something I might have overheard over a beer or in the corner of one of the hangouts along the Coronado Strand.

Wounded Warriors is the one charity I give to on a regular basis. I encourage you to get involved and tell them thank you:

https://support.woundedwarriorproject.org

CHAPTER 1

Special Operator Nicholas Dunn shed his shoes and shirt and dove into the waters of San Diego Bay to scrub the left over grit and sand of Afghanistan from his body. It was his first day back ritual. He didn't stop until he'd skinned his knee and taken a serious hit on the chin bodysurfing. The shedding of blood hammered the reality of being home straight to his brain. He'd seen way too much blood this last tour. Friends died. Innocents died too. He couldn't save them all.

And now his sister was dying at home. Not a damned thing he could do about that, either.

He'd stashed his bags at the apartment he shared with Marc "Marky Mark" Beale. Marc had been his best friend ever since they met almost six years ago at the Great Lakes Training Camp, long before they were invited to try out for the Teams. In those days, they were more afraid of marching out of step or getting written up for not having something properly polished, buffed, folded or pressed.

While Nick was swimming, Marc was out scouting for Day One dates. Day One was an automatic Frog Hogs night. Had been their tradition even when they came back from training exercises. Just like having brews at the Scupper and watching the coeds parade by hoping to snag a little Frog interest.

Although he'd agreed, Nick wasn't really sure he was up to it tonight. He looked at his cell phone. No call yet.

Girls on the beach watched him as he dried off, slipped his cargo shorts back over his wet trunks, kicked into his flip-flops and headed for his bright yellow Hummer. The attention was always welcome, and on any other day he'd have reveled in it.

He was interested, all right. Nothing wrong in that department. But the fact was, his sister—his beautiful, outgoing big sister, who loved him like the mother they'd lost to cancer when he was still in high school—his sister was dying. And there was no easy way to deal with it. Death claimed innocents as well as warriors. And all that Sophie would leave behind, thanks to her entrepreneurial streak of independence, was a failing nursery. No grieving husband. No kids. Not even parents to grieve over her. Only Nick.

He knew it would come one of these days soon. *That* call.

He'd worried about her all during his last difficult deployment in the Middle East. Every night he said a prayer for her. He Skyped calls to her as often as he could, and watched the grey rings under her eyes grow as her hoarseness increased.

He'd worried about it today as he boarded the plane to San Diego from Virginia. So he should have been prepared for the call that came as he drove along the Strand. Knew it would come. Hoped it might come a few days or weeks from now, so this one could be a casual, "Hi, welcome home." But it came today, the first day he was back, and that was bad. Very bad.

"Hey, Sis. How's it going?"

"Not well, Baby Brother. I'm in a lot of pain all the time now."

"You want me to come up?"

"Not right away. Enjoy your homecoming. You deserve it, Nick. Come up when you can. I need to make some final decisions and I would appreciate your help. I'm going to close the nursery down."

Nick was actually glad to hear it.

"But I can't do everything I used to, so need to work on it while I still can."

Nick was *not* glad to hear that.

"I'll be up tomorrow, Sophie. Hang in there. Captain America will save the day."

"Normally, I'd give you hell for that kind of sexist comment, but today I'm just grateful for the help."

Sophie was still pretending to be tough. If she said come in a few days, it meant there weren't more than a few days left. "You can nail me as much as you want on my attitude, Soph—my word choices, and my friends. But I'm coming to help you out, and there's nothing you can do to stop me."

"There's the Nick that charms the pants off all the ladies. By the way, you'll be working with a good friend of mine. Actually, you met her before. Devon. Remember her?"

Nick was scratching his head. He vaguely remembered some noodle-armed high schooler with braces. Knobby knees and ashamed of her tin grin. He was surprised he remembered anything about her.

"And why are we talking about this Devon person?"

"Because you're gonna need someone to spar with when I'm gone."

"Does she wrestle?"

"She'll kick your ass. Little bit of a thing, but I think she knows karate."

"Then she doesn't stand a chance."

If it made Sophie feel better, he'd play along. Last thing he wanted to do was start running around with a female who thought she was Bruce Lee-La, regardless of Sophie's wishes. "I'll be up tomorrow. Can I bring a friend so we can get more shit done for you?"

"You're bringing a girlfriend? Thought I'd never see the day, Nick."

Nick laughed. "Hardly, Soph. I'm going to ask my roommate, Marc. You mind?"

"Sounds good, no problem."

Sophie had never been one to depend on or need anyone, but Nick could tell she was looking forward to his visit and his help.

Yup, it was definitely time.

Nick cruised down the Strand in the Hummer, scaring birds, squirrels and tourists with its roar. He was looking for Marky, who'd said he would be at Duckies having an ice cream. When Nick found him, six blonde coeds with legs as long as telephone poles surrounded him. The accumulated glow from their super-white, perfectly straight teeth darkened his convertible sunglasses.

Marky jerked his chin in greeting. "And here he is, the stud of Coronado, ladies," he said to his harem, who obligingly parted like the Red Sea. Marc was wearing an aloha shirt and holding his favorite banana nut crunch ice cream cone dipped in chocolate with sprinkles. Some of the chocolate had migrated to his upper lip.

Nick tried not to make eye contact with any of the lovelies, but damn, it was hard. He was trying to confine his eyes to above the neck, regardless of the signals he was getting from the girls.

"Marky, you up for a road trip north?" he asked.

"North? As in LA, or north as in where you—"

"Sonoma County. Got to go up to Santa Rosa to help my sister."

Nick heard several "ahhs" in the background. He was scoring points he'd only be too happy to collect on any other day. Not today.

He nodded toward the street to give Marc the idea he wanted a private discussion. He didn't want to offend the ladies in case Marc had plans.

"Excuse me. I shall return," Marc said to the crowd.

The two muscled SEALs walked out into the sunlight and stood on the sidewalk facing Oceanside Drive. Marc planted his arm around Nick's shoulder.

"Sorry, man. She that bad?"

Nick inhaled to keep from allowing moisture in his eyes. "I think this is the beginning of the end." He tore his eyes away from the rows of Spanish-style bungalows across the street and peered into Marc's face. "I hate to ask you on our first day back, but would you go with me? She's going to close down the nursery, and I'm thinking she could use another set of arms."

"Gotcha. Well, I didn't make any plans I couldn't break. I'm all yours."

"Thanks, man."

"So we leaving tonight, then?" Marky squinted into the sun as he slurped dripping ice cream from around the base of the cone.

Nick laughed. "Of course."

"That's what I thought. Thank God I washed my underwear, at least."

The trip north was long, but Nick distracted himself with Pashto language tapes. Marc was rocking out to country music on his iPod.

Ten hours later, they turned down a dusty driveway flagged with the Matanzas Creek Nursery sign on the corner fence. They drove past rows of black plastic gallon containers filled with young grape vines and shrubs. Several larger containers held bushy, multicolored flowering clumps. Laid out on black plastic, the ten-acre parcel was stuffed to capacity with neat rows of living plant material. The office was a tin-roofed wooden structure near the back of the parcel. Connected by a breezeway in the rear sat his sister's three-bedroom bungalow.

Nick noticed only one car in the lot in the front parking lot. Sophie's.

"Geez, Nick, it's a Tuesday afternoon and I'd expect things to be slow, but damn, I'd think the nursery would have more than one customer here," whistled Marc.

"That's Sophie's car. I don't ever see any paying customers. I think she's too far out into the country, and she probably doesn't price her things like the big stores."

Nick looked at the greenish gold hills of Bennett Peak and Annadel State Park, where he used to run for athletic training in high school. The valley floor was painted with the beautiful colors and designs of his sister's nursery in a setting that looked pretty much like Heaven itself.

"I'd come for the view," he said to Marc.

"Yeah, but most people only show up for the deals," Marc said as the Hummer stopped. He got out to unkink his long frame, stretching back and then down to touch his toes.

Nick began to do the same. The long ride had been uneventful, even boring. The Hummer was so noisy it made conversation impossible, and so they'd both just zoned out on their electronic devices.

Sophie appeared at the doorway of the nursery office. Her jeans were loose and her sleeveless blouse gaped at the armpits. Nick was shocked to realize she had probably lost another twenty-five pounds. But, characteristic of Sophie, she wore a bright smile accentuated with bright coral lipstick.

She ran up to Nick and threw her arms around him. "Thanks for coming."

Nick squeezed her in his usual bear hug and noticed Sophie hitched a bit in obvious pain. He carefully released her and took a good look at her face, which was turning the color of sand. The only color was her lipstick, artificially bright, as if trying to convince everyone she was really okay.

Marc was shifting back and forth from one foot to the other. Nick saw him look down at his feet and clear his throat. Sophie looked up at him.

"Welllll… Hello there, sailor," she said in a low, sexy voice, extending her hand. "I'm Sophie. And you must be Marc?"

"Yes, ma'am. Marc Beale."

"Thought he could help out," Nick offered.

"Sweet. *Good of you to come*," she said in mock British accent. She abruptly turned to Nick and motioned for them to come inside.

Oldies music was playing in the corner, accompanying the numerous water fountains trickling in several sections of the shop. He smelled lemons and realized she was burning lemon candles in the sunny window frames. Under each candle was a mirror. He remembered her little superstition about keeping out evil spirits this way. Even the windows with no candles had mirrors on the ledges. Sophie was taking evil seriously these days, he noted.

"You want some coffee?" Sophie asked as she slipped behind a curtain into the galley kitchen.

"Whatever you got," Nick replied.

"Okay, then. I'll give you a steaming glass of fish oil. How's that?"

"Funny."

She handed him a mug of coffee. From the smell, it must have just been brewed.

"And you?" she looked at Marc.

"Alcohol. Anything with spirits in it."

Marc was served a long-necked microbrew as Sophie brought out reheated minestrone soup with French bread, and the trio sat at a rustic plank and beam table built on metal sawhorses.

"Afraid this is all I've got right now. Tomorrow I go shopping at the farmer's market."

"You make this?" Marc asked.

"I'm not very domestic. Haven't you told him anything about me?" she smacked Nick on the forearm with the back of her soup spoon.

"Sorry, sis."

"No, this started with a can, but added all my own veggies." She lowered her gaze and spoke to the soup. "Supposed to be good for me, and soup is one thing I can keep down after chemo."

The little office suddenly felt cold to Nick.

The three of them ate in silence. Afterward, Sophie gathered their bowls and plates, rinsing them in the sink and setting them on the drain board. "I'll clean the rest of this up later."

"No worries, Sis. We'll do it. You taking off?" Nick asked.

Sophie took off her blue bandana, revealing bald spots on her scalp. She untied the knot, flapped it like a wet towel, and tied it about her head with the bow on top above her forehead. "Time for my beauty treatments. But the good news is, this is the last doctor visit. You know, on the off chance I've had a miracle like the finger of God curing me. This is the last one until they—"

"I'll take you, Soph," Nick interrupted.

"Nope. I want you here in case I don't get back on time. I got that friend coming…you remember, Devon Brandeburg…she's coming over to help me put a price on this place. I want you here when she comes."

"Then I'll drive you," Marc said as he stepped toward her and extended his palm. "Come on, lady, hand over your keys," he said, mimicking a gangster.

Just as Nick expected, Sophie responded with a soft smile, and, if he wasn't totally bonkers, perhaps even a little blush.

Good for you, Sophie. He was also proud of his randy roommate for stepping up and doing the right thing.

After the two of them left, Nick had a chance to look around the place.

Though Sophie's house was behind the little shed office, it looked like she did most of her living, and bleeding, here. With a kitchen sink, a hot plate and microwave, along with a back storage room that had a cot with blankets folded on it, he'd bet that some afternoons, when she had no customers, she'd just slept here.

The space was decorated in eclectic, neo-nursery chic. Recycled timbers made up the underpinnings of an L-shaped countertop covered in hammered aluminum. Various wind chimes and bird houses hung on long fishing lines and tinkled in the breeze.

He imagined the place would be cold in winter, but noted a small potbellied stove in the corner with a neat pile of recycled magazines and shredded cardboard boxes, covered with a few pieces of kindling and several round logs.

The oldies continued playing in the main shop, making the picture cozy and complete.

But depressing. Like some of those places overseas. The battle zones.

Looking through the doorway at the nursery beyond, seeing that its dilapidated wooden crisscrossed slats were occasionally missing a piece, and parts of the dark green fabric protecting the plants drooped down in ripped sections here and there, he knew his sister had worked hard to keep this concern going.

And it had killed her. Unlike his team buddies, Nick couldn't save her from herself, rescue her from a life cut short, just like he hadn't been able to save his mom. Maybe it wasn't safe for him to get close to a woman, since all of the most important ones in his life left him. Permanently.

Sophie was one of those women, just like his mother, who refused to go to see the doctor until it was too late. Both women would not be told what to do, or how to do it. Besides being fiercely independent, they were both very strong physically. He remembered wrestling with Sophie until he was in his teens, and his mother always rooted for Sophie. The day he was able to pin Sophie was the last day. She got up and told him never to wrestle with her again.

It didn't surprise him that she hadn't settled down and had a family. She liked men, and dated a few. But mostly she said it just wasn't worth the trouble to have them around. He knew it was because she didn't want to change for anybody, or had never met anybody she wanted to change for. And love? They'd never discussed the topic.

It wasn't on either of their radars.

CHAPTER 2

Devon Brandeburg didn't see Sophie's car, but did find a God-awful yellow, totally obnoxious Hummer she'd need a stepladder to mount, parked at an angle and taking up half the parking lot. She knew right away it belonged to Sophie's full-of-himself SEAL brother, Nick. He'd driven up five years ago, right after he made it through the BUD/S program. He'd been so puffed up with hubris he pushed all the air out of the room when he entered.

The worst thing about the guy, as Devon remembered, was that he automatically thought any girl would fall down on her knees and beg him to do the nasty with her. Devon had been so bold as to ask him one time about suicides increasing in the military . She was going to do an English paper on the subject. His answer was, "Not the SEALs. Hell, why would we deprive the ladies of some fun? We're God's gift to the female population."

He'd given her that big, goofy smile, overly confident and irritating as heck. In Sonoma County she never ran across such bravado and in-your-face braggadocio.

It had turned her stomach. She'd rolled her eyes then, and when she'd looked back at him he had the nerve to wink!

But later, she'd had a hard time forgetting the sight of his hard body and muscular arms, easily twice the size of anyone else's she knew. And yes, she did dream about him that night. That really pissed her off.

All that had happened when she was twenty and completely inexperienced. Hell, she was still a virgin at twenty-five, a secret she guarded with her life. The one time she'd extended her heart to someone she thought perhaps she could love, she was hurt so badly, she never let anyone get close again. She poured herself into her work as a means to forget the whole experience.

No, sexual confidence wasn't something she'd had a chance to develop, but she'd make damned sure, if Sophie forced her to talk to him about his sister's estate, Mr. Nicholas Dunn would never learn that little factoid.

She'd become a successful realtor and made enough to support herself with a decent lifestyle. She'd mentored under Sophie originally, until Sophie gave up her career in real estate to go into the nursery business. Devon became the professional realtor, while Sophie got her hands dirty tending to a failing business. They remained best friends.

Devon parked her Lexus a safe distance away from the rock-spraying beast of a vehicle Nick was probably driving, and secretly hoped he'd not be there.

Her luck wasn't that good.

He still sucked all the air out of the room. He was standing at Sophie's little sink washing dishes. And he was singing, rocking his hips from side to side. Was that the song from *Flashdance*?

"I'm a maniac—"

She couldn't resist breaking in.

"Well, look at you...so domestic." She crossed her arms, tilted her head and enjoyed surprising the heck out of this normally self-composed brute. He to slammed the water faucet shut with his fist and dried his hands. Then he slowly perused the length of her body, leaving no part unexplored. His emerald green eyes were blazing.

Still the same cocky son of a bitch. Devon knew he didn't care if he got caught ogling her, so confident was he that a rejection wasn't anywhere in his future. He was all the kinds of maleness she'd been running from.

He leaned his butt against the tiled countertop. Then he threw down the towel and mirrored Devon's stance with crossed arms. "Been awhile, Dev."

"Devon."

"Right. Still don't like me, do you?"

"You're a good judge of character," she answered. "I'll give you that."

"You're just as scrappy as Sophie told me you'd be." He smiled as if his approval mattered to her.

"I'll just leave you to your work, then."

"Oh, the dishes are done. I was going to sweep the floor and then wash all the windows. But you go ahead and do all that computer stuff you realtors do. Way beyond me."

Devon found that comment funny, despite an internal backdrop of curiosity and fear. Attempting to focus on her work, she sat down at the plank tabletop, stacked the listing folders to the side and opened up her computer. She crossed her legs and ran her fingers through the hair at the back of her scalp, took a deep breath and logged on to the Internet to begin a property search. But Nick's presence still loomed large enough to make her catch her breath.

The soft sweeping sound of Sophie's broom against the cool concrete floor began to distract her. Didn't help much that she could see Nick wrestling the handle with nearly enough force to break it. His forearms were as big as her thighs, for goodness' sake. His shoulders moved with sinewy grace underneath smooth tanned skin. His mop of blond hair went in all directions. He tickled her ankles as he reached the broom under the table and swept the area around her.

"Does that bother you?" he asked. He'd stopped, leaning his chin on the end of the broomstick.

"As in, were you trying to?" *Why were men so obvious?*

"Nope. It was an honest question." The sparkle in his eyes made him out to be a liar. His animal magnetism was bringing up those butterflies again. She needed to get back to the cold hard facts, and the numbers. Things she was asked to do for poor Sophie. This was all about Sophie, after all.

"You want some coffee, Devon?" he asked.

He wasn't going to leave her alone, was he? "Wow. You clean the dishes, sweep the floor, *and* you make coffee? The Navy must have trained you well. What did they do, get some of the senior wives to come in and give you pointers?" She wondered where that comment came from.

"I don't need any pointers."

In spite of herself, she blushed. *Damn.* That sticky feeling of not being in control and him standing there, looking all confident and smug sent her pulse racing. She attempted to get back to her computer when…

Just then he fired up the coffee grinder, making her jump in her seat. She began to smell the glorious scent of freshly brewing coffee and her mouth watered.

When she looked up, he had his back to her. A variety of Celtic crosses and symbols poked up above the collar of his T-shirt. She could see discoloration from beneath the white cotton fabric, hinting at tats on his shoulders and lower, in places she forced her eyes not to search. One long stream of tats like footprints of a three-legged toad was inked on his right inside forearm.

It was impossible to ignore the enormous V of his upper torso leading to the small waist, his deltoids and lats so tight they looked like they'd hurt. She began to wonder what they would feel like—

He caught her staring when he stole a quick glance over his shoulder before crossing the room with two mugs of the hot black coffee. Placing one next to her computer, he took a seat right across from her like she was his entertainment.

"I dare you to say there's a better cup of coffee anywhere." His deep green eyes were almost iridescent. His smooth tanned face and full lips did cause her to blush. She quickly grabbed the mug, sipping the steamy liquid. She was going to try to ignore him by finding something of interest on the screen.

But then Nick slurped his coffee. She could feel his eyes still focused on her.

Devon didn't care how long he stared. She wasn't going to return the gaze. Didn't the guy have any shame? Or, was this little cat and mouse game a way to process the pain he must be feeling over Sophie's illness. Either way, it was making her feel like she was spinning out of control.

She frowned, consulted her yellow-lined tablet and kept tapping on the keys. Her red nail polish matched her red suit, but now she wished she'd worn black.

One of her heels fell off and plopped to the ground because her legs were crossed. She briefly looked up at him, only to see the wiggle of his eyebrows, and the unspoken offer to crawl under the table and place the patent leather pump back on her foot. That would mean he'd have to touch her calf as he adjusted the shoe. He'd hold her ankle with both his dinner plate hands, and his fingers—

Feeling very much like an insect pinned in a collection box, she inhaled loudly, stuffed her foot into her errant shoe, and picked up the pace of her typing.

He continued to watch her, occasionally piercing the quiet with his sips.

The room was beginning to heat up. The late fall weather pattern was growing hot, which meant some long, sweaty nights with crickets chirping madly, since Sophie's house didn't have air conditioning. Neither did the nursery. She sighed, blowing air up to her bangs.

"You should have worn something sleeveless."

"A fashionista as well?" She was wondering when he'd take the hint and stop trying to distract her.

"I just notice you're looking rather hot today, Devon."

No way was she going to look at him. He had her really bothered now. But then she did look up, and *damn,* he was fine. She fell into the crease at the right side of his mouth, the huskiness in his voice that made her ears buzz. She had to get him to stop.

"So you sit there and make an obnoxious ass of yourself while you watch me work? You think that's some kind of fun?" Did he hear the waver in her voice?

"I enjoy watching beautiful women."

It was getting hotter in the room. "Really? Women who don't know you? Women who don't care in the slightest anything about you? Sounds like a rather pathetic way to spend a few minutes."

"Not from over here." She could tell he was enjoying laying it on thick, and she was powerless to stop him. She had to act now or she'd be completely lost.

Devon shot up to her feet. "Enough! Nick. Go outside. Make yourself useful. I'm sure there are some weeds to pull or some walkways to rake."

He shrugged. "Suit yourself." He took his mug and swaggered outside into the afternoon sunlight. She found herself still gasping for air at the sight of him making his way lazily across the parking lot.

Devon's heart rate was thumping wildly. A bead of sweat trickled down between her breasts.

Whatever it was she'd dreamed about five years ago was still there. Lurking. Waiting to pounce.

CHAPTER 3

Nick drank his coffee and looked out over the tattered nursery. Dark green cloth covered the nursery's frame, letting only bits of light through. Nick found it depressing. He couldn't honestly understand what Sophie saw in it, except for the location—those beautiful hills beyond. He'd loved hiking Bennett Peak. Those had been happy days.

He continued to look for something that would explain why Sophie loved it so much. The state of disrepair would certainly telegraph to anyone that the nursery was a failing enterprise. He thought it was odd that now she was finally going to sell it, now that she was dying.

Sis, you should have done it sooner. You could have had a life.

But he knew that line of thinking was off-purpose. It wouldn't help him navigate the shoals of his own feelings, where the deaths of their parents still lay lurking in the deep. Sophie had been his lifeline whenever he felt morose or defeated in spirit. No matter where he went, his sister had always been the one he came home to, and now he would be completely alone.

Better buck up and get used to it. You can't afford distractions. Distractions get you killed. Make you do stupid things.

He walked under the shade, brushing the tops of green and red lettuce starts with the tips of his fingers. He looked at chrysanthemums getting ready to burst forth in fall colors of burgundy, gold and yellow. Fruit trees were beginning to lose their leaves. Rose leaves were yellowed and the roses sparse, crumbling beneath his fingers as he touched them.

He turned to face the opened doorway of the nursery office, and could barely make out Devon's red suit glowing from the shadows inside. Something about her brought out the worst in him. He had to admit, he'd been a complete dick. Yes, she had caught him in a lighter moment, washing dishes, and singing no less, trying to get his mind off his sister's all too imminent demise and the black hole of her future, but damn, Dev had to go rub his nose in it.

The pea gravel walkways crunched under his weight. Several plant flats were dried and wilted already, and Nick concluded Sophie had not done her morning watering. He found the overhead sprayer, turned on the water, and gave a good soak to the lettuces and the cole crops of broccoli, cauliflower and cabbage first, then went down the rows of other vegetables, annual flowers and some groundcover flats. The air was warming up, so he removed his shirt and worked in his cargo pants.

Next he watered the roses and several fruit trees that looked nearly dead.

He found the musty smell of the wet soil oddly pleasant. After spending months in sandy places overseas, wishing for a swimming pool or long, hot, private bath, he enjoyed the sight and smell of the green vegetation before him, covered in droplets of life-giving water.

He turned around and found Devon leaning against the doorjamb of the office, arms crossed, eyeing him. He returned to his watering and let her look. He wasn't embarrassed this time. He told himself to ignore her completely and not try to read anything into the little gesture.

Women are dangerous.

Devon watched the manly specimen before her. Not only had he sucked the air out of a room, he could do it to a whole valley. His huge tanned shoulders and muscled arms hoisted the hose and showered water over everything. He took his time. He was meticulous, filling every dry spot with moisture. She could only imagine what kind of exquisite care a man like that could give a woman, if he were of the mind to. If she'd let him.

Of course, that was completely ridiculous thought, but not entirely unpleasant. Didn't mean she trusted him, but she had to admire the view.

He clearly wasn't the man she'd expected, washing dishes and brewing coffee. And now he was tending the dying garden of her best friend. She wished she could have helped her friend in the same way. But those days were gone and those words of regret and apology had been spoken, and now it was the end of things. End of their relationship. Now Devon realized that, with Sophie gone, she'd have no one.

He'd been smiling when he turned around and caught her watching him. He'd told her he liked watching her, too, but of course she'd rejected him, and the idea. But now, just the way he turned back to his work, the light dancing through the fine water mist in the greenhouse, watching this hunk of a guy tend to his sister's heart project, the thought he might like to watch her seemed just fine.

Sighing, she removed her jacket, unbuttoning each button slowly as she watched him. He was extra attentive to the flora. Devon guessed he didn't really care if she watched him or not. Or, maybe he just hadn't noticed she was still doing it.

She laid the red jacket over a wire table. Her white shell underneath was damp from the heat. She blew down her front, holding the thin material between her thumb and forefinger, fluttering it, sending little waves of cool air to her face, and then walked outside in his direction.

Devon felt like she was a moth to the flame. He was the first man she'd ever met who literally pulled her in his direction. The hissing of the silver droplets of water mesmerized her. Watching the cords of muscles flex and extend under his smooth flesh made the tats seem like cartoon characters that had come to life. It also made her want to touch him.

She was within four feet of him when he turned quickly, hose in hand, and sprayed her. She jumped, shrieking, and saw that now her shell clung, revealing the white lace bra underneath. Then she saw her favorite pair of red patent leather shoes covered in droplets of water. She was headed straight for anger, thinking he'd surely done the maneuver on purpose. But he stopped her.

He'd released the hose, but it was still spraying everywhere, including hitting her with a second wave.

"I'm so sorry. I didn't know you were there." He was searching for a towel or something to dry her off and found a dirty rag. She got her heels unstuck from the muddy gravel ground and backed up with her hands out in front of her.

"No! Stay away. I'm fine."

Like hell she was! Her favorite shoes were ruined, her hair and chest soaking wet. She must have looked like a drowned rat. He'd humiliated her. And now he was going to try to make some lame excuse it was an accident?

Mister Masterful. Bull *shit.*

She didn't trust his pained expression. This overly-confident-testosterone-stuffed-performance-enhanced-self-proclaimed superhero was mean to women. That was a fact. He didn't play fair. And here she'd been about to apologize to him for being such a cold bitch. She would never utter an *I'm sorry* in his presence.

Ever.

She nearly made it across the driveway to the office when Sophie arrived in her Subaru station wagon. But she wasn't driving. Some guy with arms almost as big as Nick's was at the wheel. Sophie slowly got out of the car on the passenger side, and leaned against it. She was out of breath and very pale. Devon was shocked to see the change in her friend since she'd seen her only a week ago.

But then Sophie smiled that little wicked smile she used to do when she was well. The smile that told Devon they were about to have an adventure, or get into trouble, or do something they'd laugh about for years.

"I see you've started to play with my brother. Don't try to take him down. He's bigger."

Nick was having trouble turning off the water in the nursery. The faucet shut-off had dropped to the ground. Water spewed everywhere. He swore, grabbing repeatedly, but the hose seemed to have a mind of its own, walking like a cobra, drenching him and everything around him. He finally found a wrench and shut off the valve, hanging the limp hose on the overhead spray rig. He emerged soaking wet, shaking his head.

The other guy was having a hard time containing himself. Finally he began to howl, doubling over.

"You shut the fuck up," Nick said with a scowl.

The other guy was really enjoying this. "Leave you alone with a woman, and what do you do? Make a damned fool of yourself."

Nick glared at him.

"Never thought I'd see the day when a hose would get the better of you."

Devon's anger subsided a bit as she saw her attacker was bearing the brunt of so much laughter. She could almost enjoy watching it, seeing how embarrassed he was. Some small revenge.

Devon carefully helped Sophie into the house without getting her too wet, while the two men stood outside. She could hear Nick trying to explain himself. Every other word was damn, fuck or freaking.

"So you two are alone for an hour, and you immediately get into a water fight. Just like when we were kids."

"No, Sophie. It wasn't like that. He—"

"He likes you. Can't you see that?"

"What? He just sprayed me with water."

Sophie sighed and sat on a chair at the table, but her dark purple lips were involuntarily smiling. "Don't you remember grammar school? There was this one Sunday at church. My friend and I were swinging in the yard between services. These two boys we liked pelted us with plums. Stained our dresses and made us cry. We ran in to tell our teacher who laughed and said, 'Don't you know that's all boys know how to do at this age? This means they like you.'"

It was good to see Sophie laugh. It had been awhile. Devon dared a quick glance out to the parking lot where Nick was wiping away the water on his chest with a rag. She still couldn't keep her eyes off him.

Sophie had followed her gaze. "Give him a chance. He's the best thing since the Fourth of July." She put her palm to Devon's cheek. "Just a chance. Let him show you what he's really made of."

Before she could respond to her best friend, the two men entered the room.

"Ah, Devon," Sophie began, "want you to meet Nick's friend, Marc Beale. He's also one of the guys from SEAL Team 3," Sophie motioned to Marc, who stepped forward, bowed his head slightly.

"Nice to meet you, ma'am."

"Ma'am?" Devon sputtered. Nick's presence was flustering her.

Everyone backed up a step. Sophie rose to get a glass of water at the sink. Devon realized she'd perhaps been a tad loud. But her mouth was running like a wild horse and she was powerless to stop it.

"That's what they used to call my mom," she ranted. Devon knew she was doing the crash and burn, but she didn't care. "Do I look that old?" It came out of Devon's mouth before she had a chance to swallow it. But instead of being offended, they laughed.

"She's a hellcat, Nick. No wonder you soaked her. I'd have done worse," Marc said as he winked at her.

"I didn't—"

"Enough with all this child's play," Sophie interjected. "You guys are totally juvenile. Quit it." She took several sips of water and swallowed painfully.

What could anyone say to her?

Sophie set her glass down on the drain board and returned to the table. "Although this has given me some fun this afternoon. Something to break up the doom and gloom, but now it's time for a dose of reality." Sophie strained on every word. "Get yourselves something to drink and then we need to have a talk."

Devon watched as Nick's hands immediately clenched and his jaw tightened.

Marc spoke up. "You need anything at the store? I can run errands for you, since I'm not really part of this little meeting."

Devon found his cheerful demeanor irritating.

"Sis, why don't you just put up the closed sign and we'll walk back to the house, if you're up to it." Nick offered.

"No, I like Marc's plan. I haven't died yet, and I sure as hell am still open for business. I need some tequila, and I'm afraid I have no beer. You want to pick up something like a pizza, too?" She glanced over at Devon. "But you better bring a salad for Devon, here."

Nick helped his sister sit down. "Sophie, you're not supposed to drink with the chemo."

"Well, that's what I need to talk to you two about." With a great deal of pain, she tried to find a more comfortable position, then laced her fingers together, resting her elbows on the plank table.

"Sophie, let me go get some things. You don't have to pay for any of this," Devon said.

"Hell, I was hoping my brother would take care of the tab."

"You got it, Soph," Nick answered.

"And unless Marc knows about property values in Sonoma County, I think you better stay here and tell me what I can get for the place. If you're ready, that is."

Devon hadn't been thinking. Of course, this was the reason for the little meeting today. How stupid she must seem. "Yes. Completely. Ready." She turned to Nick, fishing through her purse. "I'd like to cover this," she began.

He stopped her hand. The feel of his touch didn't make her jump. His eyes were soft and his voice sent a chill down her spine. "That was really nice, Devon, but Marc and I will cover this. Maybe another time—"

"I'm off," said Marc. "Your keys to the beast, Nick?" Marc was nervously shifting from foot to foot again.

"There's a shopping center down Bennett Valley Road about four miles. There's a pizza parlor there, as well as Chinese and Mexican, and a grocery store. Go knock yourself out." Nick gave him a couple of twenties.

Marc whispered something Devon couldn't hear and then left.

Devon sat across the table from Sophie with Nick seated at her right. She swallowed hard as she watched the difficulty Sophie had with doing ordinary things like sitting, drinking water, even talking. She reached over and grabbed Sophie's hand and let her begin.

"The doctor told me today my lymphoma is advancing at a rapid pace. My chemo was ended a month ago. I guess he was hoping the markers would go down, as they sometimes do. I'm not one of the lucky ones. The cancer is too aggressive."

Nick leaned in and grabbed Sophie's hands in his big paw, catching hers as well. Devon could tell he wanted to say something, but couldn't. His fingers gave reassuring squeeze.

"I'm going to list the property for sale with you, Devon. Ideally, it would sell before I pass on. That way I can sell it to someone I like, someone who will continue my work here, not that asshole next door. But if not, I'd like you to handle it when I'm up in that big nursery in the sky, and distribute the profits, if there are any."

"Come on, Sophie. Don't do that. There's plenty of time. The market has gotten very strong lately."

"I'm not sure," Sophie said. "I'm just making plans now for every eventuality."

"Well that's nonsense, but it's your call. We can do some advance care planning. Just let me know who you want as beneficiaries, and I'll get instructions to escrow drawn up by the title company I use. You do have a will, right?"

"Yes."

"Good, I'll need to show a copy of it to title so your wishes can be carried out to the letter. All we have to do now is determine the value and get it on the market."

"Good. But before we begin, I want both of you to understand three requirements I have. I've given it a lot of thought."

Nick looked away out the window, withdrawing his hand. Devon saw his massive chest rising and falling, heard the hitch in his breath and knew he was struggling with his emotions.

"I'm not sure there is any equity in this property. But if there is, I want to leave it to *both* of you."

Devon looked at Nick, who looked just as confused.

"Sophie, you should leave it to family. Nick's your only living relative. I'm just your friend, and I'll handle the sale for you. But you don't have to leave me anything. That wouldn't be right."

"I disagree. You've been there for me all throughout my illness. Even before I became ill. I want to say thank you."

"But it isn't necessary," Devon began.

"It is to *me*. I want you and Nick to work on this together. I want you both to find the right buyer for this property. That's the second part."

It began to dawn on Devon that Sophie had a plan beyond money. She placed her hands back in her lap and braced herself. She admired how Sophie was willing to face things head-on, just like she'd lived most of her life.

"And the last part is most important of all."

Devon began to get a bad feeling in her stomach. She couldn't look Nick in the eyes, even though she could tell his face was turned her way, as if wanting to draw strength from her. The pain she was feeling was intense enough. If she saw it in his eye, her grief might spill over. She wanted to stay clear-headed to do her job, even though this was her best friend, discussing her final wishes.

"I want you two to date at least five times before I pass on. That's all I ask. A real date. A dinner, picnic, whatever you want, but not just coffee. You don't have to get engaged, married, or even fall in love. But I want you two to give each other some time."

Devon began to rise. "Sophie, how is this appropriate? I don't see why you should require that I—"

"Stop it, Devon. Don't take me for a fool. I know you perhaps better than anyone else around. If you want to sell my nursery, you'll accommodate me. And it's okay if you say no."

"But—"

"It's a deal-breaker for me, Devon. You either agree or I find someone else. If you're going to abandon our friendship over this, then you weren't the friend I thought you were."

Nick rose as well so that they both looked down on his sister. "Sophie, that's nuts. Like you're reaching from the grave to make demands."

"That's exactly what it is, Nick. You honestly going to stand there and deny me my deathbed request?"

Nick stared at the floor. Devon could see him struggle to breathe evenly. They stood close to one another, so close she could feel his body heat.

Sophie never lied. Her eyes were dead serious and unflinching, darting between the two of them. Devon dared to glance up at the man standing to her right and damn, her panties got wet.

That was a very bad sign.

CHAPTER 4

Of all the fucked up things to have to deal with. On top of his sister dying, now he was forced to "agree to Sophie's wishes" by dating the cold, uptight woman who stood beside him. Devon had made it obvious she wasn't interested in him. She didn't seem to be interested in men at all. Probably why she had that horrible reaction to Sophie's request.

He'd never been forced to date anyone in his life. He'd never had a woman NOT want to go out with him, either. Of course, until today, he'd not played "Thunder Down Under" while he sang and washed dishes, and then sprayed a woman with water. He'd never battled a freaking devil of a hose before. This was not something he wanted to get used to.

And to make matters worse, his pecker was as hard as granite and was about to pull him over and flat onto his face. He sat, attempting to get composed and tried to cross his legs, but couldn't. He sighed and drummed his fingers on the table until his sister gave him that stern look that said *be careful*.

Devon took her seat as well. Her silence was troubling. Was she going to do everything he did first? That was a cooling thought.

It wasn't fair, being made to do something this way. He never thought of his sister as a controlling bitch before. But this was...nasty. Wicked. Completely unacceptable. Beyond evil. Like showing up for battle in the Batman boxers he'd gotten as an anonymous care package from Navy Moms.

His groin lurched, reminding him his little head disagreed with him. So be it. He'd beat the shit out of it later, but right now he'd have to stay calm and

composed. Or should he give her that wolfish grin she hated so much? If he
started being all cocky and full of himself, she'd surely hightail it out of here
and that might solve the problem.

But then his sister would have lost a friend. She wouldn't have the person
she wanted sell her property. And the whole scene would just go downhill
from there.

No, best thing was to just grin and bear it. His little head liked that idea.
Shut up, you fuckin' traitor.

This was wrong on so many levels. But if the girl was willing, he could
stand a few dinners. Lord knows he'd had lots of them that were harmless
enough. Trick was to not make them so horrible she'd quit. 'Cause that would
hurt Sophie. Or maybe…

Yeah, his other part was reminding him it had been a while since his last
female contact. And it didn't count that he and Marc had ogled every decent-
looking female in the airports all the way home from the sand country, and at
rest stops along the freeway on the drive up to Northern California.

And just a week ago he'd been helping Cooper tend to the women—and
the children—having babies at the makeshift clinic they'd set up over there.
They'd done all that in a no-name village under the protection of his other
team buddies who were keeping a watchful eye out for bad guys. Their Team
3 medic even delivered a breech baby that last day to a scared girl of fourteen.

Life wasn't fair. Half the guys he'd left behind when he finished his deployment would give anything for the chance to just talk to a beautiful woman who
looked incredible in a red business suit. And here he was complaining about
it, even if only to himself.

Time to man up.

Truth was, he was more afraid of women sometimes than the battlefield.
Maybe it was the training. Maybe it was because he knew he was made for
combat. He wasn't so sure he was made to do small talk and practice patience.
He could perform sex that would blow her mind. But this wasn't sex. This was
friendship. This was being nice.

He wasn't so sure he liked this new uniform. 'Being nice' was something
you did when you were with an elderly aunt or some retired admiral who drib-
bled on himself or accidentally peed his pants.

24

He wondered if he could trust her, this lovely lady sitting on his left, the one with the red, pouty lips and the ramrod backbone that demanded he stay away. Far, far away. But just now, for that second she looked at him, he saw her innocence and her fear. She was afraid of him, probably as much as he was afraid of her.

Damn, that wasn't a very good start. Not for anyone, but especially not for a SEAL.

Devon licked her lips. She wasn't going to say anything. Was leaving it totally up to him to dictate how it all went down. Half of him wanted to beg out, plead with his sister to be released from this obligation. It wasn't fair.

But something in Devon made his chest rise, reminded him of his pride in what he did every day. He was a man born to protect the weak and innocent, the women and children and elderly. The ones who couldn't defend themselves. Part of him wanted to rise to the occasion, take her in his arms and whisper soothing things, promising it would be okay. Letting her know he'd never hurt her. Never do anything she wouldn't want. And that was the key. What did *she* want?

As if his eyes had asked her that question, she blushed and looked down at her hands. He tilted his head, surprised at that little slip on her part. Maybe she wasn't really an ice queen after all. Maybe Sophie knew something about the two of them he had yet to discover.

"Here's the deal," Sophie began. "I'm having symptoms of kidney failure. The glow on my face that might look like a suntan is really a buildup of toxins in my system. Any day now I'll have to be admitted to the hospital for some heroic stuff that won't do anything but postpone the inevitable. Once in there, I wouldn't be coming out. But I don't want to die in any hospital. I want to die *here*, where I live. My doctor was ready to admit me today and I told him flat-out no."

That's when Nick tore his eyes away from Devon's bowed head and focused on his sister.

Devon did the same.

"Oh, Sophie." Devon reached over to grab his sister's hands with both of hers. "I had no idea you were so far along."

"Well, they were trying something new, and there was a chance it would kick in. I'm afraid I don't have enough time left to find out. The plan now is just to keep me comfortable."

"So you'll need twenty-four-hour care. With the three of us, we should be able to handle that, unless..." Nicholas began as he slid his chair closer to his sister.

"I'm going to clear the decks so I'll be available to take a shift," Devon said to Sophie. Nick could see the comment was intended for him, but Devon wasn't going to look at him. He read her blush in her cheeks and knew why. She was as confused as he was, but the attraction was there. No mistaking it.

"I have no insurance. I'm on the indigent list. Can you believe it?" Sophie said with a lopsided smile. Nick noticed her teeth had started to yellow and her gums were pale.

"There's nothing we can do, except get started wrapping up this whole experiment. I'm afraid there's no silver lining or happily ever after for my story." Sophie leaned back in her chair. "Now for you two, that's another story altogether." She attempted a smile, but began coughing.

They spent the rest of an hour going over the figures on the property. Devon made some suggestions for ways to market, including holding a big liquidation auction for all the plants and equipment. Sophie said she wanted to be there, if she could. Wanted to watch it all go to good homes.

Nick objected at first, said he wasn't so sure this was a good idea, but Sophie's dream had already taken on a life of its own and he dropped his opposition.

The listing agreement was signed and Devon gave Sophie the disclosure statements to work on. "I can pick these up tomorrow. Maybe Nick can help you fill them out tonight, if you're up to it. We like to have everything complete in the file. And if I can, I'd like some profit and loss statements."

"Nonexistent," whispered Sophie.

"Then we'll make something up. It needs to be fairly accurate."

"Not much to tell," Sophie said with a shrug.

"How did you survive all this time?" Nick asked.

"I had that auto accident last year, remember? The hit and run? Got a cash settlement and used it all up trying to get this place off the ground. I was so sure I was going to be able to do it."

Nick nodded, looking over the disclosure statements. "Geez, there's a ton of stuff to fill out."

"If you have any questions, give me a call and I'll go over them with you." Devon offered. She gave him her card with her cell phone number on it.

"I guess I'll be needing this anyway," he said, and then winced as he thought better of it. Devon wasn't a piece of meat that had been auctioned off to the highest bidder. She was flesh and blood. Delicate, even if she was spirited.

"I suppose you're planning to do it the old-fashioned way? You'll call me to ask me out, too?"

That didn't sound half bad anymore. Plain vanilla sex and a big bed had never triggered such erotic fantasies.

"One other thing, Devon, I'd love it if you'd move in here," Sophie said.

At first Devon stiffened. "Oh, Sophie. I—"

"Yes, I know I have no right, but I'm asking you anyway. I think it would make things easier for everyone. I know you have to work, but I can't show the property, and I want you to be my spokesperson as much as possible. And, truth is, I'm scared, Devon."

Nick saw Devon struggle with her reply. "I'll need a day to get ready."

"Fair enough," his sister said. "Not like I'm gonna die tomorrow."

Marc arrived with the pizza and beer and a side salad for Devon. The sun was low enough in the sky that the outside lights turned on automatically and the crickets began to chirp. Several waterfalls continued to gurgle. Something about this green patch of ground was soothing and endearing.

The pizza was good, and the beer better. Afterwards, Devon rose to leave, giving Sophie a big hug while not allowing her to leave the chair. Slipping her computer case strap over her right shoulder, she waved goodbye. Nick got up to walk her to her car.

She thanked him tersely, got out her keys and unlocked the silver Lexus. She paused before sliding into the driver's seat.

"Are you sure you're up for this?" Devon asked him. "I'm okay if you're not. Your sister is a special friend, probably the best friend I've ever had. But you don't have to do this. I'd make it right with Sophie, somehow," she said.

Nick admired the courage it must have taken to say that to him. He decided to try on the Being Nice uniform. The damned thing was too small, partly because of the telephone pole between his legs. But he gave it a go.

"Devon, my goal is to see my sister die with a smile on her face, if that's possible. I think she wants us to pretend we like each other. She wants to live through us, experience something she never had herself. I can do this for her if you can."

She thought about it and slid behind the wheel.

"All right. Then it's agreed." She held her hand out through the open window for him to shake. When he gripped her fingers, he tried not to squeeze too hard, but the feeling of her soft flesh in the palm of his hand was thrilling. He started to grip for a shake, and then thought about being the Nice Guy who would do something really out of character for Nick. No one was looking. He held her fingers to his lips and kissed her knuckles.

There was no mistaking her rapidly increasing pulse as his fingers touched the delicate skin under her wrist. The scent of her hand tickled his nose. The tender kiss he placed there had no beginning or end.

And he wished it could go on forever.

CHAPTER 5

All the way home Devon found it hard to breathe. Her throat was constricted and her mouth was dry. The hair on her arms tingled and her chest was warm. She put on and took off her jacket several times on the way home, stopping by the side of the road each time, which was ridiculous. In the end, she just left it off and cranked up the heater.

She had that feeling a great adventure was about to begin and it scared her a little, but she was still excited, felt more alive than ever. Nick was the first man she could see herself spending any time with. His touch didn't make her flinch, but gave her an electric charge she sort of liked. Maybe it was because he was her dear friend's brother. Maybe not.

She still felt the firmness of his callused fingers holding her hand so carefully. Although it was reassuring to know he could be gentle, it also scared her. And dammit, she wanted him to touch her again. Just that little touch had opened something frightening, but so delicious.

She was appalled when she saw herself in the hallway mirror at home. Her hair was matted down in places, and wildly out of control in others. Water droplets spotted the white shell. Her skirt was horribly wrinkled She didn't bother to examine the suit jacket, before she threw everything into the cleaner's bin. She stripped off her underwear and took a long hot shower.

The water was warm and the lavender shower gel sluiced down her body. With her eyes closed, she imagined what it would feel like to have his arms around her, maybe even kissing her neck. She shivered and had to look behind her to make sure he wasn't really there. The new tingling sensations on her skin were alarming, but so curiously fascinating. Not at all like the feeling of dread and debasement she'd felt at the hands of someone who didn't know the meaning of the word "no." Thank God she'd gotten away.

She had always wondered if that experience had soured her on men forever. Until she met Nick, she'd been sure she would remain alone for a long time. Her therapist had said she needed to give herself enough time to allow the vivid memory to fade into the background where it belonged. And now she'd been pulled into the warm company of this handsome warrior. Something had shifted. Maybe she could explore that skeleton in her closet more closely now.

Drying off, she decided she'd do just a bit of work, and then turn in early. It had been an exhausting day. Time was certainly of the essence, so getting a head start tonight on a few things would probably help. She put lotion on her legs and arms, clipped her hair on top of her head, applied the orange night-time moisturizer to her face, the cherry gloss to her lips, and considered her bedtime routine complete.

Normally, she'd have been excited over having a new listing. Something to crow about the next morning at the sales meeting. But no, not this time. She was so distracted, her usual focus was eluding her. She found herself staring off into a dark blue window full of evening stars, chin resting on her palm. Deliciously distracted. She'd never felt this way before.

Finally pulling her wits back together, she sat with her robe loosely gaping open, uploaded the listing information to the MLS, and sent a couple of emails to commercial agents in the area she'd worked with before.

One sent back an email right away, saying he had a buyer. He asked how she'd arrived at the value, but Devon didn't have the energy to do an email exchange, so shut down the computer and decided to get ready for bed early.

She slipped off her robe and dove under the cream-colored sheets naked. She sifted through the wet strands of her newly washed hair as she lay back watching the shadows move across her vanilla ceiling, and thought about the day. She saw his naked back as he raised an arm up, spraying plants. Baggy cargo pants hanging just below his trim waist. The large muscles of his calves as they flexed and extended while he walked around the greenhouse area. She had to admit when he turned he'd looked sexy as hell. When he'd kissed her fingers he'd looked smoldering.

She closed her eyes, but the image only increased in intensity and made her gasp for air.

Devon knew he was a trained killer, a SEAL who was probably used to women falling all over him. And she admitted that a part of her did, too. According to Sophie, he was an experienced seducer.

She had never in her life simply held a man in her arms or felt one hold her in a loving embrace. Devon knew that the biggest problem with the arrangement Sophie had insisted on was that they were a total mismatch. There was no way their friendship could go anywhere, so why put everyone through it in the first place? It could only lead to awkwardness and heartache. Maybe her only option was to renege. Tell them she wasn't ready. Would that be admitting defeat?

Do I dare tell him I'm a virgin? Or about my bad experience? Would that even help? Would he suddenly find her more attractive, a conquest waiting to be captured? Or would he find her lack of skills boring compared to the many women he probably had been with? Would Sophie tell him? Should she ask her? Devon knew nothing at all about men and how they thought.

But Devon knew one thing for sure. Quitting was not in her nature. So, after thinking everything through once more, she decided she'd see this adventure through. All she needed was to set some safe boundaries and then everything would be fine. Five little dates. Throw in a little harmless playacting for Sophie's benefit. And after her friend passed on, she'd try to focus on her career again, go back to being the woman she had been before. Confident. Self-reliant. *Definitely* not one who needed a man.

She could do it for Sophie. Her own needs could wait until the right guy appeared on her radar.

But that right guy was definitely not *Nick*.

CHAPTER 6

Sophie woke up slowly the next morning. Nick and Marc had already watered the nursery and done some cleanup, then had breakfast. She said she wasn't hungry for anything but coffee, and told them she'd be spending most of the day in bed. Nick had heard her throwing up several times during the night. He planned to ask her if he could stay in her room to help out when—if—it happened again.

She was much worse today. The helplessness of his situation upset his stomach. He worked to push it down, just like he'd learned to do in the Middle East when headed into unknown territory filled with hostiles.

The house behind the office was decorated with the same recycled junk that was in the front. But the deep earth colors and a variety of metals, woods and granite provided some warmth and made it attractive. Nick thought perhaps she'd missed her calling and should have become an interior designer.

He especially liked the airplane propeller threaded with twinkle lights that Sophie had hung from the ceiling over the only table in the place. The plank table was also made of found objects, nearly twelve feet long, and made from rough-hewn beams that had at one time been stained turquoise and red. It was big enough that there was plenty of room for one end of the table to serve as a catchall for magazines and a pile of bills.

Several of them caught his eye. Final notices. Even a threatening letter from a mortgage company. He would definitely have remembered if she'd mentioned anything about foreclosure, but it looked like she was, indeed, on the verge of losing the property as well as the business.

Things came flooding back to him from that summer before he entered high school. He'd thought it odd he couldn't remember Devon being in his class and didn't know how he could have missed such a looker, but when he checked, her yearbook picture had showed her with bookish-looking glasses and, knowing himself those days, no way would he have noticed her.

Plus other things had weighed on him, and his interest in girls waned a bit that summer. His dad had been working two jobs after having been without work for nearly six months. Nick took up weeding and cutting lawns and donated his meager earnings to the family, which at first was refused. But later on, even with his father's two jobs, his parents gratefully accepted what little he could pay. He'd sometimes gone with Sophie to buy their clothes at Goodwill, and had always checked out the store to make sure none of his friends saw him there.

But as the summer wore on, the calls started coming, then strange men and women in business suits stopped by the house and spoke quietly with his parents. One day his father announced the bank was foreclosing on the house, and they had less than a week to move out. Nick couldn't remember ever seeing his father smile again. He'd been sure back then that if he and Sophie just worked hard enough, they could help rescue their home. But they'd had no choice but to move into a dirty two-bedroom apartment, and he and Sophie had to share one bedroom for a year.

It had broken his poor dad, who died of a heart attack soon after they'd moved, and then his mother got sick and was gone less than a year later. Nick stayed on with Sophie while she attended the local community college until she could transfer to Sonoma State. During her senior year Nick realized he wasn't cut out for college so he joined the Navy, and later tried out for the teams. He couldn't do anything to save his own parents physically or financially, but he could defend his country...and he had nowhere else to go. The Navy became his new family.

Stop dwelling on the past. Cut the baggage. Get your head in the game at hand. Face it. Just like the SEALs Creed, *The Only Easy Day Was Yesterday*, life was hard and would continue to get harder, and that was all there was to it.

Nick sorted through more pink specially labeled envelopes and found a delinquent gas and electric bill for nearly a thousand dollars. He folded it quickly and slipped it into his pants pocket.

"Don't go through my mail." Sophie had been sitting slumped over the table, finishing her coffee.

"Sorry, sis. Thought I saw something important there."

Marc dried his hands and walked over to Nick to take a look.

Sophie was on her feet faster than he'd thought she could move these days. "Dammit, Nick."

She elbowed him out of the way, her robe nearly falling off her shoulders. Nick let her push him aside, but he grabbed her robe by the collar to make sure her bony flesh remained covered.

Sophie jerked out of the way and glared at him. "My mail's private."

"Gotta ask you, though. Some of those bills look like they're late. You okay with the mortgage?"

"They'll get paid when the place sells. That's Devon's job, so don't fret about it."

"What if it doesn't sell fast enough?"

"It will," she said over her shoulder as she hugged the pile of bills to her chest and marched off to her bedroom, slamming the door.

Marc shook his head. "Damn shame, Nick. You think she waited too long?"

He pulled out the orange electric bill notice. "I'm going to at least keep the power and lights on. Wish I could do more."

"We should organize a work party. Get all this shit sold."

"Good thinkin'." Nick said.

"Have a big fire sale, like that rug place in San Diego that goes out of business every year. That kind of thing. Get all of it cleared out."

"I think we're gonna need more help."

"I'll go call Kyle and some others. They'd love a road trip up here, doing your sister a good turn. Word gets out a bunch of Navy SEALs are working the nursery without their shirts, selling potted plants and daisies. It's bound to bring a crowd."

"Not that high-profile shit, Marc. You know Timmons would bust us for that."

"Not that he'd ever know. Come on, give the guys a way to blow off some steam and prance around half-naked. And they won't know anyone here."

"But I do, or did."

"You mean Devon? That nice piece that's got you dreamin' in the shower? I fully understand you not wanting a bunch of horny Frogs hanging around her. Probably too much for her. Make her go off and do something unladylike and all." Marc punched Nick in the arm. "Be good for the little lady, who I think needs a little man-scent in her life. Get my drift?"

Nick put aside the comment about being around Devon and forced himself to focus on the problem at hand: time was running out for Sophie. Marc might be onto something. Maybe they could earn enough money to at least make one payment. If they were close, maybe he could make up the shortfall. And maybe this kind of team bonding project was just what they needed so soon after they got back from Afghanistan. Better to schedule it now than wait until everyone had made other plans.

Why not?

"Go call 'em."

"When do you want them here?"

"Yesterday."

Marc announced that several of the men on SEAL Team 3 would be coming up, including their LPO, Kyle Lansdowne. Nick was glad to know that Cooper had said he'd come, since he'd practically been born under a tractor in Nebraska. and knew how to fix anything. Nick hoped Coop could fix several rototillers and mowers Sophie used to rent out, but that no longer started. At this point they'd been sitting around so long they were also rusty as hell.

She also had a vintage vegetable truck in the back with four flat tires. He knew Coop would get that thing running in no time.

Now he reviewed the disclosure statements Devon had left and had some questions, so he gave her a call.

"Hey, Dev."

"Devon."

"Miss Brandeburg. How's that?"

"Nick, can we just stop this? Just call me Devon, okay?"

"Fine. So, I have questions about these disclosure papers and was wondering if I could go over them with you."

"Sophie has to fill them out."

"Well, she's not getting out of bed today. I think, under the circumstances, I should fill them out and she can sign."

"You have to know about the property."

"I'll leave blank the things I don't know. I can ask her about those."

"That would work. So, what questions do you have?"

"Well, I thought we could kill two birds, sort of do it over lunch, like a date? I think it would make her happy if we did that."

"Our first date?"

"Our very first."

"Okay. Why don't we meet at the Italian place on Fourth Street next to the bookstore? Mama's."

"Perfect. Say in an hour?"

Mama's was packed with a lunch crowd. The quaint restaurant was "noisy intimate" like some of his favorite places in San Diego. The food was tasty, with free bread sticks and supposedly the best pizza north of San Francisco. He was watching the mostly young crowd around him, waiting in a booth for Devon to show up.

When she walked in, his heart thumped so hard it made his ears ring. She wore her hair up in a clip but loose, so that silky strands fell about her shoulders and neck. She studied the room, starting on the right at the bar, and moving her gaze across the dining room until their eyes met. He tried to suppress a smile, but it was tough.

He acknowledged her with a lift of his hand while trying not to grin like an idiot. His mouth was dry even though he'd tried to swallow several times. He ground his teeth and locked his jaw. Something about her was all the right kinds of haughty and sweet. Her sexual energy was bigger than the room.

She turned every male head as she made her way to him with long strides on a straight trajectory. Best of all, she never took her eyes off his. For a second, he thought perhaps he'd been wrong about her experience with men. She was fucking killing him.

He almost forgot himself, but at the last minute stood as she slipped into the booth. Nick had no idea what to say. His tongue was stuck to the roof of his mouth.

"Sorry I'm late," she said as she picked up the menu without checking his reaction.

"I'm always early," he said and noted the croak in his voice like he was fifteen-year-old dork…again.

"And I'm usually late." She was looking over the cream and red plastic menu. Her dark eyes were made up more heavily than yesterday. He would have to say sultry. Siren. She had on her work demeanor too, another nice suit of dark blue with a sheer white blouse and a virginal schoolgirl bow under her chin. Oh the things he thought about doing with her and that bow. The places he could tie her up. The body parts he could restrain. If she was aware he was staring at her with his tongue hanging out, she didn't show it.

Nick didn't like feeling he wasn't in control. Usually after he'd spent this much time with a woman she'd be drooling all over him, hinting about going for a drive or a picnic in the woods. Sliding up to him, giving him little hints of the feel of her body. But Devon was strictly hands-off. He was going to have to play it that way, for now. He just couldn't stop his dirty mind from getting creative, conspiring with that certain body part that always gave him a hard time.

She finally looked at him and dished out a generous smile. White teeth, plump lips, and red again, with a sparkle in the eyes and tiny laugh lines that broke the intensity of her presence.

God almighty. You toying with me, kitten? Just looking at her sent his libido into high gear. Half in a state of panic, he realized he was nervous.

Nervous? WTF?

This had never happened to him before.

"So, what are you having?" she asked.

He noted she took a quick glance from one side of his shoulder to the other. He very carefully sat up straighter and took a deep breath, enlarging his ribcage. He rubbed the back of his head, exposing his right bicep.

She watched every second of it and then tore her eyes away.

"Was sort of thinking about a pizza. What one do you recommend?"

"I don't eat pizza."

"Interesting." He found himself smiling with half-lidded eyes, even while trying to reel in his reflex to pounce and possess. "What do you eat?"

That got a reaction. Her brown eyes flared and the frown lines between her brows made a brief appearance, and then disappeared.

"Green things mostly."

Nick noticed how quickly she'd taken it out of the sexual realm and made it about neutral things like spinach salads and healthy food. He was definitely thinking about steamy, sexual things. And definitely not vegetables.

"No protein?" he said as he glanced up at a young waitress passing by. The girl blushed and giggled.

Devon noticed his pass and the girl's blush. She arched her eyebrow and scanned the room. Nick knew there were more than a few women looking his way, but he kept his eyes on her in spite of the distraction. He watched the arch of her neck, the way the tiny hairs behind her ears were slightly darker and curlier than the floppy loose curls at the top of her head. Her scent was the same as yesterday, some perfume he'd not experienced before. He wondered how it would taste on her skin.

Turning back to him, she said, "Are we ready?"

He didn't answer except to nod silently. Oh, yeah. He was ready, all right. This one was special. He was going to have to work very hard to win her trust.

He loved a good challenge.

After their lunch was served they began the obligatory small talk. Devon knew about Nick's parents, of course, but Nick learned she had also lost her parents in high school, in a private plane crash. She'd known his sister originally through student government, even though Sophie had been two grades ahead. She said she remembered Nick too, but he was sad to admit he didn't remember Devon at all. That bothered him a bit.

Devon told him she and Sophie became friends through a Pilates class. Sophie had just gotten her real estate license when Devon came in one day and asked to be mentored.

"So what's the deal with my sister? Why hasn't she settled down?"

"I think all the economic uncertainty of your parents' passing made her feel like she wanted to get her career in order first, get stable. I completely understand. I'm the same way," she said.

"I guess I missed all that. I was just a kid finishing up high school. There was no college fund, so I got the Navy. Not that I'm complaining."

"Would you have gone?"

"To college? I don't think about that at all, Dev—Devon."

She smiled. "Thank you."

"Does that mean I get a treat?"

"Don't push your luck."

That spark of connection between them was brief, but very intimate. He had the urge to push his luck. He cleared his throat and tried to clear his mind.

"Is this so difficult now, being with me?" he asked.

She smiled. "No. Not what I expected." Her voice became a whisper. For a second he felt like he was in the presence of a delicate bird. Something he wanted to protect.

"I'll take that as a good sign, then." He sat back and hoped he wouldn't get a smart-ass comment in return. Hoped she'd follow along. Let him lead her just a little bit closer, and eventually into his arms.

"I think you're a nicer person than I realized. Sophie said to give you time to show your better side."

He had to look away. Did he have a better side? Why was it so important that he make a good impression on her? What did he really want? A hookup? That brought on all sorts of visions. A portion of his brain was working overtime like dancers in a Bollywood movie.

She waved her hand in front of his face. "Hello? We have some work to do, remember?"

The plates were cleared and he pulled out the disclosure paperwork. But he quickly tired of trying to explain things upside down.

"Can I sit there next to you? It would be easier," he asked.

She tilted her head, gave a lop-sided smile, and then scooted over and made room for him on the burgundy vinyl bench seat. He loved sitting on the warm spot her beautiful butt had occupied.

Her intense scent was making his nose itch, but every other part of his body was cheering with more intensity than a Stanford vs. Cal game. His thigh was close enough to hers that, even with the fabric of his canvas cargoes between them, he could feel the hairs on his legs stiffen and rise to attention. And they weren't the only things rising, either.

"Here," he said as he pointed out a couple of questions and boxes he was supposed to check off. "I'm not sure what they are asking. The place is old. How would she know if any of these things work or not?"

She leaned in and her shoulder brushed his. He let the feeling warm him for a moment, then backed away to give her space. She angled her head to look at the question, and that beautiful swan's neck came so close to him he could have leaned forward only inches to give her a kiss there. And he really wanted to.

"She just has to say what she knows. She can't be responsible for what she doesn't know. Fill it out with what she thinks is correct. Find out if she has any old reports, and I'll go back and check the old files. When she bought the property I don't think there were any reports given. She bought it in foreclosure."

"Speaking of that, have you asked Sophie if she's current on her payments?"

"Well, it's a question on this statement. You'll have to ask her."

"But do you know if she is?"

"No. You think she is?" Her brown doe eyes pulled at his heart and made it ache. Their lips were close. He wanted to put his arm up on the top of the booth, but then he'd be looming all over her and he knew it would scare her again. Besides, he'd been sweating and that was always a turnoff to women. Suddenly his arms, hands and legs were awkward appendages and he couldn't find a comfortable place to put them.

"She's gotten some nasty notices. She was trying to hide them from me."

Devon sighed. He felt it run through her body though they were barely touching. "I was afraid of that. I'll have the title people check to see if any notices were filed. This is something, unfortunately, we have to disclose to a potential buyer."

"Dev—on," he stumbled and noticed her smile again. It was getting easier to get her to do that. "There are some things I can discuss with my sister, but her financial status is not one of them. She's pretty much shut me out for years. And I've been telling her she's killing herself with all this folly with the nursery. She pretty much forbids me to ask about any of that stuff."

She nodded.

He pulled out the delinquent power bill. "I'm going to go by this office and pay this bill today."

Devon looked from the statement to Nick's face. "That's nearly a thousand dollars."

"I've got savings."

She grinned again.

"What's so funny?"

"She thinks you buy toys all the time. Guns and trucks and equipment."

"I do. But I don't spend it all." He paused and focused on her mouth. "I live a simple lifestyle." If he knew her better, he'd have told her a big bed with fresh sheets and lots of pillows and a bottle of red wine wasn't expensive, and was about the only thing he could think about right now.

She had focused on his mouth too, and, for just a second, there was the possibility of a kiss. He was hungry for it.

"Anything else I can do for you guys?" the cheerful high school-aged waitress chirped.

Nick noticed Devon had composed herself quickly, retreating into professional realtor mode. He sighed and reached for his wallet and gave the waitress his credit card. "No, thanks."

I think you've done enough.

CHAPTER 7

Devon could hardly breathe all afternoon. Being so close to Nick's body heated her blood and her pulse was pounding like she'd had three cups of coffee.

She nearly got into an accident on her way back to the office. After daydreaming in front of the computer for an hour, she realized she wasn't going to get anything done. Since she had no appointments, she decided to leave early and pack her suitcase for the stay at Sophie's.

Was she doing this for Sophie, or did she secretly want to be close to Nick? The way he moved, the way his voice sent a shiver down her spine, were all tantalizing recollections as she moved with zombie-like slowness, picking out her tops and jeans, a pair of old running shoes she knew she'd need for working in the yard, plus sunscreen and all her shampoo sample bottles.

She went to her underwear drawer and exposed the bright pink rabbit vibrator amongst her lacy things. She'd won the device at a bachelorette party. The new feelings she was having as a result of being so close to Nick were like those first stolen moments when she dared to turn the thing on and let it touch her. Closing her eyes, she imagined what it would be like if he touched her there.

With a shudder, she scolded herself to finish her packing and get over to Sophie's. Inquiries were already coming in about the property, and if Nick was right and Sophie was in foreclosure, they'd have to hurry to get it sold in time. It would be the worst thing in the world for her to have to watch the bank take it back. Devon decided she would not let that happen.

The meandering roadway on Bennett Valley was always a pleasant drive. Turning up Sophie's drive, she was disappointed to note Nick's Hummer was not in the lot. But Sophie's car was.

The sign read 'closed', which was odd. The door to the office was locked, so she went around the back. The house was also locked up.

She dialed Sophie's cell phone and got voicemail. Thirty seconds later, Nick returned her call.

"We're at her oncologist's office."

"What's going on?"

"She hasn't stopped vomiting since last night. They're giving her fluids and sending her home with some pain meds, but he thinks we need to call hospice."

"Oh, no! Already?"

"He said he was trying to get her to do it a month ago."

"That's our Sophie." She waited for tears in her eyes to subside so her voice wouldn't wobble. "So, should I get anything for her, or just wait here?"

"You're at the house?"

"Yes."

There was a pause on the other end of the line. Finally, Nick said, "I'm glad. Sophie will be relieved."

Devon walked down the rows of gallon cans set on black plastic cloth. She knew Sophie had started most of the plants either from graft or seed. At one time they had been lush and green. Now the lack of attention had created a slew of yellowed leaves and dried flowers that needed deadheading.

She wandered into the greenhouse where Nick had soaked her with the hose. There was a small wooden sign that read "Sophie's Specials" posted over a variety of unusual plants on wooden benches. Sophie told her she had collected heirloom seeds of all sorts from local organic growers, and exchanged them for grape cuttings or fruit trees she'd multi-grafted. Devon had sometimes accompanied her on her bi-weekly trips to the local farmer's market, where she always found something interesting or new. All the farmers shared a common bond: they did what they did because they loved it, not because it made any of them rich.

Devon wished one of them would be able to buy the nursery. That way, 'Sophie's Specials' would survive a few years longer.

Will anyone care about it half as much as Sophie does?

Big tires on the gravel driveway signaled Nick's return with his precious cargo. She saw Sophie in the front seat, looking even smaller than before, dwarfed by the huge roaring, snorting beast of a vehicle. She would never understand why men liked big trucks. They were expensive to maintain, she'd heard, and, like equally expensive and frivolous racehorses, broke down frequently.

Devon was smiling at Sophie through the passenger window when Nick came up behind her, put his hands on her waist and moved her aside. "Excuse me, pretty, lady, but Marc's gotta carry her."

He'd dropped his hands immediately. Marc wiggled his eyebrows and opened the passenger door. He carefully extracted Sophie, who looked a pale shade of green. Holding her under the knees and around the waist, he carried her to the back.

"Nick, I'm gonna need you to unlock the door, please, so don't get in any water fights yet," he yelled over his shoulder.

Sophie had laid her head against Marc's chest in an uncharacteristic move. Devon's eyes immediately began to water.

"Oh, God, Nick. I'm going to lose her."

He wrapped an arm around her and gave her a safe squeeze. "I'll be right back."

Devon had known this day was coming, but it was happening so fast. She thought she'd have time to prepare, to get used to the idea that Sophie was leaving this world forever. What had she been thinking? She was filled with regret for all the times she hadn't called her friend right back, for the lunches she'd cancelled because of clients. She wished she'd helped her paint or weed or run the shop, or just do *some*thing to help out. And now it was all too little too late.

Nick returned, his white T-shirt glowing in the late afternoon sun. "We've got someone from hospice coming over tonight for the initial interview. They send a caseworker first. I wish they'd just send a nurse."

"I don't know what to do," Devon said.

"Unfortunately, Devon, I do. I've done a lot of it. Except this time it will be my sister." He abruptly turned his back to her. Their shared pain was becoming unbearable, but there was also something good about being there. She could feel it, as she stood beside him looking out at the golden peaks of the surrounding hills and the big cloudless sky above. She understood she was standing in the doorway of the end of things. And the beginning of something else.

A new adventure. But this time, without Sophie.

Marc stayed with Sophie while Devon changed into her grubbies and went out to the nursery to help Nick. He had a clipboard and was making notes.

"Making a list. The guys are coming tomorrow to help get everything ready for a big sale this weekend."

"Guys?"

"From my team."

"Oh. How many?"

"Six, I think. Maybe more later."

"They'll just come up here like that?" she asked.

"Sure. It's what we do. We're family. We take care of our own. Someone leaves us, we take care of their family. Any one of us needs someone, someone is provided. We work as a team both on and off the battlefield."

"The Navy trains all that into you?"

Nick lowered the clipboard and stared off in the distance. "I don't think so. I think we were always this way, just found out after we became teammates. We have this bond, this brotherhood. We never leave each other behind. We never forget. We never stop grieving for the things we lose and we never stop rejoicing for the things we have."

"So no one's alone."

"That's right. No one gets left behind."

Nick was serious, focused on the task at hand. Devon wondered if he was annoyed with her. She followed him around, asking about what they would do with this or that. He had answers for some of her questions, but mostly he said he didn't know and he'd think of something. He kept writing, as if the writing were a mission unto itself.

She began to feel like a fifth wheel. She missed the close, intimate lunch they'd had, the way he'd looked at her and whispered his questions, the way he was careful around her. Now she was feeling ignored.

She tried to engage him one more time. "So do you want me to start picking through the flats and throwing out the dead stuff, Nick?"

He dropped his clipboard again and sighed. "Devon, you're gonna have to leave me alone for a while. I'm trying to figure it all out, and I can't think straight with you standing there so close to me."

He didn't look at her. He swore and walked away, shaking his head.

Dinner was awkward. Devon could see Marc had been greatly affected by Sophie's condition. "Can't wait for Coop to get up here and take a look at her. I think she's going to need more pain meds," he said.

The social worker arrived in the evening for a brief visit. Sophie dozed in and out of consciousness during the discussion. Marc finally went over to the couch and picked her up and held her on his lap. The social worker explained the hospice procedure.

"We want to keep her calm. No big drama. Keep things little, simple, small. Less is better."

Devon saw the two men look at each other. There was about to be an explosion of activity and a whole lot of big guys hanging around. Things would be far from quiet or small.

"She needs to eat, but of course she doesn't want to."

That got to Sophie and she sat up. "You talk as if I'm already dead. I'm right here. My name is Sophie and I can hear everything you're saying about me."

The heavyset social worker appeared rattled, but gave a syrupy smile and continued. "Well now, Sophie, I'm glad to see your spunk. You have some awfully nice friends here."

They made arrangements for two nurses to start working the late night shift on alternating days so Devon, Nick and Marc could get some proper rest, starting right away.

Marc put Sophie to bed after the lady from hospice left.

"I'm sorry I was short with you today," Nick said. "I'm expected to have a full plan lined out when the guys get here tomorrow."

"I understand," she whispered. "Thought maybe I'd said something wrong."

"You could never do anything wrong," he replied.

CHAPTER 8

The weight of all the fast-moving decisions was pressing on Nick, which was unusual, since that's what he did every day on the battlefield. But today, it was giving him a headache. He was in an unpredictable mood, one that he didn't often let civilians see, let alone his sister's best friend. Maybe it was because, for all his training, he couldn't control the outcome of Sophie's cancer. All his equipment was of no use when it came to dealing with his sister and her final affairs.

He decided to rummage in Sophie's kitchen for something to put him at ease.

"You want some tequila?" he asked Devon.

"I've never tried it."

Of course, Nick thought. "Well then, you should have just one with me. Would you do that?" He held the bottle in his right hand and two shot glasses in his left.

"I'll watch."

"Nope. Gotta participate to be on this team, Devon."

"Excuse me? You're going to *make* me have a drink? Don't you think that's a little dangerous? People can be allergic to alcohol."

He could see he'd picked a scab. "But you're forgetting. I have medic training. We all do. I can quickly assess the signs." She was getting back some of that edge, but he'd defused it a bit.

She crossed her arms and scrunched her eyebrows up into a delicious little frown he wanted to kiss in the worst way.

"I'm telling you there are some things that should just be experienced. Having a shot of tequila is one of them."

"Name some others." She was standing with her feet perpendicular, like a sensual dancer in the wings, arms still crossed, and her lips were so scrunched up they were downright hot and begging to be violated.

"Having great freakin' sex on the beach under the moonlight. Having sex in the back of a pickup truck at a campground. Having sex on a mountaintop in the rain in Hawaii. Having sex in a boat and watching the stars in the biggest sky you've ever seen." He'd forgotten who he was talking to. When he looked up at her, her jaw had dropped a good three inches.

He clicked the two little shot glasses together with his third and fourth fingers. "And having your first shot of tequila. Ready?"

"Oh why the fuck not?"

She stomped over to the table and plopped down with her elbows resting on the table.

"I like that nasty mouth of yours. You should use it more often."

"Well, I happen to talk that way all the time," she said. Her chin was raised. She looked back at him with her eyelids nearly closed.

"Well, thank God for small miracles. You looked a little tightly wound yesterday. You can talk dirty with me any time you want, Devon." He slammed down the glasses and filled them. Picking up a lemon from the fruit bowl, he sliced it into halves and then quarters and placed one piece next to the glass he pushed in her direction.

"We do this together." He grinned at her. Her scowl looked fake.

He motioned she should pick up the glass, and she followed his lead. He brought his to his lips and he nearly forgot where he was when she did the same.

"You'll drink the whole shot in one gulp and then bite down on the lemon, agreed? Or are you going to chicken out?"

"I'm not a chicken."

"I can see that."

"Ready? Go."

Devon tossed back the drink and quickly grabbed the lemon with a gasp. She bit down on it and wrinkled her nose.

Nick had gotten so engrossed in her actions he'd forgotten to take his lemon. The woman was dangerous. He could see himself spending a lifetime teaching her everything he knew about everything, especially drinking and sex. But if she didn't want to drink, well then, just the sex. God, he was easy.

"That was horrible," she sputtered.

"You did it! You conquered your fears, Devon." He unscrewed the bottle again. "Another."

"No!"

He smiled and poured himself another and downed it.

"Okay," he smacked the table with both hands. "Done. Fixed."

"You do this sort of thing a lot?" she asked.

He wiped the lemon off his hands with a damp tea towel and then came over to the back of the couch and leaned against it, reveling in her mussed-up hair and her dirty shoes. He knew she'd be a hellcat if she ever got drunk and lost control. Not that she'd be unladylike or anything, but he knew he'd have one great time if she could just loosen up a bit. She looked about as comfortable in her casual jeans and shirt as a buck on opening day of deer season. "No, but 'desperate times call for desperate measures.'"

He motioned for her to come over to him.

She hesitated at first, then stood up and meandered in his direction, swaying gently from side to side. She was avoiding eye contact.

He motioned for her to give him her hands, and this time she did it without any hesitation.

"You did real good today, Devon. You've been holding up like a champ."

He didn't want to, but he dropped her hands and placed his palms on his thighs.

He decided to wait out the little silence to see if she would shy away. She stood her ground. He could feel the heat from her body and knew she felt his. Her deep breathing told him she was excited. Maybe a there was some fear, but there was something else there too. Perhaps a tiny crack had developed in the ice queen's veneer.

The look she gave him next was all longing, pure hunger. He didn't think she realized how needy she appeared. If she could only see how desirable she was at that very moment. How much he wanted to pull her into his arms and give her a proper kiss. His little head was doing cartwheels in anticipation, but he looked away and tried to think of something besides getting sweaty in a large bed with her. He knew what she'd feel like underneath him. He knew he could awaken the dreams and desires she worked so hard to keep suppressed.

But she would have to ask for it. He was not going to force her.

Well, maybe he could do a little temperature check. He tilted his head to the side. "Can I ask you something?"

Her eyes were sending the message "tell me what to do." He was going to do the right thing, just as he'd promised Sophie.

"Go ahead. Ask," Devon said.

"When was the last time you were kissed by someone you really wanted to kiss?"

At first her eyes widened, perhaps showing some panic. But as the thought settled in, though, he saw a hint of a smile. She was shaking, too, holding herself in check, being very brave. Then she looked down again.

"Never," she said to the floor.

"Say that again and look at me this time, Devon."

She lifted her head up and he watched her search his face, give it a good look. Her eyes focused on his lips. "Never." She suddenly got shy and looked down again.

He wanted to rise and take her in his arms, but he stayed where he was. His package was uncomfortable but he dared not adjust himself.

"Would you allow me to kiss you? To kiss you that way, as if you wanted it?" he asked. His heart was pounding in his throat.

"That way. Meaning, you want to kiss me?" she said, deadpan, except her eyes sparkled just a tad too much.

"No more than you want to kiss me. It's a consensual act. Just a kiss. One little kiss. And you never have to do it again if you don't like it."

"Teach me," Her tequila and lemon breath and throaty voice were sexy as hell. The longing in her face broke his heart. He knew for certain then that Devon was a virgin. He was willing to bet she'd suffered trauma. He beckoned and she obeyed, getting near enough to touch his chest if she wanted. His knees were splayed to the sides as he remained propped on the back of the couch.

"Hands here." He placed her palms against his chest. One of his hands held the back of her head. "Head back a little." She leaned away from him and let him support her head. "Lick your lips, Devon."

She tried to lean back and pushed against his chest. He angled a look at her and she relaxed.

"Can we get this over with?" she finally said. He could tell she was feigning indifference. It looked more like she was nearly paralyzed with fear.

"We certainly can. So. Resume the position."

She put her hands on his chest again and he felt the wonderful electricity of the most beautiful woman he'd ever met. He began to feel her come alive as she touched him. She licked her lips and slowly leaned her head back into the cradle of his palm.

"Open your mouth, Devon, just a little."

She was awkward and glared at him for a second.

"And close your eyes, please."

She shut them and mechanically opened her mouth like she was a marionette. He felt her shaking like a delicate leaf.

He stood and allowed his chest to come in contact with hers. Pressing against her breasts he brushed his fingers over her cheek, following with a thumb on her lower lip. With a slow exhale, he bent down, and met the flesh of her lips with his.

He didn't press. He didn't probe. He let her feel the strength and resolve of his passion, waited for her discover her own as it rose within her.

And she did. She leaned into him, pressing their lips together as she took a breath and then pressed again. She was starved for affection. He felt her nipples tighten under the cotton T-shirt. He could practically feel the pheromones rising to her skin and sneaking around to ensnare him. He kissed his way to her ear, down her throat, and then back to her waiting lips. Her fingers had at first dug into his pecs, but now her hands slipped up around his neck as she pulled his head down to hers. He dropped his hands to the back of her waist, desperately wanting to pull her into his groin, but he stopped at her waist. If she was alert enough, and he thought she might be, she might already feel his erection looming.

He kept a safe distance so as not to scare her. They ended the kiss with her palms pressed against his cheeks as she searched his eyes. He'd opened the doorway, all right. The lady had a need maybe as strong as his own. But he had an idea she was feeling it for the first time, or just recognizing it for the first time.

He dipped his head to give her another kiss and she immediately backed away.

Damn.

She quickly turned, but not before he saw she was wiping tears from her eyes.

"You okay?" he asked.

"Wow. Just wow," she said as she stared at the door, arms wrapped around herself with her back to him. Nick leaned back on the couch and watched as she slowly turned in his direction again. "I don't know what to say."

"Thank you would be nice. But you can also tell me to go to hell if you feel like it." Nick smiled at the flush on her cheeks, the way her neck got red and blotchy, the fact that her hands fluttered in the air without anything to do. He loved watching her float on the cloud of passion, and then realize that she wanted to experience more.

And all he could do right now was watch and hope that her passion would continue to bloom for him.

CHAPTER 9

"You can stash your things in there," Nick pointed to the second bedroom down the hallway from Sophie's. "Best to rest up. Tomorrow will be a killer of a day."

She was feeling tired, and her back and neck were sore. She rubbed her shoulders and let her head roll from side to side.

"Go set your things down, and then I'll give you a neck rub, get you all ready for bed. I guarantee you won't know what hit you."

She did as she was instructed, then paused to lean against the doorway and study him. "You must be exhausted too, Nick. I think I'll just slip into bed. Thanks for the offer, though."

He was looking straight ahead, having left a spot on the couch for her to sit.

"Come here." He beckoned again with his fingers.

"I'm okay. Really. You don't have to do that."

"Remember, I can make you fall asleep so fast you won't know what hit you. Honest." He walked around and grabbed her hand, then led her to the couch before gently pushing her down to sit.

Nick sat right next to her. His hands tenderly found the top of her spine and he began to press. The pressure was so pleasurable Devon thought she'd see stars. The rhythmic motion of his fingers rolled and cajoled the soft flesh between the ridges in her spine and neck. She felt herself leaning backward and to the left. Against him.

Devon awoke sometime after midnight with a start. At first, she loved the feel of the warm chest underneath her, and then she realized she was sleeping on *top* of Nick. His hands were wrapped around her back and waist and a light blanket had been pulled over their legs.

She arched up.

"Hey there," he whispered. "Have a good sleep?"

She sat up as Nick adjusted his legs to allow her feet to hit the floor. He remained prone, one huge arm underneath his head. She could see his eyes twinkling in the moonlight, as well as the outline of his lips. The ocean she'd been hearing in her dream was his breathing.

"I guess you weren't kidding about the shoulder rubs. Sorry I doubted you," she said before she could stop herself.

"You were out in less than five minutes. And, just so you know, I didn't try anything. I was a perfect gentleman." She could see the Cheshire cat grin glowing back at her.

"How would I know?" she challenged.

"You wouldn't. But I would. I don't do that."

Well. So much for *that* conversation.

"Dev…"

"Devon."

"Back to that again? Okay, *Devon*, you have a big day tomorrow. Why don't you run to the bedroom and finish your sleep on a real bed?"

"I should." The harshness of her reaction to the nickname got to her a bit and she felt herself soften. "I'm sorry I'm so disagreeable sometimes."

"You are a handful, I'll give you that."

"I don't mean to be difficult, but I want my boundaries respected."

He was nodding in the moonlight. Perhaps he was staring at the ceiling.

"Sounds like someone with trust issues. Were you hurt by someone, Devon?"

"No," she said too quickly. There wouldn't be any further discussion of her past.

"Go run along. I'll get you up early and we'll make Sophie a nice breakfast."

She had an idea. Probably not very wise, but it was an idea. "Nick, if you promise to completely behave yourself, I mean no touchy and stuff, you can come in and sleep on the bed next to me."

"I'm fine here," he said.

"Well it can't be very comfortable, and here I was pressing against you—"

"I didn't mind that one bit."

Of course. You walked right into that one, Devon.

"Besides," he added, "this couch is way more comfortable than the cots and dirt floors I usually sleep on. Almost a luxury."

She shook her head. "How do you do all that?"

"All what?"

"All that stuff over there. The killing, the danger, all the fear. How do you sleep?"

"Very carefully. Many days we don't. We catch naps when we can, when someone is looking out for us."

"So that's how the team buddy thing works, then."

"Yup. We watch out for each other. We listen for signs of danger. We develop a sixth sense about it. If you don't feel the danger before it comes, then it kills you. So you either feel it and react, or you're dead."

"I don't understand how you can take it."

"Well, you drive along the freeway, right? You see shops and buildings at the side of the road. You watch other drivers. You look for bad drivers. You look behind you and to the sides so you know where you are at all times. You see billboards, listen to things on the radio, watch the clock, and you're alert when you drive, right?"

"Right."

"That's how we do it. Except we're trained to look for other kinds of danger, and deal with them without thinking."

"But doesn't it bother you?"

"What?"

"The killing, the stuff you've seen."

"You see stuff every day on the news and read about stuff in the paper every day that's even worse. Evil lives all over the world. We're trained to contain only a part of it. We're trained so we don't have to think about it. We just act. And hope to God we got the message in time."

"I'm not sure I could do that."

Nick smoothed a hand over her shoulder and down her back in a neutral way, without a sexual overtones. "And that's why I'm here. So you don't have to do that. So you can go to the mall, drive cars, sell houses, go to the movies and have a life. We protect that way of life. And we love doing it. For you guys."

Devon began to tear up. She was so sad that this man was going to lose the only family he had left. And in spite of all his training, his physical strength, his can-do attitude, there wasn't a damn thing he could do to prevent it.

"Offer's still open." She took his hand and held it between both of hers. "If you'll behave, you can share the bed."

"No can do, Devon." His piercing look was unmistakable. At first the realization was frightening, and then it made her glow inside.

After Devon left, Nick knew he'd get only restless sleep, if any. He programmed himself to wake up at 05:00, to shower and be ready to wake her up in case she overslept.

Then he stared out the window at a nearly full moon just beginning to slip behind Bennett Peak. He wished he believed in God. Maybe it would be a good time to start thinking about that, so that when Sophie passed, he might be able to somehow connect with her, God willing. Armando's mom, Felicia Guzman, prayed to her God all the time, and just about everything she'd prayed for came to pass. So maybe he could adopt hers.

He decided to try it.

Okay, Sir. If you're there, please get things ready for Sophie. She's a pistol and she swears too much, but she has a good heart. Protect her until I can come and relieve you, if that's how it works.

He listened and watched to see if God might give him a sign...and was disappointed to find nothing. But he felt better. Just a little. Then he prayed to Mama Guzman's God to help his heart be strong for the coming days.

And to melt Devon's.

CHAPTER 10

Nick and Marc were taking instructions from Sophie when Devon got a call about the property. It was odd that it came on her cell phone, but she picked it up anyway.

"Ms. Brandeburg, we've never met," the heavily accented voice on the other end of the line continued, "but I represent an party interested in your nursery listing."

"That's wonderful. I'm sorry, but I didn't get your name."

"Ulysses Silva. I was wondering if I could come by later this afternoon."

"I'm sorry, Mr. Silva. As the listing says, we're not open for showings until after the weekend. Right now we're getting everything ready."

"But I must insist. I believe my client wants to make an offer tonight."

"Well, that won't be possible. I'd be happy to entertain an offer, but we want to give the property the right exposure, and right now it doesn't look as good as it will."

"What if you don't have to do all that work? What if my client will do all the cleanup?"

Devon was wary of an offer from a broker she didn't know. And she never liked it when the buyer was being pushy. Sophie was, indeed, in a financial bind, as she'd finally admitted to Devon and Nick this morning, but there wasn't any reason to make her appear desperate.

"I'll talk to my client. Can I reach you at this number?"

"Please understand, Ms. Brandeburg, we are very interested in the property and are willing to pay significantly more than the asking price for it."

That got Devon's attention.

"I see. Well let me speak to her, and I'll call you back later this afternoon
if I can."

"I understand she is very ill."

This definitely raised hackles on Devon's neck. "That's not something I'm
willing to discuss, Mr. Silva. Now, if you'll excuse me, I'm busy getting ready
for our big sale."

"Sale?"

"We're having a big plant sale extravaganza this weekend. Get rid of all the
inventory and de-clutter what's here."

"You are closing down the sales office, then?"

"Well, not right away, but yes, unless a new owner wants to keep
everything."

"This is a possibility."

Devon didn't trust this caller. But she had to discuss alternative responses
with Sophie, and perhaps Nick too. This man's aggressive eagerness to buy
the property without asking any of the questions the potential buyers usually
asked—like the well output , the business profit and loss , or the inventory
value—felt off. Her gut feeling was that this buyer wasn't real. They hadn't
even gotten the pest report, or well and septic testing.

"You know we've had a lot of interest."

"That surprises me."

"Well, we have. I need to go. You will hear from me this afternoon." Devon
hung up.

She decided to go speak with Sophie, who was outside with Nick and Marc,
planning out the scope of work.

"Those annuals are looking pretty sad. We can put a little fish emulsion
on them and see if they perk up. Anything that doesn't gets put in the trash
bin behind the shop. Garbage pickup is on Fridays, thank God. Haven't filled
it in months."

She was telling Marc where to move wood-boxed trees when Nick noticed
the look on Devon's face.

"Something wrong?"

"I just got the strangest call. The guy says he has a buyer," Devon began, but Sophie overheard and had turned.

"Already?" Sophie exclaimed.

"Yes. He wants to come over today. I told him we were getting ready for a big cleanup, but he was rather obnoxious about coming over before anyone else could."

Sophie straightened, sparks shooting out of her eyes. "Did he have an accent?" she demanded.

Devon forced herself not to back away from Sophie's intensity. "Yes, he did."

"You know who I'll bet it is?" Sophie had her hands on her hips. "That dipshit neighbor of mine." She pointed to the vineyard on her right. "He's been after me to sell for a couple of years now."

"Really? Sophie, you never told me about this. He owns practically the whole valley. Having this strip of land wouldn't do him any good," Nick added.

"I've got a commercial well, hundred gallons a minute. I think he wants the water for his vineyard."

Devon nodded. "I didn't think of that. Doesn't he have water on his land?"

"You go over there and look at the wells he's dug. As close to the property line as possible. He's been trying to tap into mine for months now. I'm guessing he hasn't succeeded. And he can't improve or expand his vineyard without more water."

Nick whistled. "So the water rights are more valuable than the property? Maybe we need to rethink this, Devon."

"It's just one factor, but isn't the whole thing," Devon began. "I think we want to get ourselves as many potential buyers as possible. Putting our eggs in one basket doesn't seem wise. I say we stay the course, but Sophie, it's up to you."

"It will be a cold day in hell before I'd ever sell to that asshole. He hasn't played nice since he bought the vineyard. A bully, if you ask me."

"I'll bet that's what he's after, Soph. That might pay off for you. Why not use it to your advantage?" Nick had his hands on his hips, the sunlight doing all kinds of sparkly things to the sweat around his collar and his upper lip.

"And that means he'll level this place. I'd like to save it for someone who will work it, turn it into the beautiful nursery I dreamt of building," Sophie said.

"But Soph," Nick began, "who cares, if he'll give you a good price?"

"I don't care about a good price. I just want enough to pay the debts and a little extra for you two. It's not like I'm going to be around for another ten years to spend it."

Nick nodded his head and looked at Devon. She did, after all, have a point. Why hold out for lots of money if she wasn't going to be around to spend it? And it was the story of Sophie's life. Too stubborn and principled to live in society without rocking the boat and occasionally getting tossed overboard.

But that was why Devon loved her so much.

They'd been working all day repairing the ripped sunshade and tossing dead plants. Devon was wearing one of Nick's old SEAL Team 3 hats. The guys ordered a pizza from a local delivery, with a salad for Devon. Sophie tried a little cottage cheese, but Devon found her throwing it up behind one of the sheds an hour later.

They had a pile of plastic containers and six-packs several feet tall. Marc was shoveling the dead plant material into a wheelbarrow. Sophie had been watering nonstop, and Devon knew something was bothering her.

Devon and Nick were sorting plants and deadheading.

"Never thought I'd enjoy doing this kind of work," he said.

"Know what you mean. Even with the gloves, though, my hands are a mess."

"I rather like your hands, Miss Devon."

"So now it's Miss Devon?" she said tilting her cap up off her forehead. "I guess that's a good compromise. Better than Dev, anyway."

"Sort of makes you sound matronly, though, doesn't it?" Nick said.

Devon threw a dead plastic pony pack at him that hit him squarely in the middle of his back.

"Watch it," she said. But then she smiled and was rewarded when he returned it.

"So, does this count as one of our dates, Devon?"

"I'd say no."

"Ah, so she wants to spend more time with me. That's a very good sign."

She stopped at that one. They were having fun together. The banter was easy. The work wasn't exactly romantic, but she was actually having fun getting dirty and doing physical labor. And now Nick was hinting that he'd like it if she wanted to spend more time with him.

Is this what you want?

Yes, something like that, she thought. Someone she could just be with without pretense.

"So, are you available for dinner tonight, Miss Devon?"

"I think it could be arranged."

"You pick the place. So much has changed here in Sonoma County, I wouldn't know where to take you."

Marc had come up behind Sophie and scooped her up. Now he was wheeling her around the nursery in the empty wheelbarrow. Sophie was screaming at the top of her lungs, and laughing. Marc wheeled her around back and out of sight.

Devon and Nick exchanged glances. "Did I miss something while we were working?" she asked.

Nick took off his gloves and walked towards Devon. He stopped a little closer than he would have before, thighs touching hers. In a swift move, he'd removed her cap, allowing her hair to fall all about her shoulders. "I feel the need to continue your training, Miss Devon." His voice was low and hoarse.

Devon's heart picked up and a thrill tingled down her spine when he placed his big arm around her waist and drew her to him, into him, fully pressing all of her against his firm body so gently, but with such confidence it made her knees wobble.

"Lesson number two," he whispered to her lips just before he claimed them.

She nearly lost her balance but it didn't matter. He wasn't going to let her fall. She clung to him as she feasted on his passion. He was being so careful with her, while showing her his strong need. Her lips opened and his tongue slipped inside, finding hers. She couldn't help but moan and sink into him further.

Their lips parted but he remained holding her pressed against him. "I just couldn't help myself," he said as he kissed her neck. "Do you forgive me?"

With her arms wrapped around his neck and her face pressed against his, she realized she was delighted this big, strong man wanted to kiss her. "Only if you'll agree to kiss me again."

"Gladly," he said as he examined her face. He stroked her cheek with the backs of his fingers. Slowly he inhaled and lowered his lips onto hers.

So many things tumbled through her mind. She thought about how safe she felt for the first time ever. Something about the chemistry between them made her want to please him. She'd been stealing glances all afternoon and a couple of times she'd caught him doing the same. The ache deep down inside her was hard to miss.

His left hand rubbed down her waist, and lower. He gently caressed her bottom and then pressed her closer to his groin. His hand slid up and down her thigh, then up to her waistband and under her shirt. She felt the warmth of his fingers as they squeezed her breast through her bra. His fingers went to probe under the silky fabric. He found her nipple and squeezed it. He was kissing her neck as she found herself whispering, "Yes." She rubbed her face against his cheek, and then whispered again, "Yes, please," into his ear.

She knew that when she didn't make him stop she'd opened the doorway to more experimentation, and the idea thrilled her. Everything about him told her she could trust him. She could rely on him. She could—care—for him.

Was that the word?

Maybe tonight it would happen. That milestone in becoming a woman, the one they say everyone remembers. She'd never felt so ready.

His hand slipped down the front of her jeans and she jerked.

"Sorry," he whispered. "Got a little ahead of myself," he said as he removed it.

She took his hand in hers and kissed it. She placed it back on her breast, outside the shirt. "I'm not used to this. It's all new, Nick."

They stared into each other's eyes. She knew she could trust him.

"Teach me, Nick. Show me."

She saw he understood her meaning. His smile started with the little crease to the right of his lips, then spread to the other side. His eyes danced as he said, "With pleasure."

She halfway expected that he would pick her up just like Marc had picked up Sophie, but the sound of tires on the gravel got her attention.

A sleek, black S600 Mercedes barreled up the road and parked at an angle behind Nick's yellow Hummer. The windows were tinted. A man in a tailored business suit got out and opened the rear door for someone.

Nick and Devon dropped their hands and stepped apart. She put her hair back up under the cap and brushed errant wisps of hair from her face with her fingertips.

The short man emerging from the car had mean eyes. A small pencil moustache accentuated thin lips. His black hair was worn slicked back and was a bit too long over the collar for his expensive midnight blue business suit. The top button on his shirt was undone and he didn't wear a tie.

"Am I interrupting anything, Ms. Brandeburg?" the man said in the clipped accent of the broker who'd called her this afternoon.

"I'd say you're trespassing, Mr. Silva. I told you I'd call you."

"I have my client in the car. She'd like to see the property right now."

"She?" Devon wondered if Sophie had gotten it right about the new owner. She hadn't said anything about a woman owner.

"Miss Chun?" he called to the passenger side of the back seat.

Devon stepped forward and held out her palms. "Wait just a minute here. You have not received permission to look at the property."

"But it's listed."

"Read the remarks. You subscribe to MLS, I'm sure."

"I told you she wanted to see it today. I think it could be worth your while to let her do so."

"No," came the sound from Devon's right. "Get the hell off my property. Devon, I don't give you permission to show it." Sophie was mad, something Devon had rarely witnessed.

"Miss Dunn, please, we're trying to help you out here," Silva said with syrupy sweetness.

"I don't need your kind of help." She was holding an aluminum baseball bat, raising it high and ready. "Unless you want to get a couple of your windows broken, stay off my property."

Silva was pissed. Sick or no, Sophie raised the bat with the full intention of bringing it down on the car, or its passengers. The muscled driver looked uncomfortable and Devon noticed he'd unbuttoned his jacket. Silva slithered back into the passenger seat and closed his own door with a slam. The driver got back behind the wheel and started the engine.

As the shiny obsidian vehicle began to pull out of the driveway, Silva rolled down his window. "I don't have time for stupid games like this, and neither do you."

Sophie took off after the car, screaming at the top of her lungs, surprising everyone who stood behind her. Devon had never seen her so fired up.

With that, the car sped down the road and onto the highway.

CHAPTER 11

Sophie nearly collapsed. Marc ran down the driveway, grabbed Sophie under her shoulders and knees, and carried her inside. Nick understood the *no drama* thing clearly wasn't working. He had recognized that the driver was also an enforcer, even wore the military shades, and from the little Nick had seen of his movements, Nick knew the man had some serious training. Probably ex-military.

"I'm not happy with this turn of events," he mumbled under his breath. He scanned the area to his right, looking to see if he could locate a black vehicle making its way to the property next door, but he saw nothing.

"Sophie never told me much about her neighbor, except that there were some disputes. The guy used to run his tractor over part of her property and had the gall to keep moving the fence inside her property line every time he went back to 'repair' his mistake.

"I know fighting him cost her money," Devon continued. "Surveyors and engineers aren't cheap. And she doesn't trust real estate attorneys.

"Then that's one of the first things we're going to do, make sure the fences are on the property line. Think we can hire an engineer to get this done fast?"

"Our office uses one who seems pretty good. I'll call him and ask. Cost is an issue, Nick."

"Not really. Sophie's not paying for this. I am."

"Let me share in the cost, Nick. I can afford it."

Her offer bothered him. His hands immediately went into fists as he realized she probably made way more money than he did. He'd always told himself that was no problem. Wasn't what he did his job for, but today it kind of sucked.

He had to work on himself to soften his tone, but it came out a little bitter anyway. "No, Devon. When I say I'll pay for it, that's what I mean. Don't question me about something like this."

He finally looked at her face and, yes, he could see she was grappling with what he'd said, and probably about his tone, too. She took several deep breaths and crossed her arms, but remained a bit out of arm's reach.

"Sorry, Dev—on. Didn't mean to offend you. It was a nice offer." Inside, he was wincing. This *being nice* thing, while it was the right thing to do, was eating at him a bit.

Maybe it was because he cared about what she was feeling right now.

In a moment that he knew would feel like some kind of bridge crossed, she said the perfect thing.

"Then, Mr. Tough Guy, I pay for dinner tonight. And I'm not backing down on that one, sailor."

While Devon was checking on Sophie, Nick had a private talk with Marc.

"This is fucked up, Nick."

"Sorry, wish I'd known about it sooner. I apologize for getting you involved in this mess."

"Like always, the messes you get in are my messes, too. Not sayin' I don't tend to aggravate it a bit." Marc's smile was what got him all the attention. That, and his stunning physical condition. He knew Marc had formed some sort of attachment with Sophie, which would have been a no-no at any other time. Most team guys guarded their sisters around their friends like guarding Fort Knox. But this was different.

"That aggravation happen to have hair falling out and sleeps a lot?"

"You got it. She's an incredible woman. And I know the rules. No problem there."

"Not sure, in this situation, if there are any rules anymore. Except I don't want her heart broken."

"I got you. No worries. We've snuggled and fooled around a bit. The woman wants to feel like a woman and not some piece of—sorry, Nick. I just…"

Nick punched him in the arm. His eyes had teared up. "Hey, I'm just glad you're here. Gives me a little alone time with Dev."

"She's off the charts, Nick. And she has the hots for you something fierce. Better slow down or that complication could come at the wrong time, get my drift?"

"Can't. I don't think I can stop it now."

Marc returned a slow glance. Yeah, his buddy knew what was going on inside him. Men didn't talk about their feelings, but the look they shared was completely understood. When a man started to feel territorial over a woman, it meant he was beginning to think of sacrifice and being willing to become something he wasn't before. That was a big step, especially for an elite warrior. Nick knew he had all the symptoms of falling in love.

Marc punched his shoulder. "Well, good luck with that, Nick."

They went outside to organize last-minute details so the team could get it all done tomorrow.

Their attention was sidetracked to a noisy old Toyota driving up the road. The light green dented and faded paint reminded Nick of Gunny's old beater 4-door ex-Parks Department truck back in Coronado. Fredo had one just like it.

A very rotund woman barely five feet tall and nearly that wide extricated herself with difficulty from the car. Nick ran over to be of assistance, but got hit in the chest with her Playmate lunch pail, and it smarted.

"I'm Emma. I'm your hostage nurse," she said in broken English. Her face and dark skin identified her as a Pacific Islander. Marc was smirking with the mis-spoken word.

"Hostage? You take hostages here?" Marc said.

"Hossss-piss!" she corrected herself.

"Welcome, Emma. I'll take you inside and introduce you to Sophie." Nick gripped her lunch pail as he watched the old Toyota barrel back down the driveway. Opening Sophie's door, he found Devon curled up next to his sister, both of them sound asleep. Sophie had her arm around Devon like she was the healer and Devon was the patient.

"Sophie," Nick whispered as he came over to the side of the bed. "Emma is here," he said. Then recognition flooded her face and she stirred, waking Devon.

Nick studied Devon as she sat up, tried to put her hair into a clip and rose to stretch. Her soft gaze fell on his waist and traveled lazily up his chest to meet his eyes. He felt all the spark and excitement he'd felt as a boy going to Disneyland. He'd never wanted anyone so much in his entire life.

"I'm your hossss-pisss nurse, Sophie. My name is Emma," the woman barked.

Sophie struggled to sit up further on the bed. Marc was at her side to pull out the pillows and reset them behind her back.

"Nice to meet you, Emma." She turned to the three of them. "You guys get out of here now. I'd like to take a shower, if you don't mind, and I don't want any curious onlookers." She raised and lowered her eyebrows, finishing on Marc.

"All right. Let's do what the lady says," said Marc.

They closed the door behind them as they walked out. Standing in the middle of the living room with Devon, Nick was sure Marc could feel the intense attraction between the two of them, and Marc confirmed it by excusing himself to go outside. Just before he got through the door, Nick called to him.

"You okay if Devon and I go for some dinner?"

"Sure. Knock yourselves out." Marc saluted and was gone.

"I'd like to freshen up," Devon said to him, her eyes moist and searching.

"I'd like to help you do it, Dev—on."

"You have to wait. You can use the shower after me."

"What about Sophie?" Nick asked.

"There's another shower in the office. I'm going to go use that one." She stepped closer and let her hands travel up his chest. "You'll have to wait until I'm finished. Then you can shower. We'll have dinner, and then let's see what happens."

He bent down and kissed her, clutching her hair in his fingers as he held the back of her head. Holding her face between his palms he whispered hoarsely, "Can't wait."

It was awkward driving in the Hummer with the center console between them, but Nick figured it also heightened the anticipation. They held hands like they'd been doing it for years, he thought. He liked her relaxed style, when she revealed it. But he also liked her tough side. That was what was new for him. He almost liked her tough side better.

He'd been ready to beg her to cancel the dinner plans and just go off with him someplace where they had a roaring fireplace and a big bed. Then she'd stepped outside, ready to go. She had on little dangle earrings, a low-cut, simple black dress that fit all her curves and showed off her flat tummy. The dress stopped just above the knee, so her long legs tempted his soul. She wore more makeup. She smelled great.

Best of all, she'd dressed up for him.

The bumpy ride made the tops of her breasts bounce and he managed to steal a few peeks. He'd adjusted his position several times, but his little head was doing cartwheels again and poking him in the gut with pitchforks. Her bright red lips smiled one time when she caught him.

She directed him to the garage next to her choice of restaurant, a new Tuscan/American bistro. After parking, he got to her door just before she managed to finish her exit.

"This is my job," he whispered as he lifted her down, conveniently "forgetting" the plastic step so he could hold her tiny waist and let her slide down his body. She didn't weigh anything at all, so he drew it out as long as he could, and she didn't squirm to be released any sooner. Her face was flushed when he set her on her feet.

So far so good.

Devon obviously wasn't used to being waited on, and for the life of him, he couldn't figure out why there was no one else around to do it. She tucked under his arm easily as they walked to the restaurant in silence. It was beginning to feel like it would be the longest meal of his life.

Inside a gentle samba was playing. With the tall ceilings and bright artwork everywhere, it felt like an upscale gallery, except for the smell of food and hickory from the wood-fired pizza oven. They were ushered to a table for two in front of a raised fireplace hearth. The waiter removed the reserved sign and scurried off.

"Nice," he said as he held out his hands and she placed hers inside. He rubbed them with his thumbs and fingers as he watched the fire dance in her eyes. Her breathing was erratic and she swallowed a lot. She was nervous too.

"So, help me order. What's good here?"

They opened their menus.

"Anything. It's all good. I usually have the wedge salad and the Mediterranean chicken. Comes with garlic mashed potatoes."

The waiter stepped up to describe a couple of appetizer specials, completing the spiel with, "We also have Hog Island oysters tonight, very lightly salted and sprinkled with mango salsa."

Devon looked up at him and blushed.

"You want some?" he asked, returning a smile.

"Whatever you like. Remember, I'm buying."

"Sort of feel like a kept man." He meant it as a joke, but her eyes turned to lead and her smile evaporated. She lowered the menu and leaned back in her chair.

"A few minutes please," she said to the waiter. She gulped some water and leaned forward on her forearms. "So, just to clear the air here, you are *not* a kept man, and I *resent* any inferences to that effect. I'm not doing this for *you*. I'm doing this for Sophie."

Of course, she hadn't said she was doing it for her, either. And that weighed on him.

The old fear came back. *God, I've blown it.*

She was gulping her water, chewing ice. Yup, she was still nervous. Angry? He tilted his head and examined her. He wondered if it was smart, but he needed to stand up to her or he'd never forgive himself. If there was anything but three more dates and a funeral in their future, he'd have to use this opportunity to tell her the truth.

"Devon, some day you're going to have to trust someone. I just hope you make the right choice, because your radar is all bass-ackwards."

She started a reflexive glare and then stopped herself.

"I'd never do anything to belittle you, hurt you, or intentionally cause you any kind of pain. But you're going to have to give me the benefit of the doubt and quit judging me like I'm some ogre with malfeasance on his brain. You're a lovely lady, but no honorable man appreciates having his intentions questioned, his words dissected or his mannerisms criticized."

He wasn't sure she'd gotten the message. Hell, he wasn't sure if he'd delivered it clearly enough. He wasn't sure exactly what he'd wanted to get across, actually.

The silence between them was killing him. He wasn't going to tone down his statements, though. She'd have to take the whole enchilada or—*Or what?* He could tell she was struggling with something. After a big sigh, she answered him.

"I apologize," she said curtly. Almost too neat. Those red lips were tempting him.. Maybe she was a little more fun when she was angry, but fuck, it wasn't the way he was supposed to act around a lady. Wasn't fair to her. It wasn't what he really wanted, either.

In her occasionally miraculous way, she broke the ice, and he was grateful for it.

"So you won't misinterpret *my* intentions, then?" He could see she was trying to be very proper. No smile on that flawless face. Did he see something devilish lurking there? Or was he seeing what he wanted to see? Her dark eyes and lush lashes glistened in the dimly lit room.

He decided to play along. "What intentions?"

"I want you to start with the oysters."

CHAPTER 12

Devon wished she'd requested a dark corner instead of the fireplace front and center, where everyone's eyes landed when they entered the restaurant. They had no privacy as their legs locked under the table, and they ate holding hands as much as possible. He watched everything she did during dinner with rapt attention. Every time she licked her lips or closed her eyes when she savored something delicious he stopped and watched her, and smiled.

The pressure deep inside her belly grew into a dull ache that demanded release. Her body was giving her all the signals that life for her was about to change. She would no longer be the same woman she was tonight. She would feel the touch of a man's hands on her body, a lover's touch. She wanted him to be the one. What happened in the future would have to take care of itself when the time came. She was going to make this night a gift to herself. An indulgence she'd never allowed herself to dream might happen.

Outside the restaurant he walked her to a nearby park bench. Sitting down, he patted his knee. "Let's talk, Devon."

She did as instructed and sat, leaning her head into the firmness between his neck and shoulder. His arm was wrapped around her, holding her tight against him. Every time she inhaled, she absorbed the scent of him. She heard and felt the steady thumping of his heart, matching her own.

"Where would you like to go?"

She sat up. She'd not thought about that, but of course he had.

"I want it to be special," he whispered into the side of her face as he kissed her hair.

Special? How could it not be special?

"We can go back to Sophie's—"

"No."

Just the way he said it made her panties wet.

"I didn't bring anything. I mean I was expecting we'd go back there."

"Were you, really?" His thumb and forefinger held her chin. His lips rubbed against hers. "I want to make love to you, Devon Brandeburg, and I want to do it right."

His warm lips tasted of the delicious Merlot they'd had with dinner.

"I can't think, Nick. You're going to have to do that for the both of us." She looked up at him and delivered a message she hoped he'd like. "I trust you."

After another lingering kiss, he got up and took her hand. "I have an idea."

They'd entered an intimate reception area with walls decorated with maps and drawings depicting early California history. Artifacts of early settlers in the Sonoma Valley were displayed in glass cases throughout the lobby area. A fireplace large enough to stand up in was at the end of the room. Nick checked them in and told the evening manager there was no luggage. That elicited a quick glance toward Devon.

Beyond the handmade metal doors, the courtyard was filled with the sound of water. They followed a paver-tiled walkway up around the side of a building in back and walked past a water wheel slowly pouring buckets into a koi pond. The pond overflowed into a series of moats and rivulets that circulated all around the courtyard area.

They mounted steps to a pair of hand-hewn doors with a stucco wall separating them. Nick inserted a skeleton key into the doorway to the left and opened it, escorting her into a large room with tall, rustic-beamed ceilings. Centered on a wall covered in old paintings, maps and hanging tapestries was a huge four-poster bed. Directly across the room was a roaring fireplace.

Devon was suddenly shy and her hands felt cold. She went to the fireplace and extended her hands to warm them. Nick stepped behind her and embraced her waist, resting his chin on her right shoulder.

She closed her eyes, reveling in the feeling of his strong arms about her body. The breakneck speed with which she had fallen for this guy worried her a little. But then she remembered his words, "I'd never do anything to hurt you." She did trust him, and knew he spoke the truth.

"You want anything?" he whispered.

"No. Well, yes, but nothing you can fetch. It's right here." Her hand reached back behind his head as she arched into his upper torso. His long fingers migrated up from her waist to the bodice of her dress and breached the low neckline to find her. She loved the sensation of his hands exploring her body.

When she turned, his green eyes were alight with the fire's reflection. The orange glow highlighted golden strands in his hair and his reddish stubble. She lay her head against his chest and listened to his heartbeat. His hands lazily sifted through her hair, rubbing her shoulders. She liked that he was patient, not urgent, though she knew he felt the same intense anticipation she did.

He brought her over to the bed and sat her down. Dropping to his knees, he removed both her high heels and smoothed his palms up her calves to her thighs. His thumbs crossed over her flesh until they met in front. He hooked his fingers on her panties and removed them under cover of her dress.

He stood up and lifted her to him, unzipping her dress while kissing her neck. Her hands felt the muscles in his back ripple as he lifted his arms and removed her dress.

Her shyness came back as she locked her fingers together covering the apex of her legs. Naturally, that was where his eyes focused.

He licked his lips and said, "I'll take it very slow, Devon. You tell me if you want to stop, and I'll stop."

She nodded, putting her forehead just under his chin. His fingers played her spine and migrated down to squeeze her bottom and gently press her against his erection.

Devon began to unbutton his shirt, kissing down the center of his sternum. The light dusting of hair smelled musty and sweet. She continued unbuttoning his shirt and pulling it out of his jeans as their kiss became heated, as their tongues intertwined and she tasted his passion.

He quickly threw off his shirt and unbuttoned his pants, letting them fall to the ground. His penis rubbed against her lower belly and he guided her hands to him, moving them along his shaft. She was surprised at the texture and feel of him, the delicate skin and tracery of veins on the underside.

She wasn't afraid.

Last article of clothing was her bra, which he removed, bending to kiss each of her breasts, one at a time. She kissed the top of his head and soothed his temples with her fingertips.

"Come," he said as he pulled back the coverlet. Large satin pillows fell to the floor. The cream sheets were cool as she sat, then slid under the covers. Soon he joined her and their bodies lay stretched out flesh to flesh, touching the full length as much as possible.

He moved on top of her and they kissed. His pushed a knee between her legs and she found herself straddling his thigh. She clutched him with her knees and felt him press against her sex. A dull ache made her gently slide up and down his thigh, pressing herself against him in an attempt to relieve it.

One of his fingers found its way up between her nether lips, rubbing her clitoris in circular motion, which made her jump. He rimmed her opening, massaging and spreading her folds. He slowly inserted his forefinger inside her and watched her arch up and roll her head back into the pillow.

He kissed her body from her belly button down to the beginning of her mound.

Raising his head up, he said, "I want to taste you."

"Yes," she had no choice but to say, "yes, please."

She raised her knees as his tongue found her nub, which he sucked. Then he slowly delved his tongue into her opening, alternately kissing and sucking her labia. Instantly she was wild with sensation and began to thrash from side to side as he stimulated her clit and feasted on her sex.

"Tell me if you want more, Devon," he whispered as he came up for air.

She was rubbing the top of his head, massaging his temples.

"More," she sighed.

He continued to lap her most sensitive region, patiently stopping to kiss and then alternating with a biting nip on the inside of her thighs.

Something was building deep inside her and suddenly she wanted him buried deep inside her. "Please. Please, Nick. Come here. Show me. Teach me."

He stopped and wrestled with something in his pants, which turned out to be a foil packet. She sat up to watch him place the condom over his cock and smooth it down to its base. Her fingers moved over his tip and down one side of him. His rigid member was now engorged.

Nick crawled over her and pulled her body down the bed, pinning her hands above her head with one of his own. He angled his penis at her entrance, rubbing back and forth along her labia. On one pass, he pushed through inside her, slowly and insistently pressing into her core. She expected to feel some pain but there was none.

He was moving in and out of her slowly, skillfully alternating between rubbing up and down against her sensitized flesh, pushing slowly into her and pulling back out.

He put his arms under her back and pulled her down on him by the shoulders, and that's when she felt the pain of him thrusting deep inside her. Her little moan brought kisses to her neck and breasts. He pulled back and went deeper still, and again she whimpered involuntarily. His rhythm was slow and deliberate. Each stroke filled her and then left her vacant, wanting more.

At one deep thrust, she felt another sharp pain.

"You okay?" he said as he stopped.

"Don't stop."

Nick chuckled. "Who knew the ice queen could be so insatiable? I love being inside you, Devon."

"I don't feel like an ice queen. I feel like your woman."

He hesitated for a second. Devon wondered if she'd said the wrong thing.

"You are."

He pulled her legs up over his shoulders and pumped in a gentle motion until she thought she'd explode, he was so deep. Every stroke made her see stars. Suddenly in a burst of spasms, she felt like she'd been turned inside out. Every part of her sex was tingling and inside her muscles clamped down on him. She was sure it was an orgasm.

Nick's control left him and he began to spasm in concert with her.

"Baby, baby," he whispered.

As their breathing slowed, she cradled his head on her chest, loving the feeling of him covering her body, their legs tangled, sheets mussed. His kisses continued between her breasts and up under her chin, and then slowly they ceased.

Minutes went by while she played the scene over and over again in her mind, knowing it would be something she would never want to forget. And then when she heard him breathing heavily, she realized he'd fallen asleep.

She didn't want to move. He was still barely inside her, so she was careful as she lifted the comforter back over them both, hoping he'd stay there.

Where he belonged.

CHAPTER 13

Nick was dreaming about walking through the Souk in Tunisia, brushing through silks and other soft fabrics with little beads and coins sewed on them. He'd been following someone down into the bowels of the old city. He dared not look at the female shopkeepers shrouded in fabric, their eyes darkened with kohl. He was focusing on the man he needed to take back for questioning. It was an unofficial mission.

As he parted the fabric and entered a doorway he found a red satin pillow with a naked woman waiting for him. At first he couldn't see her fully, except to notice her beautiful white thighs and ample breasts with rosy nipples. She ran her fingertips over them and then gave them a squeeze. Then he realized it was Devon, her body calling to him. Her arms came up to beg him to join her on the bed.

He covered her body. He felt her legs around him, as she arched and pressed herself against him. Her fingers held his cock as one encircled his tip.

She smelled of lemon and cloves and something else spicy. He kissed her lips and felt her tongue inside his mouth. He wanted her.

Then he realized it wasn't a dream. Devon was wrapped around his hips, moving in a slow rhythm, waking him up and reviving his soul in their room at the Waterwheel Inn. His callused hands smoothed over her forehead as he bent down and kissed her hungry lips.

"Hey," he said.

"Hey yourself," she answered. "I've heard sometimes men have to wait a bit to have sex again." She was massaging the hair at his temple and he could see her eyes sparkle in the moonlight streaming through the window. Sounds of the waterfall outside made him feel like he was floating on a mattress in a cool lake. Her supple body melted into him as he felt the softness of her belly, the smooth, creamy surfaces of her inner thighs.

He could tell she wanted him to touch her there again, so he brought two fingers to her sex and massaged her swollen lips.

"How do you feel?" he asked as he bent down and kissed her neck, then grazed her lips, licking and sucking her bottom one.

"You didn't answer my question, Nick. How long?"

"I don't think it's going to take very long, the way you smell, the way you feel under me." He pushed two fingers inside her gently and saw that beautiful arch in her back again, lifting her breasts closer to his mouth. He kissed her there as his fingers moved in and out in slow rhythm.

"Do you like this?" he asked.

"I want you to teach me to be a great lover for you, Nick. I want you to show me how I can make you feel as good as I feel now. Teach me, please."

He groaned and lost himself in the hollows and arcs of her neck, nipping her ear and tasting the soft flesh under her chin, and then her lips.

"I couldn't feel any better, Devon," he whispered.

"I want—"

"Shhh," he interrupted. "We will. In time we'll do it all. There's no race here."

He removed the spent condom and had reached down into his pants for another.

"I think that's sexy as hell that you planned ahead. And you brought more than one."

He smiled as he tore open the packet with his teeth.

"Let me put it on."

She rubbed his shaft and squeezed him at the base. His penis began to grow and harden again as she rolled the condom down, covering him. He enjoyed the feeling of her fingers on him, her tentative explorations. She'd said she wanted to do it all, so he decided another position might suit her.

"Let's try something, baby," he said after she'd fully sheathed him fully.

Coming up to a sitting position, he lifted her body up over his legs, which dangled over the side of the bed. He gently set her down on his lap, positioning her on her knees with her legs on either side of his thighs. He held her by the waist and raised her up over his groin, seated his cock at her opening and pulled her down on him.

Devon's delicious moan made him practically come on the spot. She ground her pelvis into him as he raised her again and then felt himself slide into her deeply.

She tucked her knees under her and quickly discovered she could increase her pleasure, and his, by clenching over him and moving her body up and down, her breasts bouncing with the slapping of their thighs as their speed increased.

"I want it all," she whispered.

He was emboldened again, his cock getting thick and ready to explode.

"Fuck meeeee," she moaned.

He picked her body up and threw her on the bed on her side and entered her from behind with one of her knees bent up, hugging her chest. He seated deep, pushing through her tight opening again and again.

She was coming unraveled and it spurred him on further. She gripped a pillow to her chest as he bit her neck from behind while he plunged in, gripping her hips and slamming her into his groin. He felt her internal muscles contract as she began to whimper out of control. Her back glistened with sweat. He squeezed her bottom and separated her cheeks and dug himself into her deeper to spend as she pulsed under him.

She lay like a limp rag doll under him as he covered her back with his chest. He extended his arms the length of hers, weaving into her fingers as their hands squeezed.

"Oh, God. Nick."

"You okay?" he whispered into the side of her face.

"More than okay," she said into the mattress. "I never knew this is how it would feel. I've been misled. It's way better than it was described."

He laughed and she picked up on it and began to laugh too.

"Who knew? I thought the stuff I read in romance novels was just fantasy. This is even better than that."

"I like fulfilling all your fantasies, Devon. I love bringing you pleasure," he answered.

The sight of her plump bottom thrilled him. He caressed each of her cheeks, reaching around to the front of her and gently rubbing her clitoris, feeling how his cock completely filled her entrance.

"Let's take a little nap, sweetheart."

"Yes," she said, just before she dozed off.

"Sleep well, princess. And we'll see what tomorrow brings."

But she didn't move. He rested beside and against her, spooning to fit into all her delicious curves. He was glad the fireplace embers were still hot. He wanted to watch her naked body rise and fall with each breath, restore itself.

Until he could make love to her again.

Nick saw the rosy beginnings of a new day creep through the windows and wished he'd pulled the curtains shut last night. He wasn't done with the evening. He'd never felt this kind of intensity, been so completely addicted to anyone before.

He'd brought her back on top of him as he lay flat against the pillows, his arm tucked back behind his head. Her head was snuggled up against his chin. Her arm has extended the length of his at the side, with their fingers entwined. Her soft body melted perfectly into his, her legs caught between his, her hip against his. She'd draped her other arm over the pillow next to his ear.

He smiled at how willing she was. How she threw herself into things, especially new things. Her appetite for sex was new, and yet she wore it like a glove that was made for her. He loved being tender with her, and yet couldn't wait to push their boundaries, explore more of her body as her new world opened up. He was glad he was a part of it, at least for now.

Something inside him had shifted. He was standing in a doorway, saying goodbye to his precious sister, and saying hello to Devon. He wasn't sure where it would all lead, but being with Devon seemed so natural. It had happened so fast, but seamlessly. One minute almost sparring partners and the next lovers in one of the greatest nights he'd ever spent.

She'd honored him with her trust. God, he hoped he could live up to that trust. Right now, all he wanted to do was spend the whole day in bed with her. And that wasn't possible. There was lots to do if they were going to be organized enough that the guys could get everything accomplished in the few hours they had before Sophie's closing sale.

Devon stirred. He probed her scalp with his fingertips, massaging her neck and the back of her head. Her silky mahogany curls covered him. Her breasts pressed into him as she slept. She stirred and he felt her satin flesh brush against his chest.

He rolled his palm and felt her fingers cling to his. He massaged the back of her knuckles with his thumb. Small, dainty hands, with red nail polish. What those fingers could do to him. He was a killing machine but could be felled by the touch of her fingertips on his body.

Bending his forearm at the elbow, he lifted her hand to his lips. She arched and raised her head, reading his eyes.

Heaven help him, he thought as he looked into her eyes, he had fallen in love. It was more than a complication. It became something he needed more than just about anything else. The day brightened just seeing her smiling face close to his, feeling her body nestled against him.

They'd barely had a few hours' sleep, and he knew he'd pay for it later, but he realized it was nearly six and time to get up and get ready for the day.

"Glad you're awake," he said.

"But I'm not." She kissed his sternum, moved over and laved his left nipple.

His fingers stroked her backside. He slid his forefinger up her spine and she shivered.

"I want to stay in bed with you all day, Nick."

He chuckled. "It is a wickedly wonderful thought, but honey, we have to get up."

"Make me."

"You mean to wrestle? Challenge my prowess?"

"I could never do that. I like that prowess. But I do like to fight." She kissed his neck and scooted up, her delicious sex rubbing against his thigh, and he was only too happy to press her down to increase the friction. "Love wars. That kind of wrestling."

"I like how you think."

"I love how you feel deep inside me."

Her eyes were lit with a low orange flame he could feel all over his body. He wanted her more each minute they were together.

She came up on her elbows, resting her forearms against his shoulders. The arch reaching up from her firm little bottom to her mid back was smooth, but his hands soon found their way to her rear as he squeezed her against his growing erection.

She slid one knee to the side of his thigh. He massaged her rump and guided her to cover his cock. Holding her gently by the waist, he lifted her up, positioned her for his penetration and slowly let her slide down the length of him.

She closed her eyes as he entered her. She bit her lower lip and winced. Her shudders of pleasure and pain spurred him on. Her lips had formed an open "O" as she rocked against him while he raised and lowered her effortlessly.

He realized he hadn't put on a condom. He stopped.

Her eyes flew open as she looked down on him with concern. She leaned forward, positioning herself on her palms, and kissed him.

"Devon," he said to her hungry lips. "I have no more protection."

"I don't care." She'd migrated to his neck and was kissing under his jaw, licking a tiny trail up to his ear.

"But you should care. We shouldn't—"

"Shhh." She put her fingers over his mouth, and then smiled, tracing his lower lip. She ground down on him, covering his mouth, seeking his tongue with her own.

"Devon," he tried to say between her kisses. "This isn't smart, honey."

"I don't want smart. I want you," she whispered.

He stiffened, not sure he liked the implication.

"Right now, I want your cock, not your brains."

God, he was lost. Pinned by a little bit of a thing, and powerless to get her off him. His little head was having a field day and would be celebrating soon. But something bothered him.

"Am I—" he thought better of it. The realization hit him that he cared for Devon, actually cared for her, while she was thinking he was her first lay. He'd wanted it to be special. Perhaps it was too special. Perhaps she thought it was all in the act and not about caring.

For Nick, making love to Devon was an expression of his intense feelings for her. Not just her body, but also the real flesh-and-blood woman who'd captured his heart.

And apparently it wasn't that way for her.

She was bouncing on his shaft, balancing herself with hands planted on his shoulders. In spite of himself, he arched up with each downward stroke she made, ramming deep inside her. As she orgasmed and pulsed all around him, he held back.

He doubted she knew the difference yet. In time, she'd recognize the signs. But Nick was having second thoughts. He'd been so hot to have her, he hadn't thought about what was right. What was smart. What was worthy of a SEAL's honor.

And this was not it.

CHAPTER 14

They'd showered and Devon used everything she had to get him to make love to her again, but Nick had retreated someplace she couldn't reach. Putting it out of her mind, she decided he'd lighten up later on.

She thought it might excite him seeing her in that pretty little black dress she'd worn last night. When she turned around to have him zip her up, she expected his fingers to find their way inside the fabric to her front side, but he was chaste and just zipped her up, patting her shoulder when he was all done.

He avoided eye contact, too, while they had breakfast in the downstairs courtyard. Engaging him in small talk was useless. He answered, but kept it clipped, as if he was just walking through the motions with her. It finally began to bother her.

So, on the ride back over to Sophie's, she decided to ask him. She'd made sure her dress was pulled high above her knees, and she crossed her legs. But he didn't seem to notice and didn't even take her hand like he had the evening before.

"What's up, Nick?" she finally ventured. The long pause was worrisome. She reached over and grabbed his right hand from the steering wheel. "Did I do something wrong?" She placed his palm on her chest and made his fingers squeeze.

It didn't help. He did smile back, but his eyes focused on their hands and not her face. He pulled his hand away and focused on the road.

"I think we might need to slow things down a bit, Devon," he finally said.

She was shocked. She hadn't considered this. Thinking perhaps she'd misunderstood him, she asked for clarification.

"Slow things down, as in you think I'm asking for some kind of commitment from you? Anything wrong with just enjoying the sex? I can handle *that*, if that's your worry."

It was getting worse. He almost turned green as he winced.

Great, just fucking great.

Then it hit her. He'd gotten what he wanted, and now he was cooling it down. The hunt was over. The rabbit was captured, the warriors had celebrated over a big bonfire. No more game, no more challenge. She was like yesterday's news to him.

"Nothing to be mad at, Devon."

Easy for you to say. She glared back though watery eyes.

"What? What the fuck's wrong with you?" he asked. His head was turning from the traffic back to her face repeatedly, annoyance showing in his tight jaw and lips in thin line.

"You've been quiet and sullen all morning," she started. "Not the Nick I fucked all night long." She couldn't help it. She wasn't going to pretty up her words, since he'd already used the f-bomb. Her emotions were running the show now.

"That's right. I'm not the Nick you fucked all night long." He swerved, almost sideswiping an oncoming car.

"Something wrong with all that? Terrible timing for an attack of conscience. After you've gotten what you wanted."

"Me? You mean after *you* did. In case you didn't notice, Devon, you were the one directing things. All of it."

"What? And you were an innocent bystander?"

"I supplied the cock. Remember? It wasn't my brains but my cock you wanted this morning. I just figured that out. Thanks for the not-so-subtle hint. And, for your information, that was *after* you'd thrown yourself at me and you had me practically trapped. Pinned, as I recall."

That comment made her laugh. "Wait until I tell Marc about this," she said with evil intent.

"Don't you fuckin' dare."

"Oh, Marc, she seduced me," she said in falsetto. "She doesn't love me for me. She only loves me for how many times I can screw her in one night."

He shook his head, mumbling something under his breath. "I knew it was a mistake to get involved with you. I should have listened to my brain and not my..."

Over a span of three or four minutes they rode in silence while Devon realized that perhaps he was right. She'd been so focused on her first experience, she hadn't considered him in the least. She'd lusted for the man in the iron body. She'd demanded he perform the consuming acts of passion with her that she'd dreamed about ever since childhood. And yet, she'd had no regard for him or his feelings.

She flopped back in the seat. "Oh, God," she moaned. With her fingers over her forehead she allowed the tears to trail down her cheeks. How could she have blown something so beautiful?

And now he was totally turned off by her.

"Say something, Devon."

"I think you're right. Maybe we went at this all wrong. It was a mistake."

But her insides were shredding. If she'd known it would hurt so bad the morning after, she'd never have gotten into his bed in the first place.

She closed her eyes, telling herself that was the truth, but all she could see and feel were the colors of his flesh and the ripples in his arms and back, the taste of his kisses and how absolutely wonderful he made her feel.

Maybe it had been worth it, after all.

When they entered the house, Sophie glanced up at her, looking years younger. She'd been cutting up fruit, sitting at the table, while Emma was folding clothes. Sophie glanced over Devon's black dress and her eyes danced as she threw a look at her brother. In spite of her disappointment and pain, Devon found herself blushing and looking at her toes peeking from the sling-back spiked heels he'd so lovingly removed from her feet last night.

Last night! Her stomach ached again. She still felt the tightness and swelling, reminding her how often and how intense their lovemaking had been. She squeezed her hands into fists and didn't want to hear his explanation to his sister.

"I'm going to go change. Be right back to help out," she said as she slipped into the guest room. Even with the door closed behind her, she could hear the discussion in the front room.

"It was a date, Sophie, what can I tell you? He said in low tones. "We're a couple of healthy, red-blooded, American horn dogs. Things happened."

Sophie said something she couldn't make out.

"She's more than fine, Soph. I like her a lot. But I think we got a little carried away."

"Who got carried away?" Devon heard Marc's voice as she slipped off her dress and grabbed her jeans.

Don't think about it, Devon. Get him, get the whole experience out of your mind until you can look at it later. In the meantime, pretend like it never happened.

She put on a red tank top and pulled her hair up in a clip, replacing her dangle earrings with studs. She added some powder and lipstick and a spritzer of perfume and donned her running shoes. They had a lot to do today and there wasn't any time for regrets, or crying over things she could not control.

She joined the little group. Nick gave her a respectful nod but Marc threw her a wide grin, showing his perfect white teeth.

Frowning, Nick consulted his clipboard and went over the to-do list. Most everything that needed doing was outdoors, making Devon glad she'd brought her sunscreen.

"Sophie, can I borrow a hat?" she asked.

Nick was quick to present her with the SEAL Tem 3 cap she wore yesterday.

"No thanks," she said without looking up at him. "You have something with a wide brim, Sophie?"

"Several. Hanging on the back of my closet door," Sophie said as she pointed to her bedroom with a wet knife.

Devon found a large floppy hat with ridiculous flowers all over the top of it. She would not normally wear such a display of nonsense, but today she decided to put on her big girl panties and do all sorts of things that were out of character. Perhaps wearing the stupid hat would take her mind off what was going on inside her.

When she walked outside, Nick threw a pair of gloves at her that hit her squarely on the chest. "I got you pink ones," he said and walked away.

Marc called her over to the greenhouse. "You're on the water detail, missy. And, for what it's worth, I think he needs to be hosed down." He pointed to Nick, who was carting off cinder blocks with a wheelbarrow. She couldn't help but notice the bulging muscles of his shoulders and arms and the trail of sweat already dampening his T-shirt down the middle of his back.

Sophie yelled from the house. "Hours for the sale should be like ten to three? What do you guys think?"

Nick turned to Marc and they shrugged in unison.

"I'm thinking all day," Nick hollered back, "like ten to five. And you're placing the ad for Sunday, too?"

"Nope. I say we sell it all on Saturday. Sunday maybe we can use the guys to haul off what didn't sell, and get everything cleaned up and cleared out," Sophie shouted out the door. "Devon, that work for you?"

Devon nodded and picked up the hose to begin her chores.

She welcomed the almost mesmerizing sound of the water as it sprayed out and gave glistening sustenance to the plants underneath. She'd never wanted a yard and had an upscale townhouse in a trendy part of Santa Rosa, close to dozens of boutique shops and gourmet restaurants. But she felt the pulse of living things as she tended Sophie's garden. In only a few days all of this would be gone. A few weeks and Sophie would be gone as well. Thinking about life's fragility and the temporary nature of things gave her a hitch in her throat.

Nothing lasts forever.

Virgins don't stay virgins forever. Friends die.

Devon got a call from her manager an hour later.

"You working today?" he asked.

"Sort of. Helping Sophie get ready for the cleanup and big plant sale this weekend."

"That's the nursery property on Bennett Valley?"

"Yes."

"I've gotten a couple of voicemails from a Mr. Silva—"

"He has a lot of nerve. Tried to show the property yesterday, brought his client and everything without calling ahead of time."

"He says you aren't returning his calls. He wants to present an offer with me and make sure I get it to the seller, bypassing you. So, Devon, I gotta ask, what's going on? You two have some history?"

"Sophie has some history with him. It's a long story, but Sophie doesn't want him on the property."

"She can't exactly do that, if it's listed. He's talking discrimination, due to his Hispanic surname. His client is minority as well."

"He's bad news, Joe."

"But we can't violate the law just because someone's a creep."

"I put a notice in MLS about showings starting Monday. If that doesn't work, I'll just withdraw it until Monday."

"I think I'd rather have you do that. Put a note it will be re-listed on Monday. But keep that Agency Disclosure on you at all times. Sounds like he might force the issue."

"Force the issue on a dying woman, Joe. There has to be a law protecting Sophie from harassment."

"Then you call the police, understood? Next time he shows up there, you inform him that's what you're going to do. I'm going to call him back right now and tell him the same thing."

She hung up and removed her gloves. Dashing into the office, she got her laptop out and logged in, pulling up the MLS information on the property. She checked her briefcase for a change order form and found one wrinkled and folded at the bottom. Taking the paper and pen, she bolted to the door to look for Sophie, and ran straight into Nick's chest.

His familiar smell, the rivulets of sweat coming down the side of his neck, and in damp patches under his arms, added to the sheer masculinity of his size compared to hers. He'd grabbed her waist, which was good since she probably would have lost her balance.

The paper was jammed between them and the pen went flying. She got her balance, and scurried after it.

"Excuse me," she said as she walked around him. "Need to find Sophie."

"She's over by the water tank, but Dev—"

She didn't want to wait or look at him, and walked a determined straight line towards the tank. Not seeing her friend, she walked round the side and caught Sophie in an embrace with Marc.

Before they could see her, she backed up and again came in contact with Nick's granite torso.

"I tried to tell you," he whispered.

Devon's cell phone rang again and she swore.

"Joe, I'm getting a change order signed right now. I'll change the status in two minutes. Be patient with me," she said to her manger again.

"Not why I called, Devon. Forgot to remind you tonight is the company awards dinner. I'm just making sure you're coming. You're getting an award, you know."

At first the thought of the awards dinner turned her stomach, but suddenly the distraction of being anyplace but here at Sophie's, in Nick's company, felt welcome.

"I'll be there."

"You bringing anyone?"

"Nope," she said as she watched Nick's sweat-stained back retreating from her, "I'll be coming alone tonight."

CHAPTER 15

Devon left just as the sun was sinking low in the sky, casting a golden glow over everything, even the dilapidated but remarkably sparse greenhouse site.

With Sophie's blessing, the listing had been temporarily withdrawn. Then she sneaked off to leave without saying goodbye. Nick knew he was part of the reason she'd pulled away from all of them, so he caught her just before she left.

"Devon, you still sore with me?"

"Shouldn't I be?"

"I think we should talk about it."

"Yeah, whatever *it* is," she said sarcastically.

"I still think we should talk."

"Well, I've got dinner to go to and you have all your buddies arriving at any moment, so we'll both be busy."

"Are you coming back here tonight?" he asked. He wished she'd asked him to go with her.

"I'm wondering if I should. But I promised Sophie." Her eyes held pain and sadness, or was it fear? He'd been hoping that keeping his distance would soften her stiffness, but he could see it hadn't.

"Well. It makes a difference to me. I want to talk to you."

"Fine. I'll be back here around nine or so. Will that fit into your schedule?"

"Don't do this, Devon," he begged.

"I'm slowing things down, just like you wanted."

"Right." He stepped back and waved to her. "Have a good time, then. See you later. And please be safe."

He watched the Lexus as a cloud of dust trailed behind it all the way to Bennett Valley Road, and then disappeared into the early evening. Part of him wanted to go follow her. He hoped she'd be safe.

It hadn't been more than a few minutes when the boys from Coronado showed up. They'd managed to drive straight through. They were hot and dusty from the long trip, and Nick was glad Devon wasn't around for the room full of eau de armpit. She'd been so quiet and into herself that no one, not even Sophie, had been able to engage her in conversation. He wondered how she'd handle the crowd when she got back.

The parking lot looked like a Hummer road rally. Kyle's black one was pulled in right next to Nick's. There were two others, plus Fredo's beater, which was the only vehicle that looked like it belonged at the nursery.

Sophie eyed the beater with lust. "Now we're talking. This is a truck you can actually use for work."

His LPO shook Sophie's hand and stepped aside, waiting for the rest of the team to do the same. Cooper's six foot four frame towered over her, but his voice was gentle as he told her he was the fixit man.

"Sophie, Cooper was born under a tractor. He sleeps with parts," Nick informed her.

"But I like my wife's parts way better," Coop said. He got some catcalls and punches in the arm for that remark.

Fredo stepped forward, "Yeah, some of those parts is toys, too." He grinned and greeted her. "I'm Fredo."

"Sophie, this here is Malcolm, we got Rory here, Ty, Armando and Grady."

"Geez," Sophie said. "Is San Diego still safe when all you guys are up here?"

"Think the question is, are the ladies of Sonoma County safe with us here?" someone quipped.

The general mumble and laughter were just what Nick needed to feel around him. Things would finally be okay.

Pizza delivery was arranged and the group began to set up sleeping bags around the living room. Malcolm and Tyler took over the office. Sophie had a fire pit out back and a hot tub off the back deck, so several guys were soaking while others had pulled up black plastic five-gallon plant containers and wine barrel halves to sit by the fire. Fredo was giving Cooper a hard time about the news his wife, Libby, was pregnant.

"I was wondering why it took you a whole six months to knock her up, man," he said.

"I was practicing for the kill shot, Fredo. You know I have to practice."

"Training is everything. Here's to being perfect," Malcolm Jones said and raised his long-necked beer to the stars. Those who could clinked glass on glass.

Sophie was resting against Marc's chest in a lounge chair. Marc was without alcohol, but sipped on mineral water like Coop, who never drank.

Nick went over plans for the next day, using the list he and Sophie had created. Within ten minutes all the assignments were delegated.

"So Nick, where's your lady?" Fredo asked.

"She's not my lady, you dickhead. She's Sophie's best friend."

"So, where is she?" Cooper asked.

Marc piped up. "She's at a company dinner."

"She's being given an award," Sophie added.

"Really? That's cool." Fredo said.

Soon the fire pit in the center of the back yard began to die down to orange embers, illuminating their faces like the pits on the beach in San Diego they frequented with their families. They'd brought several cases of beer, and nearly all of them were gone already. Bottles littered the ground, but Nick knew they'd be stacked and stowed before the team hit the sack.

"I appreciate all you guys coming to help out." Nick said.

A series of grumbles and expletives littered the evening air. But there was no objection. A road trip was always something the guys enjoyed.

"Like I told Nick several times, I was willing to pay for a motel. You don't have to hang out here."

"Shit, Nick never told us that," Kyle blurted out. There was multiple agreement. Sophie cast a panicked look to Nick, who waved it off as a joke.

"No, Fredo here was the only one who wanted the motel, but he was outvoted," he said.

Emma demanded Sophie go to bed, and came out with the wheelchair. Marc picked her up and carried her to the back bedroom. Emma followed huffily, pushing the empty, squeaking wheel chair and scraping it on the woodwork as she rounded the corner.

Several low whistles traveled through the crowd.

"Marc's being a real hero. He know what he's doing?" Kyle asked Nick with concern.

"I'm cool with it under the circumstances," Nick answered. "Distraction can be a good thing for pain."

That had a sobering effect on the group.

"So, Kyle, I was surprised Timmons let you all come up here together."

"You complaining?"

"Not at all."

"I have to check in with him tomorrow night. He doesn't know Tyler and Malcolm came. I'll let him know then."

Marc returned and grabbed a beer, taking up a seat by the fire.

"Guess who else wanted to come?" Fredo asked.

Nick stared back at him.

"Gunny and Sanouk," Fredo said. Former Gunnery Sergeant, "Gunny," ran a no-frills, rusty old gym in Coronado where the team guys like to hang out. He had recently been reunited with a son he had fathered in Thailand, the first he'd ever met of his many offspring that littered the globe. Gunny was known for doing the right thing and marrying the woman first before he'd have sex with her. But, while he believed in marriage, he didn't believe in divorce.

"Sanouk's mother's coming out, and it's got Gunny in several shades of panic. He's even hired cleaners to polish up his gym," Coop informed him.

"No shit. This must be serious," said Nick.

"He's got a little time to make it right. Gunny's not doing well, Nick," said Kyle.

"Sorry to hear that."

An hour later, Nick heard Devon's car pull up front and soon she walked through the back door, clutching a large crystal shard on a pedestal in her right hand. She was done up in the little black cocktail dress Nick remembered peeling off her the night before. He blushed as he looked at her delicate ankles and toes strapped up in the high heels he vividly remembered slipping off her sexy feet. Her dark brown curls cascaded over her head, held up with little crystal clips that sparkled in the moonlight. Nick could smell her perfume and wished he'd been allowed to accompany her. She was a goddess, a vision. His gut was filled with regret at how they'd left things earlier. And she was scoring major points with the guys.

Instantly, all the men rose to attention. It made Devon step back in a brief moment of panic.

"Wow. Easy there," she said. Nick loved the nervous lilt to her voice when she was on new territory. "Should I be scared?"

"Devon this Kyle, my LPO—Lead Petty Officer, sort of our leader," Nick said. He hoped he'd get a smile from her, but she remained cold.

Kyle stepped forward, extending his hand. "Only when we're getting shot at and shit. Around women, they're all on their own. Nice to meet you, Devon."

"This is Cooper. He's our medic," Nick said.

"Nice to meet you, ma'am."

"There's that term again. What am I fifty years old?" Devon had gotten all prickly.

Nick knew her nerves were getting the better of her.

"You have a problem with your age, Dev?" Marc asked.

"Devon. It's Devon."

Several of the guys chuckled.

"What's so funny?" she demanded. Nick was in a bit of pain, seeing the pit she was digging.

Kyle gave his silver-tongued version of the facts, which was something he was really good at. "Devon, it's a term of respect. We call each other's wives ma'am, their mothers, their sisters, all ma'am."

"And we don't talk to their daughters if we can help it." Jones said.

That brought laughter again.

"Whatever," Devon said as she cut off their laughter with a little nervous one of her own. "Please, don't stand up for me. I'm not the queen here. Sophie is."

The men sat. A somber tone had permeated the group. Nick knew they were all assessing, evaluating, checking their surroundings, and looking for signs of something from each other.

The silence appeared to flummox Devon a bit.

"Well, I thank you for coming. Sophie and I, and—" she glanced at Nick and Marc nervously, "are thrilled to see she has so much help."

"You're welcome," was the answer, almost in unison.

"So, let's see, I haven't met you yet," she walked over to Fredo, who stood.

"I'm Fredo, this here is Rory."

"Dev—on. If this property doesn't sell, Rory here is an expert at setting things on fire," Marc volunteered.

"Excuse me? Why on earth would I want to have you burn down this property?"

Nick decided he had to explain. "Rory here had a few rocky teenage years in foster care, didn't you, Rory?"

"Fuckin' system—pardon me, ma'am," Rory said as he nodded to Devon. "Every time I went to a new foster home I hated, I'd burn their garage down."

Laughter bounced around the group again. Nick could see a scowl creeping over Devon's pretty forehead.

"That's illegal," she said.

"Yes, ma'am. I was counting on the authorities to take me away. Juvenile Hall was way better than some of the foster families I had to stay with."

"So I suppose you set things on fire now, is that right?"

"Damn straight. Courtesy of Uncle Sam."

"He's one of our explosives experts, Devon," Nick added.

"Great," she said. "Anything else I should be aware of about this crew of yours, Nick?"

"They're an acquired taste," he answered. Everyone laughed again.

Emma, the hospice nurse came barreling out onto the patio. "Please, you must stop this at once. You have awakened her." Emma's rotund body shook as she delivered her huffy proclamation. "I must ask you to leave."

From inside the house, Nick could hear his sister's voice, screaming, "Eeeemmmmmaaa! Get me the fuck out of this bed!"

The SEALs laughed but Devon wasn't in the mood.

"She needs to rest, guys. Come on, this isn't like party time, here," Devon said.

As the men started to clean up their bottles, Marc brought Sophie out to the patio in his arms. Emma followed behind with the wheelchair, and a disgusted look on her face.

"Hey, Devon."

Devon gave Sophie a kiss on her cheek after Marc deposited her on the lawn chair. "Glad you're back. Can you get a load of these guys? You and I and all these hunky men? I'm going to die a happy woman."

They paused at first, but since Marc and Nick were laughing, the rest of the team did as well. Devon remained icy, with her arms crossed over her chest.

"I seriously wish I could entertain you, but I just can't. I do appreciate the help."

"No problem. We do this all the time. Help out," Kyle said.

"Marc, sit with me for a bit," she asked.

Emma left the wheelchair and stormed back into the house.

Devon sat down next to Sophie on the lounge before Marc could get there. "You like that woman?" she asked. "She's mean."

"Nonsense, Devon."

"Well, Sophie, I'm picking up that Emma doesn't want you to stay up too late, so, if you don't mind." Kyle began as he stood. The other team members stood as well.

"No. Don't go. I have something I want to say to all of you, now that Devon is back," Sophie started. "Sit!"

Immediately everyone sat back down.

"I want to thank all of you for protecting my little brother here. And for supporting him with your presence here tonight. It means a lot to him, and it means a lot to me."

"No problem."

"One other thing," Sophie continued. "I want to thank you for taking my brother and turning him into a man. For making him the fine man he is today."

"Sophie, he's been there for us, too," Armando said. "We're family, and family comes first."

Sophie was letting tears stream down her cheeks. Nick knew no one was going to wait around much longer. "Devon here," she placed her hands on Devon's shoulders and shook her slightly, "doesn't know much about your ways, but I've heard the stories Nick has told me. So, go easy on her, okay?"

"Yes ma'am," came the unison response. Nick could see Devon's nervousness. She glanced up at him, and then lowered her eyes. She was clutching her crystal award in her lap.

"We're going to sell every plant we can, the equipment, carts. Everything. What doesn't sell, we'll stack up neatly and take to the dump, or find some place to donate it," Sophie finished. "It's going to be a red-letter day."

Kyle stood, as did everyone else but Devon and Sophie.

"So, we'll see you tomorrow at oh-seven hundred, Sophie," Kyle said.

"What about breakfast?" Devon asked.

"We'll be going out for breakfast at six. We'll make it back over here by seven. That work for everyone?" Kyle asked again.

"No." Devon said. "I'll have breakfast ready here at six."

"That's not necessary m—Devon," Kyle answered softly.

"But I want to. And I think Sophie would enjoy it...right, Soph?"

"If I'm up. Why don't you guys do that? Least we could do for you."

"Well thanks. A home-cooked breakfast would be nice."

"What do you guys eat?" Devon asked.

There was shuffling and mumbling back and forth. Nick spoke up, "Scrambled eggs, orange juice, pancakes, biscuits, sausage, bacon and fruit, plus lots of coffee, and perhaps a couple bloody Marys."

"And cinnamon rolls," Jones added.

Nick saw the resolve in Devon's jaw. "Done."

The men said their goodbyes. Sophie whispered to Devon. "You're holding out on me. I didn't know you could cook."

Devon whispered back, "I can't cook worth a damn. Only breakfast. I only cook eggs, bacon and such. I'm hoping I can help someone else with the pancakes."

Sophie beamed. "Good girl. Thanks for being the hostess I can't be right now. We'll have fun tomorrow."

After the guys left, Emma wheeled Sophie back to her room. Nick, Devon and Marc went back onto the screened porch at the back of the house. Sounds of the guys getting their bedding out and settling down drifted through the doorway.

"Okay, so I better get to the store," Devon whispered with a sigh.

"Not a chance. I got this. Keys, please?" Marc said to Nick.

While Nick was fishing in his pants for the keys, Devon took sixty dollars out of her purse and handed it to Marc. He backed away with his palms out.

"Nope. Put that away."

"Please, I insist. I know I can afford it, especially with what they pay you in the military."

"Wouldn't even consider it," Marc said stiffly and walked out. He slammed the front door behind him.

"He pissed at me?" Devon asked.

"What do you think?" Nick was sitting on the porch railing. "Come here, Devon."

"No."

"Come here. I want to say something to you." He tried for a warm smile, but Nick noticed she didn't want to let her guard down. She walked to within arm's length of him. Nick wiggled his fingers to ask her to come further forward, and she took one small, deliberate step closer. "One thing you need to know about these warrior types. Maybe it will help you in the future, if you ever actually want to score some points with them. Maybe not." He shrugged. "But I feel compelled to tell you that if they offer their services, you always say yes. Always."

"What if those services are something you don't think is morally sound?"

He could tell she was embarrassed, fearful of revealing too much about her feelings. But he could tell what was on her mind, just under the surface of her consciousness.

"Dev." He looked up at her and put a finger to her lips. "I like calling you Dev, and I don't think that shows you any disrespect."

He took both her hands in his. "I'd like to negotiate a truce. Start over. But I need you to do your part. Don't ever question the integrity or honor of these guys again."

"But I just wanted to pay for—"

"Shhh." His finger went to her mouth again. He wanted to rub it along her lower lip, but her sharp inhale made him realize he had to be careful with her right now. "What you offered to do was real nice. Real nice. You cook, and you can order us all around the kitchen and demand we do the entire cleanup. But don't stop us from being who we are. And do not question our intentions."

CHAPTER 16

Devon was alone in the guest room after Nick said his gentle good nights. She leaned against the door, her insides doing flip-flops. Tonight had been confusing. She'd been so sure she was justified in her anger towards Nick earlier, in spite of his efforts to speak with her before she left for the awards dinner, but now she was halfway hoping they could have that talk.

She thought about everything that had happened tonight. On the way to the dinner she'd gotten another call from the broker representing the owner next door, and even though she reminded him the listing had been pulled from the market temporarily, he let her know he wasn't going away. The speakerphone was loud, so she'd adjusted it down.

"I don't think you understand. Miss Chun—"

"You mean Mr. Rodriguez." Devon knew the owner of the winery next door was the real force behind the interest.

"Well, yes, he is involved too, yes. But it would be so much easier if Miss Dunn would just cooperate."

"Or what?"

"I'm sorry, but it would be to her advantage."

"Are you threatening me, Mr. Silva?" she asked.

He nervously chuckled. "Of course not, Miss Brandeburg. What a preposterous idea."

"Then stop calling me. You and your client will have the same opportunity to buy the property as anyone else. That's the way I do things. That's the way it's going to be."

She'd hit the end call button on her steering wheel and decided not to pick up if he called back.

The rest of the long country road journey had a chilling effect on her, until she reached the city limits and the safety of streetlights and well-lit intersections.

The awards ceremony had dragged on too long. All evening she'd kept looking at the vacant chair next to her, which had been provided by her broker. Nick could have been sitting in that chair. Nick could have twirled her around the dance floor. Even though she had still been angry with him at the time, she also knew he would have made her feel safe.

After the presentations, she was honored with the overall top producer award for the previous year. The clear leaded crystal triangle was engraved with her name and the company logo. It stood nearly a foot tall and was rather heavy. She begged out of staying longer, saying goodbye to several of her co-workers who were beginning to make a spectacle with alcohol. It was time to leave.

The nervousness had returned on her long trip back to Sophie's, because she knew something was very off about the neighbor and the odd broker call today. Even the jazz station she'd turned on didn't help as her Lexus traveled over the near pitch-black country road back to Sophie's. Every little spark of light caught her attention as she imagined a car darting out from one of the blind driveways she passed. Even the headlights of oncoming traffic made her jumpy. She worried that the distant lights behind her belonged to someone following her, and was relieved when they turned off on a side road.

The scene in Sophie's parking lot, which resembled a Hummer convention, made it clear there would be no private talks with Nick tonight, and maybe never, since they obviously would not have any privacy.

Nick's little lecture just before they'd said goodnight also bothered her. Tomorrow was going to be a long day. She knew she'd probably step on toes again. For being such a bunch of tough guys, they sure had thin skin. Why was it *her* job to walk on eggshells? What was wrong with a girl asking to pay for things if she wanted to? Was that not her right to spend her hard-earned money how she pleased? Some of her anger returned. She sighed and tried to put it all out of her mind.

She shed her clothes, listening to the sounds of men showering and walking back and forth outside her door as they readied for bed. She wondered where Nick was going to sleep tonight. She remembered the big bed, and the fireplace, as she slipped between the cool sheets of Sophie's guest room. Missing was the smell of his chest and the feel of his arms around her.

Someday. She'd had a taste of something wonderful, and she wanted it again. If it could happen once, it could happen again.

Am I waiting for Prince Charming…or waiting for Nick?

Her heart gave a big shrug.

Light streamed into the little bedroom early. Checking the clock, she panicked. It was already 5:30. She heard noise in the kitchen.

Pulling on her jeans and T-shirt, she glanced at herself in the mirror. She'd forgotten to take the clips out of her hair, and it looked like the pelt of a wild brown bear, done up in sparklies. Quickly she removed the rhinestones and pulled her hair back in a scrunchie. Adding some lipstick, she dashed into the hallway and ran into someone who knocked her back into the doorway.

His familiar scent had sent a chill down her spine even before their bodies collided. His gravelly whisper was soft and sensual.

"Sorry, Devon. Didn't mean to—"

"Oh, don't worry about it. After all—" She was suddenly remembering what they'd done in the motel and she couldn't finish. Looking up to his face, she softened. "I'm good with the truce thing." She felt short of breath.

He sighed. "That's good to hear."

They stood awkwardly until Marc appeared round the corner. "Ah! There's the cook. Your services are needed, ma'am," he commanded.

Devon smiled back up at Nick this time. She placed her palm against his chest in a small farewell gesture. He was quick to give it a squeeze. Just that little touch of his hand on hers brightened her spirits as she turned to follow Marc. And then she heard something that sent her heart racing. Nick stepped to her backside, his chest against her. The rumble and vibration of his voice set her on fire.

"Um, Marc, buddy. I gotta have a little chat with Devon for a sec. Can you cover for her?"

Marc gave them an appraisal with full approval. "Sure, man. You got it. Half these guys aren't up yet anyway. Go have your talk."

Devon felt Nick's large paw grab her hand as he wheeled her around and drew her into the guest bedroom, closing the door behind him. Her chest was pounding as he pressed her against the door, his big shoulders and arms completely encircling her body, holding her tight to him. He bent down and gave her a deep, penetrating kiss.

Coming up for air, he whispered, "Sorry, just had to do that, baby. I couldn't help myself."

It was exactly what she wanted to hear. "Nick I'm so ashamed of how I've acted. Like a child."

"Sweetheart," he whispered while he layered kisses under her chin, under her ears and down her shoulders, "I love the way you act. The way you smell. I love watching you get mad, I—"

She was aware he was stopping himself from saying something he might regret. She was sliding into the pool of warm water where it didn't matter anymore what they said. She'd gladly follow him anywhere right now.

His hands roamed over her breasts. He lifted her T-shirt, and the feel of his tongue and lips on her nipples made her sex tingle with anticipation. She needed the feel of this man's fingers, his mouth, all over her body.

He hitched her up and placed her thighs above his hips, wrapping her legs around his lower torso. She moved herself against the buttons of his jeans, squeezing with her thighs, telegraphing her wanton need of him.

"I want you inside me," she whispered between kisses.

Nick's gentle moan was his answer. "Baby, this will have to be quick."

"I don't care. I need you."

He arched back to look into her eyes with a frown line in the middle of his forehead. "You need me or my cock?"

Her hands smoothed over his bulging shoulders and up his neck. She pressed her breasts into him. "I need you *and* your cock, and I am totally unashamed to say it. I need you to make love to me, make me feel the way you did before. As only you can do."

He let her slide down as he urgently removed her pants, then got to work on his own. With his cargo pants down at his ankles he turned and they nearly fell onto the bed.

"Baby, baby, baby, I haven't been able to think of anything else but you."

"Me, too."

"You sure?" he said as he positioned his penis over her wet opening. He was without protection.

She placed her hands on his buttocks and pulled him into her. He gladly rooted deep inside, angling up, raising her thighs over his as he sunk in deep, gripping her hips.

She was delirious with pleasure. He filled her, warmed her, and ignited her insides. Everywhere he touched and kissed and sucked she gave back to him willingly. Her body was his completely.

"I need you," she said again. "Is it possible to need someone too much?" she whispered to his neck and the side of his face. "I've become addicted to you. Tell me that doesn't scare you. Please."

"Baby," he said as his cock began to lurch. "Nowhere else I'd rather be. This is my world, right here. I want—" his seed began spurting just as Devon's insides clamped down and she began a rolling orgasm to his tempo. "I want this to last forever."

It was a spur-of-the-moment comment, and for a second she felt the panic of commitment sizzle through her. But his scent, his soft moans into the pillow, the feel of his damp hair at the nape of his neck and the way his hands kneaded her buttocks as he filled her, urged her to step through the doorway she'd avoided before. She gave her whole body and soul to him in that moment. He had claimed her as much as she now claimed him.

She wanted to belong to him.

Forever.

Fresh from the glow of their quick lovemaking, Devon and Nick entered the kitchen.

Marc had made a bowl of drop biscuit batter and preheated the oven. He shoved three dozen eggs into Devon's hands and gave her another wink. "Go crack some eggs, lady," he said. Devon got to work after Nick kissed her neck and sent a warm blush back to her cheeks. She couldn't help but smile and decided not to hide her feelings for him any longer .

Exactly at oh-six-twenty a breakfast feast was laid out on the plank tabletop. Several under-the-breath comments were made about what had delayed the cook, and Devon's cheeks flushed, but she didn't care. Eight hungry sailors devoured three pounds of bacon and sausage, two fresh pineapples, two pitchers of orange juice, homemade biscuits with real butter, pancakes and syrup, three dozen scrambled eggs, and a pint jar each of Sophie's salsa and orange marmalade. Hardly a word was spoken. They were eating machines, reaching over each other without asking to help themselves to whatever they wanted. There were smiles all around and appreciative moans of approval, especially over Sophie's homemade marmalade and salsa.

Never in her life had Devon seen so much food consumed so quickly. In barely a half hour nearly everything was gone. Fredo and Cooper cleared the table. Nick began washing dishes and Devon grabbed a couple of tea towels and started drying, placing the cleaned plates on the table. By seven everything was put away, cleaned, floor swept, counters wiped down and the crew was outside ready for work.

Devon asked Marc how Sophie was.

"Still sleeping. Got the evil eye from Emma." He shrugged. "Think I'll make sure I stay useful."

Devon stopped him from leaving the kitchen. "Marc. Thanks for this. For what you're doing for Sophie, and Nick. For me."

"You got it, kid. She's a lovely lady. She deserves way more out of life, but I can't do anything about that. So I'm here now."

"Just thank you, Marc. Really."

"You're a doll, Devon. Take good care of my buddy's heart now, will you?"

"No worries there."

He lifted her chin with his thumb and forefinger. His azure blue eyes were warm and gentle. Not the face of a trained killer. He was a man, as they all were, who understood what life was, because he had an up close and personal relationship with death. "He's a good man, and I'll kick your butt if you do anything to hurt him. He's pretty snagged."

"Snagged?" she asked.

"As in you got the golden cuffs on him and he wants to be captured. Get my drift?"

Devon smiled. "Yes. And that's exactly where I want him to be."

"Okay. Just be sure you know what you're doing. It's an intense thing getting wrapped up in our community. I won't lie to you, some women can't take it. Watch yourself, Dev."

"Devon," she corrected him.

He smacked her on the butt, turned and left the kitchen.

Devon started dragging an ice chest outside, but got barely two feet from the door of the office before the tall one, Cooper, was there to pick it up. While Coop was several inches taller than Nick, he had the same muscle mass in his shoulders, and sported a variety of unique tats, including the same frog prints that Nick had going up his right forearm from wrist to inside of his elbow. He looked up and gave her a respectful grin.

"Where you want this, darlin'?"

"Just put it inside the greenhouse there to the right under that platform. I'll fill it with ice."

"No can do." He set the chest down and whistled to his cohorts. "I need two able-bodied frogmen to help this little lady out," he bellowed.

Shovels and rakes were dropped and soon there was a line of hunky guys standing at perfect attention, chests out, staring straight at her.

"You're gonna have to choose, Devon," Coop said.

She walked up to Nick and placed her palms against his chest, slid them up the luscious territory to the back of his neck, weaving fingers together and pulling his head down. "Well, this one," she said on tiptoes as she pulled him to her, "I've already chosen."

As soon as their lips touched, Nick's hands migrated to her butt and he lifted her, wrapping her legs around his hips. The line went crazy with whoops and catcalls.

"That's what I'm talking about," bellowed Cooper. "Damn, I'm getting homesick."

"I think you guys better go inside and get the ice," said Kyle. "In fact, I'm making that an order, sailor."

"Yessir," Nick said as he kissed her neck.

Devon looked over his shoulder at the admiring crowd and was caught off guard when Nick hoisted her up over his shoulder and ran for the office door with her slung over like a sack of potatoes.

She watched the men go back to work as Nick carried her into Sophie's sales office. He pulled her off his shoulder and slid her down his torso slowly. With his hands entwined in her hair, he removed her clip and bent down and gave her a mind-numbing kiss. Devon's insides turned to flames.

"We're supposed to be getting the drinks and ice."

"I can use ice," he said as he kneeled and kissed her belly under her T-shirt. "You want some ice, baby?"

"Sophie's going to be up soon."

"We seemed to do pretty good before breakfast. How about a round two? Just another quickie."

"Hardly seems fair," she gasped as his fingers slid down the front of her pants to find her. "Everyone else is working so hard outside, and here—" She gave another sharp inhale as two of his fingers found their way into her opening.

"I'm working hard too, Devon."

She glanced outside. No one was paying attention to them, even though the doorway was open. While she was checking to make sure the coast was clear, Nick had unbuttoned her pants and had removed her T-shirt. He stood.

"I've got an idea." He led her around the bench table to the storeroom where Sophie's cot was. He slid his cargo pants down, sat on the cot, let her pants fall to her ankles. She stepped out of them and stood before him fully naked. He guided her over to sit on his lap, legs spread to the sides. Holding her waist in his massive hands, he adjusted her to slide down his shaft.

She gripped the tops of his shoulders as he bounced her up and down on him, her knotted nipples rubbing against his warm chest. He was so deep, and she still wanted more. Her swollen tissues were sore, but she wanted him any-way. He adjusted his pelvis, leaning back and bracing the weight of both their bodies on his palms gripping the edge of the cot. He rolled his hips and ground into her in smooth movements that were urgent, demanding, and relentless.

Her orgasm was quickly coming on her. "Oh! Niiiick!!"

He sucked her breasts, teasing her nipples with a little bite that made her jump. She held herself against his chest, wrapping her arms around him as her muscles milked his cock. As he lurched and began to come, she drew back to watch his face, then softly leaned back into him to nibble on his lips.

"Love this, baby," he said between kisses.

"Yes," she sighed. "I want you more each time we—" Her orgasm sent the delicious shudder down her spine. When she opened her eyes, the look he gave her showed his need. It was something she wanted to remember forever.

Nick hauled two bags of ice to the cooler while Devon brought a case of bottled water. She placed them in the ice while Nick brought out some sodas and beer Marc had bought the night before.

The radio was blaring out a country western station, and soon all the SEALs were topless. With each new song, which was always someone's favorite, there was an outburst of air guitars and karaoke routines. She hadn't seen so much undulating at shovels or rakes and pole dancing of two-by-fours in her life.

When one song came on, it seemed to erupt in a dance free-for-all.

The way I see it,
The whole wide world has gone c-r-a-z-y,
So baby why don't we just dance?

Cooper was dancing with Kyle. Fredo grabbed Malcolm's elbow and they did a do-si-do. Rory Kennedy put his T-shirt over his head and paraded around like on a runway with his shovel, sticking his chest and his butt out with affectation. He got sprayed with the hose.

Devon was clapping her hands and enjoying the spectacle, when several of the men came towards her and took turns twirling her around on the gravel floor of the greenhouse under a liberal sprinkling of water from the overhead wand. She wound up dancing with Nick last, and realized it had probably been designed that way.

By the end of the day the plants were trimmed and sorted. An enormous pile of discarded plastic containers was stacked neatly behind the water tank beside a pile of debris and dirt. Sophie sat in her wheelchair and wrote prices on plastic tags that Devon placed according to her instructions. Cooper managed to get two high weed mowers oiled and tuned to perfection, as well as six rototillers.

He even serviced Sophie's small tractor with the front loader on it. Fredo and Malcolm replaced missing slats in the walls and the overhead canvas sun cover was replaced with new fabric Sophie had stashed somewhere.

They made a large PLANT LIQUIDATION SALE sign for the end of the driveway to put out in the morning. Wind chimes, garden tools, fertilizers and statuary were displayed inside the office at 50% off. Sophie had a few items she wanted to keep, and Devon took them to her bedroom. Everything was dusted, swept. Team guys washed windows and removed cobwebs from the eaves inside and outside the little structure. They raked the gravel parking lot last.

Emma's brother had offered to help out, so Emma drove off in his car. Charles was also from Fiji, but was easily as tall as Cooper and built like a linebacker. He liked working with the SEALs, and demonstrated some of his island dance moves for them. At one point, he started a line dance that went viral and snaked around the property with all the Frogs in tow. Devon got some pictures none of her friends would believe and decided to post them on Facebook as proof.

Sophie came out to look over the place as the sun was setting. "Can't believe how beautiful this is. Just like I'd pictured it could be. Makes me wish I didn't have to sell it. Sure none of you wants to go into the nursery business?"

Marc agreed to stay back with Sophie while the rest of the dirty crew decided to clean up and go into town for some pizza and more beers. Devon hung back, not sure she was invited.

"You're going with me," Nick said. "I intend to keep my promise to my sister, and this will make date number three, if I'm not mistaken."

The pizza parlor was filled with Friday night revelers. They took a large round table in the corner and ordered several pitchers of beer, watching the local "talent" as Rory called the girls who ogled and drooled over the team guys.

Devon didn't have much appetite, so ate a few bites of her salad and sipped from Nick's beer glass. As the minutes went by, he slid closer and closer to her, at first tracing the arc of her right ear with his forefinger, which tickled, and then discreetly exploring the nape of her neck in a dark corner away from the eyes of his friends.

His seduction became more obvious, and it quickly became time for them to leave the party. Taking her hand in his, he addressed Kyle and the rest of them, "Don't wait up for us."

"Careful, Devon. He's got that look," Malcolm said.

Inside, Devon was beaming.

She could hardly wait.

CHAPTER 17

Nick knew where he would take her. The lights from Neverland, the legendary place where many of his high school buddies had lost their virginity, were stunning, and he knew she'd love it. They climbed the steep off-road drive, and as they came around to the flat area Devon gasped. Twinkling lights spread before her across the expansive Santa Rosa plain that stretched fifty miles. He angled the car pointing west, pulled onto a gravel shoulder and shut down the engine.

"Beautiful."

He was looking at her profile, thinking the same thing. He traced the line of her jaw, slipping his fingers around the top of her neck and pulling her to him across the console. His lips sipped from hers. Devon opened to him as his tongue found hers and coaxed her to return the favor.

The cab was feeling cramped and his erection was getting painful.

"Come on." He grabbed a blanket from the second seat, coming around to lift her out of the car. They walked through the dried grasses to a perfect view, where spread the blanket and invited her to join him. Their shoulders touched as they watched the lights, felt the gentle breeze, and listened to the crickets. The fragrant wild grasses and the sounds of traffic in the distance always soothed him. Tonight, it felt like magic.

Nick had never felt this way about anyone in his life. He had thought of himself as immune to love. He had been so certain that his loyalty to his team-mates and his country would forever be most prominent in his life.

But now there was Devon, and it just felt so natural to have her beside him. There was a lot he didn't know about her. Could she handle a long distance relationship? Playing around with his buddies was one thing, but could she hold up during his difficult deployments? Would the intensity of their feelings survive being apart, with him living in San Diego and her in Sonoma County?

"Thank you for bringing me here, Nick. I can see this is a special place," she said.

Nick had to smile. "They call it Neverland."

"Really? Why?" Her eyes sparkled in the reflection of the lights ahead of them. Then she put her hand to her mouth. "Oh. A make-out place, right? Like a *legendary* make-out place?"

"I'm surprised you haven't—" He suddenly realized he shouldn't have said it.

She touched his lips with her fingertips. "No. I never even got close to making love with anyone. I've barely been kissed."

"That's all in the past, baby."

"Yes." She looked down, shyly.

"I can't believe no one tried to get close to you, Devon. You're beautiful, smart. You're a good friend to Sophie. Girls like you don't come along very often."

"Thank you for saying that, Nick. I have to admit, I've never met anyone like you, either."

The doorway was being breached. Surrender was imminent. But whose? He wanted to give himself to her as much as he needed her to fill all those raw spots and holes in his soul.

"I'd like this to continue after I go back to San Diego. Can you ever see yourself—what I'm asking I have no right to ask. You don't even know me."

"I know Sophie and she's told me some stories. Sophie doesn't lie."

"No, she doesn't. So now I'm afraid of what she said."

She looked back out to the lights. He saw the moisture on her lips as they began to curl up at the ends. "She said you don't let anyone in. Ever."

"Until now, Devon."

Her sparkling eyes lit up his heart when she turned to face him again. "I was hoping to hear that, Nick. For me, all this sex, it's something more than just that. I feel like I belong here, beside you."

"You do, baby."

They kissed as he lay her down into the blanket. He nuzzled under her ear and spoke the words she wasn't sure she heard at first. "I'm falling hard and I don't want to stop. You'd have a terrible time getting rid of me if you change your mind."

She laced her fingers through his hair, moving on to his temples and caressing the sides of his face. "Don't stop. I don't want you to stop. I don't want to lose this feeling—"

Before she could finish he stopped her as he brushed her lips with a soft kiss and slid his hand up under her shirt. He pulled the cotton fabric off, bending to penetrate the top of her bra with his tongue. She arched to him with a moan that nearly made him come. He removed her bra, then worked on her pants, sliding them down her thighs. Her white lace panties glowed in the moonlight.

She waited and watched him as he shed his own clothes. Then, raising one of her knees over his shoulder he bent down and licked the inside of her thigh. His tongue snaked its way under the elastic of the panty to seek and find her slit as he dipped the tip inside her warm opening. Devon grabbed his hair, clutching with her fingers wildly as her hips writhed, presenting her mound to him.

Watching her face under the stars, he slowly pulled her panties off and slipped two fingers inside her. It was heaven to watch her melt with desire. He and only he had opened the door to her garden of delights. It had never been important before, but tonight it was. He vowed he'd be the only man to ever make love to Devon for the rest of her life. If she'd have him.

He sucked her clit as he moved his fingers in and out of her.

"Please," she moaned.

"Yes. I'm here, Devon."

"Please, Nick, I need you inside me."

"Yes," he whispered. "I want—"

Should he say it? Was it wise?

"Please, need you," she was moaning.

"I want to be the only one, Devon."

"You are."

"I want to be the only one, ever," he said as he mounted her. He'd brought protection and quickly slipped it over his engorged shaft. The delay sent her into a frenzy.

"You are the only one. I don't ever want to let you go."

Nick entered her as she exploded all around him. Her warm sheath held him, pulled him deeper. Her breasts shone in the silvery night air, the red peaks of her nipples knotted with pleasure. Nothing in the world compared to the beauty of this woman surrendering fully to him under the night sky. She loved with complete abandon, and he vowed he would never leave her.

Somehow, they'd figure out a way to make all the pieces fit, just as their bodies fit together.

Somehow.

Devon stroked along Nick's back, felt the circular scars that reminded her he'd faced death more than once. Another long, thin scar inched from his hip nearly to his spine.

His callused fingers were rubbing her chest, squeezing her nipples as he laid his head against her to listen to her heart. There wasn't any part of Nick's body she didn't love. His thick thighs draped across hers, his steady breathing warming her. She ran her hand down his sides, reveling in the weight of his body on top of hers, right where he belonged.

They had not spoken of love, but she knew what this was. And she was sure he felt the same. She felt protected, honored to be loved by such a beautiful and powerful warrior.

She wanted to spend her life pleasing him. If he'd let her.

CHAPTER 18

D evon awoke to the feel of Nick's body spooning behind her in the guest bedroom.

Thank God it wasn't a dream.

They'd not gotten much sleep, but in spite of the lack, she felt energized. They showered together and barely made it to the kitchen in time to join Marc and the others at breakfast.

"Sophie, you got howler monkeys around here?" Kyle asked her. Sophie nearly dropped her spoon of oatmeal and darted a glance at Devon, whose cheeks immediately warmed in embarrassment.

The catcalls and whistles were making her nervous. Nick wrapped his big arms around her waist and kissed the side of her face. The whole table watched his affection for her, studying every detail unabashed.

Are they like this all the time? Isn't there anything they don't know about?

"I think I heard an old hound dog howling last night," Cooper added.

"No, Coop, that would be the sounds of my tractor giving up the ghost of its formerly inoperable self," Sophie interjected.

"Yup, Coop sure knows how to make the equipment purr," Rory added.

"How's Libby feeling?" asked Nick as he returned to his breakfast.

"Puking 24/7. But I don't care. On the bathroom floor or anywhere, she's still the sexiest damn lady I've ever met in my life," said Coop.

After breakfast, Sophie checked Craigslist as well as the Press Democrat ad and found everything was up, as planned. Kyle and Fredo had no sooner placed the liquidation sale sign at the end of the driveway when an old Jeep turned up the drive and beat them to the office.

A young woman with long blonde hair and an infant sleeping in a sling across her chest, followed by her skinny husband, exited the Jeep. They began to wander through the greenhouse and protected plant area, looking over the signs on the rototillers and stopping to examine the tractor. Sophie joined them. Devon was right behind her.

"You're our first customers today. Lots of great deals. What can I help you find?" Sophie asked.

The husband shoved his hands in his jeans pockets and shrugged. "I used to come in here and drool over this place. I've heard you're preparing to sell. Would you consider working out something with us? I'm David Hallberg, and this is my wife, Donna."

Sophie and Devon exchanged looks as if Divine Intervention was a fact.

"We would, as a matter of fact," Devon began as she grabbed Sophie's arm in an effort to silence her. "But we're asking one point one. That's a very fair price, and we were hoping for multiple offers."

The couple looked at each other for a moment, and then the woman spoke up. "My grandfather has just passed away and left me some money. It's always been our dream to own a nursery, especially here in the Valley. We have a good amount of cash to put down, but we'd need a loan or have to have you carry a note for the rest of it, depending on your sales price. Is that possible?"

"Getting a commercial loan would be nearly impossible, I'm sorry to say," Devon replied.

"We'd have over half in down payment," the girl said, juggling the baby in her sling.

"I'll take the difference in a note," said Sophie.

Devon nailed her with a stare telling her to shut up. She continued, "If you qualify, it looks like Sophie would consider it."

Before a handful of people arrived at the sale, Devon had written a contract for the nursery. Although she knew darned well there were many hurdles and inspections to sort through, Sophie was showing them around as if it was final. Devon knew she'd have to counsel her friend to be careful not to place too much reliance on the young couple, whose funds were not even verified. Devon had seen it dozens of times before.

Sophie had also promised the tractor and several pieces of equipment, furniture and statuary inside the office to the young couple, placing red SOLD stickers on them. Devon finally felt she had to draw her aside.

"You've got to stop this, Sophie."

"I can give it away if I want to."

"But that's not the point. We're here—everyone's come here—to help you liquidate, to earn enough money to buy you some time. You remember our discussion about the notice of default?"

"I saw that in the contract."

"We had to disclose it. We have to disclose it to anyone making an offer."

"Not the asshole next door. Can't wait to see his freakin' face—"

"Sophie, listen to me. You're not being smart. Don't count your chickens until they hatch. Let's be conservative."

Sophie angled her head and gave a wry smile. "That what was going on all last night?"

Devon was embarrassed again. It did draw her back to the lovemaking and how he commanded every cell of her body. It was hard not to grin. She tried and failed. "Okay, so your brother is a good kisser."

The two women shared a laugh.

"I'm so happy for you, Devon." Sophie gave her a hug. "I've never seen him so totally bonkers. He's running into things and can't concentrate. You've done a good job tying him up with those golden handcuffs Marc keeps telling me about."

"Well, we'll see. We're taking it one day at a time. First thing is to see this job done right, and get you into escrow, raise some cash, and make sure everything stays on track. That's my job. You're going to have to listen to me and let me handle this sale for you. Don't get your hopes up too much, okay? I don't want to see you disappointed."

"Hell, Devon, all I got left is hope."

Sophie's coral lipstick looked ridiculous this morning, Devon thought. She'd applied more makeup than she could remember seeing Sophie wear, ever, especially her attempts to cover the grey bags under her eyes.

"No, you've got us. All of us." Devon pointed to the shirtless SEALs who were escorting customers and carrying flats of plants like waiters in a fancy restaurant.

By noon, Rory and Marc were out by the highway, swinging their shirts and directing traffic up the driveway. A steady stream of cars was directed up the hill and customers parked all over the property. The event was starting to take on a carnival atmosphere. Country western music blared, waters and sodas were generously handed out, and sales went through the roof.

A television truck from a local station made its way up the driveway and a camera crew filmed the event. The SEALs posed behind dark sunglasses for the woman reporter, who also interviewed them. The reporter didn't bother to interview Sophie, even though she tried to interject herself.

Devon had posted the work crew antics on her Facebook page, sending a link to her office inviting other agents to stop by. She continued taking pictures of the crowds and uploading them throughout the day. The numbers continued to grow until nearly everything was cleaned out.

Devon watched Sophie walk unsteadily, but on her own, through the vacant racks and inspect the black plastic that used to be covered in five gallon containers of cuttings she'd started and plants she'd started from seed. Devon knew the reality was sinking in that her dream of supporting herself by creating a boutique nursery was coming to a close. When Sophie leaned against a post and wept, Devon started toward her, but Marc came to her side and carried her into the house.

Devon announced they'd made nearly fifteen thousand dollars, which would be more than enough to cover four months' payments, late fees and reinstatement costs that Sophie had finally confessed were piled up, including the notice of default she'd received the day she'd called Nick for help. Devon knew he was relieved that he wouldn't have to add any money from his own savings in order to buy his sister more time.

The SEALs were going to leave tomorrow, so they ordered takeout and everyone ate together at the large plank table one last time. It had been a very successful day. They were all in good spirits, but Sophie couldn't eat and went to bed early, saying her farewells and thanking the team guys for all their hard work. Marc joined her for a bit, and then came back out.

Kyle's phone went off. He answered, and then quickly held it away from his ear. Someone on the other end of the line was yelling at him. He put the phone on speaker and set it on the table for everyone to hear.

"And I couldn't believe when he walked in and showed me this goddamned Facebook posting by this Devon Brandeburg. You know this person?"

"Yes, Chief. She's right here. You want to talk to her?"

"Fuck no! Don't you guys understand this little caper was a shitfaced idea?"

"Just helping out Nick's sister."

"Fuck Nick's sister."

A collective "wooo" went through the group.

"Sir—"

"You listen to me, Lansdowne, you get your butts back to Coronado, and I don't want to see anything else on the Internet or anywhere. What about face recognition software do you not understand?"

Devon panicked. Had her postings gotten them all in trouble? It had never occurred to her. Of course, they would have to keep a low profile, and that's exactly what they hadn't done today.

"I'm sorry sir. We didn't know about that." Kyle made a face at Devon in mock anger. He waved his hand to indicate he was just joking. "And we didn't ask for the TV crew either."

Several of the guys began shaking their heads as they anticipated the reaction they got.

"What? What the fuck? You had TV cameras out there? Are you fuckin' *insane*, Kyle?"

"Sorry, sir. We didn't give our names. We wore sunglasses all day. I doubt they'd be able to identify us from our naked torsos."

The expletives on the other end of the line were escalating. Devon heard rustling and what sounded like furniture being forcibly relocated. Then she heard a tinkle of shattered glass.

"He break a window?" she whispered in Nick's ear.

"Chief, you okay?" Kyle asked.

"Oh, I'm okay. I'm just fine, but your fuckin' frog statue is in pieces."

"I'm sorry it got knocked down. We'll get you another one."

"Don't fuckin' bother, Lansdowne. It didn't fall. I threw it." He abruptly disconnected the phone.

"Looks like we need to take up another collection," Rory said.

Nick explained to Devon, "We bought a frog for Chief Timmons when we joined Team 3. We've had to replace it four times now, I think."

They built a bonfire again out back, by the hot tub and water tank, and Devon sat on Nick's lap as the team sat around the fire and told stories about the customers and the day. One by one men peeled off, said their goodbyes to Devon and Nick, and hit the rack for the long trip home tomorrow.

Left alone with Nick under the night sky, she realized she wanted to discuss future plans. Although she didn't want to initiate it, she had to.

"You never said when you were going back. I'm guessing you have to leave tomorrow as well?"

"Yes."

Her insides tightened. She was glad she'd have to throw herself into making sure the escrow went smoothly. It might help with the missing him part. She wanted him desperately to say something she could hang on to.

Her wish was granted.

"Devon, after this closes, I'd like you to come down to San Diego and stay for a little while. Try the place on. See if you could find yourself—" Nick's eyes sparkled.

She leaned into him and kissed him on the lips.

"Find myself what?" she teased. She wanted to hear him say it. Her sanity depended on it.

"See if you could wrap your head around maybe being with me."

She could tell he was struggling with the words. It delighted her to needle him further.

"But, Nick…" she said as she slid her hands down to his crotch, "I've already *been* with you. Almost more times than I can count. I think that part of us works just fine." She kissed him again and saw him crack a smile.

"Little did I know when I met that kid with the braces and scrawny arms that I'd feel this way."

"Feel what way, Nick?"

He sighed. "Devon, I'm in love with you."

She wanted to wait, to savor the echo of those words in the night air. But she couldn't hold it in any longer.

"Thank God!! 'Cause Nick, I fell in love with you five years ago. My brain just figured out what my body knew way back then. And nothing would give me more pleasure than to be with you in San Diego."

"I warn you, it's a different world down there."

"I'm up for it. As long as you're there."

"I don't deploy until next year, but I start workup in five months. Doesn't give us much time to—"

"It doesn't matter. We have what we have. I'll get the property closed, and then I'll come down and—"

He cut her off with another kiss. "And then we'll see what happens."

CHAPTER 19

Devon got a text from Nick the next afternoon after he'd left for San Diego with the Team.

Miss you already. My bed sucks.

Devon smiled as she looked at it in the middle of her office meeting. She didn't care that her cheeks felt hot and her panties were damp. She crossed her legs and enjoyed it. All kinds of fantasies went through her mind. She texted him back.

I like sucking. I like watching you suck. You got someone else in your bed Nicky?

Not thirty seconds went by before she got his response.

Okay, I'm on the next plane up there. I'm going to prove to you no one else is in my bed.

She smiled and crossed her legs the other way. God in Heaven, she missed him. How would she be able to abide the weeks before the escrow would close and they could be together?

And then she thought of Sophie. She hung her head in shame, felt her whole body go limp. Nick's happy text pulled her out of the sad mood she'd sunk into.

Baby, did you hear me? I'm going to come up there and suck you dry?

She sighed so loud a couple of the other agents looked at her with concern. She lovingly looked at the phone and rubbed her finger over the screen.

Wish it were so, Nick. I don't think I can last thirty days without you.

He was right back at her.

Then don't. Come down here. I suck just as good here as up there…

Her response was given before she'd had a chance to think about it. *Done. I'll make some arrangements. But Nick, you do everything perfectly. You don't suck at all. Will be in touch.*

He instantly sent back, *I like the in touch thing too. Plan to do some of that when you're here too. Let me know the instant you arrange it. Make it soon, baby. OXOX 696969 Nick.*

She went over the inspection dates with Sophie that afternoon.

"God, I sort of feel like my little property is naked in the doctor's office, waiting for a PAP smear. They going to look everywhere?" Sophie scowled.

"Better for you that way. We want to give them full access to everything so they are making informed decisions. You're more protected if other professionals give their opinions as to the condition of the property." Devon had delivered that line hundreds of times over the years, but it was even more important now than ever before. She wanted to protect Sophie the only way she knew how.

"Not that I'd be around later on to get sued."

Devon felt her stomach clench. "You have time."

"Not much, sweetie. But time enough. Guess it wouldn't be good to land the two of you in a mess when I go, though."

"Don't even think about it, because it's not going to happen, Sophie."

"Well, Devon, they always say there are two things certain in life, death and taxes. I don't think any of us will escape either of these two. My time will come soon enough, and thank you for doing a good job for me."

She decided to bring up her planned trip to San Diego.

"Ah, that's nice, Devon. I like the two of you together. See, I told you Nick would show you his good side, if you'd just give him the chance."

Devon *had* given him the chance. She'd always wondered if she could feel anything sexually for anyone, the way her past kept creeping up into her future. But with Nick, she felt safe. She trusted him, probably more than she loved him. That was a good thing.

"I am planning just a short trip down there, and I'll be back for the inspections next week. You be okay with Emma and Charles?"

"They're great. Yes."

"And you'll call me if anything changes, right?"

"Absolutely. Besides, if I don't, I know Emma would call you."

Devon made her reservations and texted Nick.

Coming Thursday Flight 2469, arrive 6:21 pm. That work for you?

I like the coming part. Plan to do some of that too. Works for me, baby. Can't wait.

The San Diego airport was three times the size of Charles Schulz International, but she wasn't interested in anything about the beautiful space. She scanned the crowds and found him standing in a pair of blue jeans and light blue shirt, his hands tucked into his pants shyly. He beamed when their eyes connected and Devon's heart pounded. Her mouth was dry but her panties were good and wet with anticipation.

She ran to him, her bag slung over her right shoulder.

His big arms encircled her waist and he squeezed so tight, lifting her off the ground. His lips were all over the side of her face, her neck, his strong fingers rubbing through her hair, sending her clip onto the floor somewhere at their feet. When at last they kissed, his tongue went deep and she had to restrain herself not to jump her knees up around his waist. She could hear the chuckles of some onlookers, but she didn't care.

He'd made arrangements for them to stay at the Hotel Del Coronado. Devon knew what that must have cost him. She'd started to ask when he put his forefinger to her lips.

"Remember what I told you about us SEAL types?"

Yeah, how could I forget? "When they offer, just let them do what they do."

He responded with a full smile that made her heart glow. "Exactly. I'm glad to see you're learning."

She wanted to learn everything about loving this man.

The little room was in the vintage section of the hotel, but it didn't matter. Once the door was closed, it could have been a closet, for all she cared. He'd leaned against the door, holding the keycard in his hand and flipping it against the fingers on his other one. She dropped her bag and purse and just watched him, allowing the delicious wave of anticipation to take her away. Postponing what they'd be doing shortly, but enjoying the excited pause between them. After taking in a deep breath and letting it out, he slowly perused her body from the ground up.

"God, Devon, I've never wanted anything more in my whole life. I've been a mess these last two days,"

It thrilled her to see the spark in his eyes, the lust behind them, even as it was a bit scary. He was a powerful man and he would always do everything with that same intensity and power.

Always.

Nick closed the distance between them in seconds. She felt his kisses on her neck, the feel of his coarse hands as they peeled the layers of her clothing away to expose her flesh to him. It sent shudders down her spine to feel how tender, but how urgent he was. His breathing was controlled, but his masculine scent, the way his muscles bunched and flexed under her palms, and his soft growls, sent her into outer space.

"Missed you," she whispered before he covered her mouth, sliding his tongue over her lower lip.

"Me too, baby," he returned and accepted her little sigh, pressing her harder against him. "Me, too."

She whimpered again and he answered with a deep growl from somewhere deep inside his chest. His hot kisses traveled under her chin and past her collarbone to between her breasts.

She wanted him deep inside her, but she was loving that he built their anticipation by taking his time. The ache between her legs throbbed and left her deliciously breathless.

It drove her nuts. And she loved him all the more for it.

"God, Devon, I've thought about this, dreamed about—" He squeezed her ass with one hand, the other slipping underneath her lace bra. Then he sank to his knees, worshiping her, placing his mouth over her knotted nipples, teasing first one and then the other with his tongue, biting down just enough to make her jump with pleasure. The sucking sounds he made with his lips fueled the fire of her libido.

"Me too, Nick, I dreamed of this every night before I went to bed." She wanted to say more, but held back. She answered his kisses softly with a long moan.

He moved his palms between her thighs and spread them apart, watching her face as his fingers breached the elastic of her panties, caressing, teasing, and asking for permission to invade. She answered him by moaning, rocking her pelvis back and forth to the gentle strokes of his fingertips against the pink satin fabric of her panties. Slowly the fingers found her flesh. Her breath hitched and she stood still as he bent forward and kissed her opening while his two fingers tucked inside her wet channel.

She was going to explode. As he lapped her clit and stroked her insides, her breathing got ragged and her knees began to wobble. When his fingers pulled out she felt hollow and even more needy than before his ministrations.

He peeled down her panties, kissing her thighs all the way down, exposing her nude sex to the cool air. Gripping her hips and pulling her towards him, his hot lips found her core, no longer impeded by her lacy satin panties.

He looked up at her, eyes twinkling in the dimly lit room. "You taste so good, Devon." He massaged her sex with his fingers, watching her face as he lazily traveled the length of her slit from her clit to around her opening and back just enough to run into dangerous territory. She closed her eyes and arched back as his thumb pressed against her nub and then slid back to insert into her in a circular motion, driving her wild. Two fingers again slipped deep inside her and spread the walls of her channel while his thumb coaxed her honeyspot into a tight peak.

Her knees began to buckle, her bones melting, as her full attention went to the feel of him exploring her, kissing her, rubbing his thumb over her clit and sucking all the places his fingers had been. His tongue penetrated her wet, hot core. She placed her palms on his shoulders to brace herself as her muscles clenched in a smooth, early-rolling orgasm he lapped up eagerly.

"Yes, baby. Love how you taste, baby," he whispered as he kissed her nether lips, spreading them apart.

"Nick I want you inside me," she gasped. He answered her with a husky groan and lazily finished with his tongue, then stood. He smirked as she frantically began removing his shirt. He had his pants and shoes off in one smooth stroke until he stood before her naked, his huge erection touching her before their bodies met. She felt the bulge of him pressed against her abdomen as he slid over her mouth kissing her deep. She tasted her own juices and she felt the hitch in her breathing at her heightened arousal.

The thick muscles of his neck were taut. Her fingers found a joyful path up the sides into his hairline. Her breasts were pressed against his chest so hard her stiff nipples ached. His large palms gripped under her butt as he raised her and she threw her legs around his hips and waist. She dragged her wet pubic area over his hardened shaft and he hissed in pleasure. Neither one of them used their hands to help his shaft find her. The rubbing of flesh on flesh, and the waiting, the glorious anticipation of the cure for her need, stoked her burning insides. The pain of vacancy waiting to be fully occupied sent flames up her spine all the way to the back of her neck and skull where his hand had fisted her hair.

"God, I need you, Nick."

"Baby, I'm here," he said to the side of her face. He squeezed her ass with both palms, massaging and pulling her cheeks aside and apart. "I'm all here for you, baby."

She ground herself against him harder and moaned. His cock wedged into her opening and she angled her pelvis down against him as he slid in slowly. She opened her eyes and watched his clear green eyes look into hers as he whispered, "Love this, Devon. Only place in the world I want to be."

Her thighs gripped his hips as she rocked back and forth, arching back and then pressing her chest against his. The slow friction between them and the look they shared spoke volumes to her.

He walked them back to the bed. He turned and lay her back on the mattress as he knelt on the ground in front of her and spread her knees apart again.

"Can't seem to get enough of you."

"Please love me, Nick. I ache for you." She was going to say something else, but stopped herself.

Nick smiled and put a finger to her lips, then went over to his pants and pulled out a condom, quickly sheathing himself. He kneeled on the edge of the bed, placing her thighs against his chest, the backs of her knees propped over his shoulders. She followed the lustful look he showed her as he watched his cock slide inside her half way. Then he pulled out and then plunged in again a little deeper.

A smooth rhythm of back and forth penetration, his thick cock spreading her, ramming deep inside her, made her more urgent. The deeper he got, the more she needed him. She felt the tip of his shaft press against her cervix inside and she began to spasm. She pulled his butt cheeks into her as her thighs slapped against his lower torso. He was so incredibly deep. But she still needed more.

Her ears began to buzz as she felt the orgasm begin to take her away.

"Give yourself to me, baby."

She was wild for him, her internal muscles clenching against him, milking him, her fingers digging into his butt cheeks, stopping to feel the depth of him. At last, like a rag doll, she let her arms fly back above her head. He leaned over her, pushing himself deeper and gripping her shoulders from underneath, pulling her torso onto him. His knees slid under her backside as her sex was raised, giving him full access.

There was no holding back, no holding on. She flew into another dimension as her body rocked with pleasure she never wanted to end. She felt his rigid member root and spasm against the walls of her sex as he groaned and shuddered in unison with her.

He leaned over her further and, after tenderly unwinding her knees from his shoulders, rested on his forearms on each side of her head. His soft lips caressed her cheek, blew cool air into her lashes and along the hairline down to the back of her neck. He kissed her ear and she could hear his tongue lick his lips as he whispered,

"You're incredible, Devon."

It was her turn to run her thumb across his lower lip as she positioned her palms at the sides of his jaw and sucked in his liquid kiss. "I've been thinking about this. Read it in one of my books," she said.

He arched up and looked at her inquisitively. "What?"

"The part where you don't have to use your hands. Where we just…" he'd begun kissing her neck and under her ear, "…find each other without using hands." She smiled and could see it register in his eyes.

"I'd like to try everything in one of those books, if this is the result."

"I can read to you at bedtime."

"Yes, you most certainly can. Until I have to toss the book aside jump your bones again."

"Oh, that sounds like so much fun," she said. Her heart was light. He was still inside her and all was right with the world.

"Fun isn't the half of it. I'm going to demand a sexy read every night."

They looked at each other, the word *every* hanging in the air, more obvious than an elephant on a trapeze. It warmed her that there could be an every night in a string of every nights. She would gladly share her bed with him, her books with him, her body with him, and just maybe her heart.

He adjusted himself and, without pulling out, leaned his side onto the bed, pulling her thigh up on his hip. He glanced down at the place they were still joined and she had to look too. "I like the way this looks, Devon."

"Yes." She did too.

His callused palm ran over her butt cheek and then he squeezed her. She pulled her sex tight and squeezed him from inside in return, feeling his response. Another erection was looming. The dull ache of his cock against her cervix felt so good she closed her eyes and savored it like a delicious dessert.

His fingertips moved up her spine, over her shoulder and his thumb traced a line under her chin to her mouth where she pulled it between her teeth and then sucked it, rolling her tongue over it and flicking the fingernail, probing.

"I want to do this all night long, Devon," he whispered.

"I'm sure you can. Teach me, Nick. Teach me how to stay awake in your arms with no rest, like in your BUD/S training."

"Honey, this isn't anything like BUD/S."

"I know. We're not getting wet and sandy," she smiled as his eyes lit up and his lips curled in a smile.

"How do you know about wet and sandy?" He traced her hairline with his large forefinger. A forefinger that still carried the scent of her arousal.

"I don't read just romance books. I've read some books about you."

"Me? Not fair. I'd love to watch a movie about you. When you take your clothes off, when you shower, when you sleep, and—" he pushed his growing erection deeper into her, "when you come."

She moaned as he began the in and out action again, filling her, spreading her beneath him. She allowed him to place her arms above her head and he held her wrists in one of his giant hands, his fingers lovingly encircling and immobilizing her. He positioned his hips at nearly a forty-five degree angle to hers, and the new sensations on parts of her channel stimulated for the first time sent a shiver down her backside and heated her thighs. His persistent penetration matched his breathing, which had begun to rumble again in his chest, sending her into a tailspin.

He growled as he pulled at her behind with one hand, still holding her arms above her head with the other. His grip on her ass forced her into his groin so he could spear her deeper. Her nipples swelled and knotted from the friction of his chest. Her mouth needed his tongue, and when he at last gave her what she wanted, she loved how he covered her and drank from her husky moan-laced orgasm while shooting his seed deep inside her.

She arched rigidly, breathing herself out of the exquisite sensation of him filling that space between her legs no one else had ever filled. It was right that it was him. It was all she'd ever wanted. And she hoped it would last forever.

CHAPTER 20

Nick woke up to the blush of a new San Diego day, and as he felt Devon's soft satin skin draped across him like a delicate comforter, he lost all thoughts about his lack of sleep and instead remembered Devon beneath him, shattering. He remembered the way she'd looked at him, the way she'd reached out for his hand as she rolled her tongue over his shaft. He remembered how she'd looked like a perfectly formed, live Grecian statue rising and falling on him, squeezing herself as he drove his hips deeper into her core.

He'd loved her little comment about the wet and sandy he was all too familiar with from his BUD/S training. It touched him that she'd read about the SEAL training, SQT, and started using phrases with him. It didn't matter if she used them incorrectly. He just enjoyed hearing her try—trying to get inside his world.

Girls in the past had attempted this, of course, numerous times. It had always been something that turned him off and set off his internal alarms. He didn't want any women to feel like they knew everything about the SEALs community, because there was no way they ever could. Not in the same way. He would never talk to Devon the way he would with another team guy. It just wasn't possible. Never would be. But she was the flesh and blood and soul of his soul now, and about as important as the guys who had his back overseas or on training missions.

A trickle of fear coursed down into his belly even as his cock began to stir, trying to remind him of other pleasures awaiting him. Was it a good sign that he now knew he needed her? Was she ready for his kind of intensity? The hurt and pain and fear of the unknown, when he wouldn't be able to talk to her for days or even sometimes weeks on end, weighed on him like a dark shroud. It was tough on the guys as they worried about their loved ones waiting at home. But it was always tougher on the women and folks at home.

He'd trained to tune out the distraction, and he knew he would be able to do it again when he was back in the theater. Back to the killing fields, where he could smell the danger as he first stepped out of the vehicle, or that first jump at midnight. Going to a place where he wasn't wanted, for what he hoped was a mission that would not fail, with men around him he could count on one hundred percent, more than he could count on his own sanity. Together they'd get through it. Together they would be the only family that mattered.

Yes. He could do that and lock the image of Devon from his mind temporarily.

But not this morning. Thank God there was this morning.

The top of her head where it rested under his chin smelled glorious. Some flowery scent he inhaled as a few mahogany strands lay across his cheek and tucked around his neck. Her soft breasts pressing against his chest made his groin lurch, but he was careful not to wake this goddess who shared her bed with him. Her left thigh rode over his and he could feel the soft lips of her sex, swollen and wet from their night of lovemaking, press against his hip as she breathed.

He focused to breathing in unison with her. He decided their lovemaking would start even before Devon woke up. She inhaled and he mirrored the fullness of her intake, and then breathed out at precisely the same time. He would keep perfect pace with her in everything this morning, because he wanted to do everything possible in tandem with her.

She must have sensed something, or maybe his timing was slightly off, because she inhaled deeply and her back began to arch. As she came to, she purred and squeezed his thigh by pressing down with hers.

"Morning sunshine," he said as he kissed the top of her head.

She rose up, bracing her forearms against him, hands on his jaw with her thumbs smoothing over his bottom lip. "Morning, handsome."

His fingers sifted through her hair as he enjoyed the sight of her sleepy face and her dark brown locks that went everywhere in sexy disarray. He like that she still wore that hungry look, even after a night of heavy lovemaking. Too little sleep, but the body wouldn't deny the pleasure of their passion.

Nick brought her by the Scupper. Kyle, Cooper, Fredo, Marc and several other Team guys were eating breakfast on the patio. She gave a big hug to Marc and then sat down next to him. Marc slung his big arm around her shoulder and said to her loud enough so everyone else could hear, "You smell real nice, Devon. But then I'm thinking you were told that a bunch already."

Devon blushed. Nick took a seat on Devon's other side, peeled off Marc's arm and replaced it with his own. The other guys nodded and snickered affectionately.

"So," Marc started, staring down at his food, "How's Sophie holding up?"

"You should know. Probably talk to her more than I do, Marc," she answered back.

"Sexting. They're sexting," Fredo quipped. "I told him, Dude, just go up there and see the lady. She'd love to see you."

Marc hung his head a bit. Devon could see he'd thought about it. And decided against it. Was it because he was concerned about his own feelings of attachment, knowing Sophie would be gone soon, or something else?

"I'll get up there next week, I think," he said. Kyle winked at him and Devon picked up there'd been some private conversation between the two. "Help her with some stuff."

Devon put her palm up on Marc's massive back and gave him a pat. "She'll love that. Thanks for being there for Sophie."

The patio got quiet.

Nick took Devon to the yogurt place, the other hangouts he'd talked about. They walked along the Strand and she bought some tee shirts to wear at home. Got a SEAL Team 3 sticker for her car, and a hat. He showed her his BUD/S graduating class logo, introduced her to other Team guys and showed her the beach where they had trained, just down from the Hotel Del.

She'd read about the boat crews and how they had learned to work together, their mission to get the inflatable rafts up and over sharp craggy boulders.

Over and over again she watched in silence as Nick cheered the guys on and catcalled a couple of the instructors he knew.

She heard one instructor yell out to the recruits, "You see that guy over there and that fine-looking lady? That's what real Team guys get to have, but you won't have any of that. All the best lookin' women go to the real Team guys, not you sorry assholes."

Devon didn't mind the appreciative smiles coming her direction.

"Don't you look at her. She doesn't even want to be on the same beach as you baby tadpoles. You guys is pussies. Not men. You're pussies. That guy, he gets that pretty little thing over there you can only dream about."

The instructor had a couple of men fall into the surf on their backs, covering themselves with wet sand, letting the waves lap over them, getting saltwater in their eyes and everywhere else.

Nick turned to Devon. "Now, that's wet and sandy."

"Why did he make them do that?"

Nick slipped his arm around her waist, under her shirt, his palm just barely touching her beneath her bra without being too obvious. "Because they smiled at you, babe."

Devon frowned feeling sorry for the young recruits.

"Or because they were slow, or didn't answer back loud enough, or hit someone with an oar, or got sand in one of the instructor's eyes when he ran past. Any one of those could earn them that." Nick searched her face, placing his palms against her cheeks as he tenderly kissed her. "Don't feel bad, honey. The right ones make it. And for those few, it's good for them."

Their kiss warmed her. Standing on the sunny beach with the wind whipping around them both, she tucked her head under his chin, and snuggled in the safety of his strong arms. She looked at the ocean, the beach, the Hotel Del in the background.

Maybe someday this all could be part of her life.

Because part of it already was.

Sunday went by faster than Saturday had. Nick took Devon to Christy's office and the three of them had lunch together nearby.

Devon was more than intimidated by the blonde beauty Nick seemed so comfortable with. It didn't matter that she and Kyle were married and had a child. Didn't matter that Kyle had put his arm around Devon several times, they'd even danced during the liquidation sale when he was in Sonoma County. Devon didn't like to see Nick's hands on her, even if it was an innocent squeeze or a quick peck on her cheek.

Christy was tall and blonde, with a model build and gait. She was confident, and Devon could see she was well liked. She knew this extended beyond the obligatory respect their LPO's wife would get. She was the one who usually took the newer wives under her wing, Nick had told her. When Nick got caught up in a conversation at the bar with another retired Team guy, Christy smiled. "You have any questions you want to ask while he's out of earshot?"

Devon was taken aback by her frankness.

"I just never knew about any of this. All new to me."

"We all feel that way at first. You get used to it." She looked into Devon's eyes without smiling. "It's a lot for a woman to take in. Some can't make it. It's very hard on everyone, just like in other branches. Gone for long periods of time. Arguments that flare up don't get resolved for months at a time."

Devon watched Nick put a foot up on the chair rail and take a sip of beer with the bartender and the other man.

"People get lonely. Babies are born while on deployment. Birthdays and anniversaries, Valentines days are missed. Recitals and graduations happen without the whole family being together. And then, some come home damaged. Wounded in other ways." She looked across the room at Nick. For a second, Devon saw a shadow cross her face.

"You know what cures them?" Christy said with her smiling eyes.

Devon shook her head.

"You just love them the way they are. You don't expect them to be anything other than what they are. You just smooth all the rough spots away and you never forget to let them know how much you love them. That's the cure for all of it, really."

Devon could see Christy's eyes tear up.

"I have to say that before I met Kyle, I didn't know what a real man was."

Devon knew she would never forget that statement.

Christy took them on a tour of the real estate office. She caught Nick watching as she examined the private offices and the conference rooms. Christy introduced her as a top-producing agent to the manager, Mr. Sims.

Devon could see the real estate small talk was boring Nick, so she thanked Christy and Mr. Sims and left.

They called Sophie. "I'm being fussed over, poked and prodded. And Devon, what do I do when people want to come over to the property to look?"

Devon took Nick's phone and answered, "You tell them to call me. It's marked as pending, and we've made comments in the listing there is a medical issue, so they shouldn't do that."

"Okay. I'll try."

"Anyone from next door?"

"God, I don't know. Emma said someone keeps calling and hanging up. She's got the ringer turned down so it doesn't wake me, so I don't know how many calls she's getting, but a few. Not sure about Rodriguez, though."

"Well, I'll be home tomorrow. Get some rest, because we have all those inspections to complete this week."

After she'd hung up, Devon was ashamed to realize that she didn't want to go home. She became quiet, saddened by the parting that would happen tomorrow.

"What can I do to cheer you up?" Nick asked.

She knew there was one thing they hadn't done. She smiled, looking out the window to the side.

"What?" he asked with a laugh.

"I'd like to see your place," she said. It didn't have the effect she'd expected.

Nick took in air and shook his head. "Babe, we have a very nice room at the—"

"I want to see *your* place, Nick. I want to see where you spend your time when you're here."

She could see he was nervous.

"The decorator is very cheap."

"Good. I'm glad she isn't spending very much time there, then," she returned.

"You know, we don't really spend very much time there."

"Good. So you don't bring girls home, then?" she said with her eyebrows raised. She loved making him squirm.

"Of course not." He had started to say something else but kept it inside. "You're not going to be impressed." His gaze swept between her face and the road ahead. "Really, it's not impressive at all."

"Why don't you let me be the judge of that?" She could tell how nervous he was by the fact that he hadn't stopped squirming in his seat, glancing out the side window, glancing back at her.

"What's so important about my place?" he finally asked. Devon thought he might refuse her.

"Your bed. I want to see your sucky bed."

"I think you have a very smart mouth, missy," he said after he parked and feigned yanking her arm as they crossed the parking lot. Nick was in a hurry, and she liked that. He zoomed to his place faster than she'd ever seen him drive.

"I thought you liked my mouth," she whispered.

Nick was laughing softly, pulling her urgently. "Five minutes. You get to see my place for five minutes and then we're going back to the Hotel Del. Agreed?"

When she didn't answer, he stopped.

She examined her toes. "It might take longer than five minutes, Nick."

"Man, are you going to get it," he said as he resumed his pursuit of his front door.

"I'm counting on it, Nick."

They ran up one flight of steps in the Spanish-styled apartment complex, down a red-tiled outdoor hallway and stopped in front of Apartment 42C.

He slipped his key inside the door lock as she snaked her palms under his shirt. Before he opened the door, he turned and covered her mouth with his. "You might have to be punished for your transgression," he whispered.

CHAPTER 21

Nick was hoping Marc had left the place clean enough. It had never mattered before, but suddenly now, holding Devon in his arms, about to bring her into his place, a place he never brought women, suddenly now it was important.

But not as important as feeling her come to life under his kiss, hearing her little sighs and moans as he slipped his tongue along her lower lip and fed from her in a long, wet kiss. His need was off the charts. His fantasies were soaring.

"So, welcome to my humble apartment and my sucky bed."

Devon squealed. Suddenly he wanted to tie her up with things and make her beg for him. But he doubted she was ready for that sort of play. And he preferred the beautiful room at the Hotel Del, but damn, he was hot for her.

He stood behind her, folding her backwards into his chest and groin, just in case she had any concerns he wasn't aroused. She took one bold step inside and he closed the door behind them, keeping it dark.

Marc had done a decent job. No dirty dishes in the sink, no dirty laundry or clean unfolded laundry anywhere. It actually didn't smell half bad, either, since Marc had left the sliding glass door open a crack.

He took her hand and gently pulled her across the living room. "Kitchen, living room, Marc's room," he pointed as they walked. "And my room," he said as he opened his bedroom door.

"And the sucky bed?"

"And yes, my lonely bed, where I sleep. And dream of you." He kissed her again.

He'd forgotten to make the bed, but it wasn't too bad. She stepped inside and her fingers traced over the top of his dresser, over the picture of Sophie, one of their parents she recognized from Sophie's place, and a picture of her. It had been taken the day of the sale, with Sophie's floppy hat. She was stained with water from one of their frequent hose duels. He'd looked at that picture ten times a day. It was the way he always thought of her. He liked her disheveled, non-professional, and all his.

His fingers stroked over the soft flesh of her most fine butt cheek under her skirt. "You see, there's really nothing to see," he said as he dropped to his knees, turned her so he could kiss the insides of her thighs under the cotton fabric. He deftly slipped her panties down until they dropped to the floor like tissue paper. Parting her knees and letting his fingers slide along her velvet flesh, he found her core as he kissed her belly button.

He inserted two fingers inside her after rubbing down the slit of her sex, focusing on pressing on her nub with his thumbs. Devon groaned and leaned into him further, reaching around to sift through his hair.

Nick felt her shaking with what he hoped was anticipation. He removed her top, undid her bra and looked at her fine body in the shadows while he quickly got rid of his own clothes. He drew her back towards his bed. The length of their bodies touched. He turned her toward his single mattress on the bare bamboo floor, gesturing down.

"And this would be the sucky bed," he said in a whisper. He thought she'd like that, but she was quiet.

Then she answered him. "Show me, show me what you dream about doing in this bed. I want to make it memorable."

Memorable. Here?

"When I think about you at night, when we're separated. I want to think about us together. Here."

Okay.

"Oh, God, Nick. Surprise me."

He had to laugh to himself. After all, everything he did to her was new and *thank God* it had been a surprise.

"Make love to me, Nick."

"With pleasure." But he hesitated because he couldn't get her comment out of his head. He was such a dumbass, because she saw the smirk on his face and she stepped back and frowned. He was on the verge of laughing and he knew it could cost him greatly, but he couldn't stop.

"Nick?" she said, starting low and slow and her voice rising.

Oh what the fuck! "It's just, well when you made that comment about surprising you, well—"

"How would I know the difference? she finished for him. "That what you mean?" Her voice was not at all soft and friendly. Boy, had he blown it.

"I'm sorry. It was just a stupid thought," he said, leaning on one hip and holding out his arms. "Sweetheart, I love doing anything, everything with you. I love that it's new for you. I mean, I *really do.*"

His treading water thing wasn't working. He could see by the expression on her face that he was drowning, and any minute she'd decide to hold him under. He could see the *Oh Shit* moment coming—and yup, she didn't disappoint.

"So I'm not as experienced as other women you've been with? I don't know how to do certain things you like, that what you're saying?"

"No! Fuck no, Devon." He tried to walk over to her, but she backed up and kept an arm's length away. "I love everything you do, the way you do it, too." He knew it was bad, really bad when they started comparing themselves to other women. But before, when these little discussions came up, he was halfway out of a relationship and sort of grateful. He even liked it when the girl broke up with him, because it was easier on him that way. And yes, there was the wonderful makeup sex when they changed their minds, but hell, women were complicated. If they wanted sex, give it to them. As long as there weren't any strings.

What the fuck are you thinking? He could not believe he was actually having this conversation inside his head. He didn't want to break up with Devon. He wanted—he wanted—Oh crap, here he was about to go down the rabbit hole.

"I love everything you do because I love you. You are what makes it special for me, unlike anyone else I've ever known."

Part of him was proud he'd finally said it to someone. The other part of him was holding tight to the edge of his imaginary flak vest.

Devon turned away, exposing her utterly perfect, velvety ass cheek and the profile of her flat tummy and heaving chest. He was used to controlling himself, but damn, it was such a turn-on to see her stand here in his room, his inner sanctum. He should have said something, because she folded her arms, rounded her shoulders and stared at the ground.

Come back to me, angel.

He knew whatever he did wasn't going to help. He also knew that if she was going to be someone he could build a life with, she'd have to take him the way he was.

She turned back to him and he could see her eyes were filled with tears.

"It hurt."

"I know, sweetheart. If you could see inside my heart, you'd know it wasn't anything—I didn't mean—"

Christ Almighty! He'd yelled instructions to a bunch of young Marines who were too scared to move a muscle but were going to get blown up any minute. He'd watched people literally explode in strings of red spray right in front of him, and he knew what to do, what to say, who to grab and how to protect himself. Standing here, naked, in front of Devon, he did not know what to do. He just wished she'd come back of her own accord, because that's the only thing that would work.

"I didn't need to be reminded."

"I understand, baby." He wasn't going to ask her to come over. He was just going to be there in case she wanted to come back. It sucked, but that was the way it had to work.

She looked up at him like a scared little girl.

"What is it, Devon? What's going on?" He could not understand why she wouldn't let it go.

"I have a hard time trusting men."

He wasn't going to ask, but there was something there she'd not told him. Something lurking just below the surface.

"I had a really bad experience with someone I thought was really nice."

"Go on."

"He turned out to be a monster, Nick. I thought he was single. One night he tried to—"

"You don't have to tell me, baby." He was shivering. He waited a safe few seconds and then asked her, "Are you cold?"

She just stood there, focused hard somewhere he wished he could go. He wanted to relieve her pain. He wasn't sure he should force anything. She appeared to be in a delicate place.

Oh, fuck it. He didn't want her to suffer alone, leave him out of her private thoughts. "Let's just sit down and walk this back a bit, okay? Take it slow?"

She nodded her head.

He sat on the edge of the mattress, and extended his arms out to her. He wanted to give her as much space as she needed. He was rewarded when she sat her sweet little derriere on his thighs and leaned her face against his chest. He enveloped her in his arms, stroking her hair.

"I met him at a nonprofit fundraiser. He was a local attorney in town. Very successful. I thought he wore a wedding ring when first I met him. I was in college. I didn't date at all in high school."

"Um hum."

"But we talked about things, and I just fell in love with the guy, or thought I did. He had a way about him, and I just thought he was you know, special. I thought he really cared for me."

She arched back and looked deep into Nick's eyes. "I *thought* I was in love, Nick, but I wasn't."

Nick liked it that she wanted him to know that she didn't consider the infatuation love, that it would make some difference to him.

And it did.

He waited.

"Before we could—Nick we hardly even kissed, I was so scared. He was a lot older than I was. He just knew how to play me. I think he was grooming me. I think he did that kind of thing all the time."

"I'm sorry," he whispered as he looked into her beautiful dark eyes.

She inhaled and placed her soft face against his chest again, her hair tickling his chin and neck.

"He'd been very patient. He'd rented a room I didn't know about. We had dinner downstairs, he invited me up to show me something. I should have known what he had in mind. I barely got out of the elevator before he was on me."

144

She paused, tears softly travelling down her cheeks.

"He'd drugged me at dinner. I was getting light-headed, but still I fought him off. He dragged me to the room. Somehow, I screamed. He got angry. My clothes were in shreds."

Nick rubbed the back of her neck, kissing the side of her face. "Go ahead, tell me. Did he rape you, Devon?" He braced himself for the truth he hoped would not be.

"No."

He was relieved, but now he wanted to kill the son of a bitch who had done this to her.

"Someone heard me. Nick, I was naked. He'd tied me up. Thank God security broke in. I didn't stop screaming until they'd hauled him away."

She was sobbing against his chest. Nick's heart was breaking for her. No wonder she'd turned into an ice princess. It should never have happened to her.

"So what happened to him?"

"I had to endure the whole trial. In the end, he was convicted. I had to testify, staring into the faces of his wife and her sister. It was awful. They said horrible things about me, things that weren't true."

"And so you saved yourself for me, baby."

She placed her hands on the sides of his face. Her delicious scent surrounded him, wove inside and through him, around him, everywhere. She was all the good things he'd ever imagined in a woman. The look of love itself. He wanted her more than he'd ever wanted anyone. But he'd have to be patient, wait for her to learn to trust.

And that was definitely something new. But not anything he'd be able to tell her right now.

"I can only give you what I have to give you, Nick. No more."

"And that's all I want, sweetheart. That's all I want."

He kept the kiss tentative, proper. She pressed against him and quickly moved to a deeper place. Her mewling sounds drove him crazy, especially with her little ass on his thighs.

"I'm here, baby. I'm not going anywhere," he said.

This ignited something inside her because all of a sudden she was all over him. She moved her knees to the sides and sat straddled over him. He brushed the tender skin on her rear, feeling her silk healing everything inside him that hurt.

"God, I'm sorry he hurt you, baby," he whispered back.

She leaned back onto the mattress, looking up at him. Her soft eyes were filled with pain, but he could see her spirit, the bravery in her soul. She must have been scared to death of him, the way he'd come waltzing into her life like he was the only thing that mattered on the planet. He suddenly realized she'd been damaged, and was bravely trying to deal with it all. He saw her need in the darkness, felt it as if they shared a sixth sense.

"You tell me what to do, and I'm here for you, baby. We can slow it down. What do you want?"

"I don't want to slow down. I don't want to hide anything from you ever again. I was afraid you wouldn't want to—"

"Shhh. Nonsense. You are more beautiful to me now than ever before. Thank you for telling me the truth, baby. I'm still here. I'm not going anywhere."

She rose up, climbing on top of him slowly, carefully, like the delicate creature she was. He let her take the lead but helped her, raising her hips, rubbing her nub. As she sat back down on his girth, she kept her fingers there at their joining. She encircled him tight and he thought he'd explode.

He allowed himself the luxury of letting her pleasure him. He could feel how important it was to her that, even with all the pain she was in, she needed to give him something special.

Her trust.

As they rode the ship of their pleasure together, he matched her. Danced with her, gave her back the pleasure she was giving him unselfishly. No fancy room with an ocean view. No fancy sheets smelling of lavender and vanilla and candles flickering. That's when it hit him. He loved her more than he wanted to have sex with her.

CHAPTER 22

Devon was happy Marc came to visit because it took her mind off her missing Nick. She'd gone to San Diego to see if there was a place in her life with him there. Odd that she found that in his bed, in his plain apartment, she found the real Nick that she knew she loved. She'd shared the one thing in the world she was most ashamed of, and he'd listened. Didn't force himself on her, and that brought out all the best in her. It was like her soul had walked through some little doorway to the rest of her life.

But she still missed him terribly.

The property inspections were conducted without incident. She kept looking around her, expecting something unexpected to happen, but, to her great relief, nothing did.

Marc was tender with Sophie. Devon tried not to listen to them when she was alone in her room at night. How Sophie chose to spend her last days was her business, Devon thought. Was something private she would only share with Marc, which was as it should be. What exactly went on between them was something that meant a great deal to Sophie, and Devon was grateful Nick's honorable friend could be there for her.

So much was already being taken away from Sophie. Devon was glad she was granted the dignity of a very private and loving farewell relationship.

Marc had to return to San Diego at the end of the ten-day emergency leave. It was a more tearful farewell than she'd had with Nick. That's when she realized Sophie wanted to say goodbye to Marc now, rather than on her deathbed.

Devon wondered if she'd have that much courage, when her time came.

It had been three weeks since Nick and the team had gone back to San Diego, two weeks since her trip to visit him. She was excited now that the escrow was nearly ready to close. The Hallbergs had just a few more inspection reports to review, but the loan was conditionally approved, since the appraisal had come in higher than the purchase price.

Sophie's condition seemed to stabilize, but Devon was grateful for the hospice care, which allowed her to wash and have a clean bed to rest in. Devon didn't have to worry about her condition as she worked. The brother and sister from Fiji had become like family.

The moon was high and stars made a fine blanket background when Devon turned into Matanzas Creek Nursery's long gravel driveway. Devon had been rushing. Her clients had made her a full two hours late. She'd tried to text Sophie, but she didn't get a text or call back.

She's probably asleep.

Gray-white smoke hit her windshield. Little pieces of ash stuck and then were sloughed off to the sides by her wipers. The light rain that fell added to the visibility problem. Hair stood out on the back of her neck and she felt a chill down her spine.

Something was very wrong.

The front door to the nursery office was open, a golden glow inside and tendrils of fire popping up behind the glass windows of the showroom.

Devon's heart caught in her throat as she gripped the steering wheel.

Where is Sophie?

She hoped to God she was at the back house safely asleep. Her car was in the driveway, but the hospice nurse's car wasn't anywhere.

Devon pulled into the parking lot, grabbed her purse and keys and locked the car. She got as close to the office as she could, but everything was fully engulfed in flame. She called 9-1-1 and reported the fire. The dispatcher said someone else had already called and they were on their way.

With sirens going off in the distance, she ran around the burning structure to Sophie's house. In the distance, she saw two shapes running down rows of vineyard on the neighbor's property.

The house shone in the moonlight. Nothing appeared to be disturbed, except there were no lights on anywhere, which was odd. Sophie always left the kitchen light on so she could find her way for a glass of water. The hospice nurse usually stayed up and half-read, half-dozed with the light on.

Devon tried the front door and found it was unlocked. Inside, the house smelled of lemon candles, but nothing else. She flipped the light switch, but nothing happened. She ran towards the hallway where Sophie's bedroom was, and nearly tripped on a body on the floor.

Falling to her knees, Devon recognized her immediately.

"Sophie! Oh. My. God. Sophie, are you hurt?" she asked as she tried to arouse her best friend. Then she heard the welcome groan and felt movement. Sophie rolled to the side and retched.

"Help is on its way. Sophie, are you hurt? Did anyone hurt you?"

"They're trying to kill me, Devon."

"Who?"

"You know, that asshole next door."

"Where's Emma?"

"She never showed. I tried calling her, but then I fell asleep."

Devon knew this was not a random act of violence. The property was in escrow, but not with the neighbor Enemorio Rodriguez. His broker's threats now came to mind. Devon hadn't believed he'd resort to this level of violence, but now she wasn't so sure.

"Did you see who set fire to the office?"

"Fire?" Sophie tried to get up. Devon stopped her. "Wait. You might be hurt."

"Of course I'm fuckin' hurt. I'm fuckin' dying and they're still trying to fuckin' kill me," Sophie spat out as she used Devon to right herself. Devon had to scramble to catch up with her. She ran behind, asking questions.

"Did someone come into your house? Did Rodriguez come into your house?"

"No, the coward sent a couple of goons. They knocked me around a bit, and then I just started to fall." Sophie was outside, headed for the office, her pajama top up over her mouth to protect herself from inhaling the smoke. "They fuckin' drugged me or something." Sophie's legs were wobbling and Devon was afraid she'd fall again.

"We need to stay away. Nothing you can do now, Sophie." Devon tried to restrain her but, though emaciated from the cancer, Sophie was still strong and stubborn as an ox. Her bony arms pushed off Devon like she was a paper doll. All Devon could do was slow her down.

Devon thought the two men she'd seen when she arrived had perhaps intended to ignite Sophie's house—with Sophie in it. She decided not to mention it until the authorities arrived.

The sirens got louder and she could see a red flashing glow in the night sky as two fire trucks arrived at the scene. Devon had restrained Sophie from going inside the office, which was in imminent danger of a full collapse. Parts of the metal roof began to twist and curl like the dried pods of a pepper tree. Glass exploded out into the night air as, one by one, the windows gave up their defenses.

As the water began finding its way into the burning rubble, Sophie turned and buried her head in Devon's shoulder. She bawled like a girl of ten.

"That bastard. That bastard," she repeated over and over again, shaking as she gulped for air between sobs. "If I had a gun, I'd go over there and blow his fuckin' brains out."

"Stop it, Sophie. You need to shut up." Devon hoped her stern countenance would bring Sophie back to her senses. A fireman in a rubberized yellow jacket and waders appeared through the smoke like an apparition from outer space, his shiny visor reflecting in the moonlight. Devon wondered if he'd heard Sophie's remarks.

"This your place?" he asked.

"Hers. Belongs to Sophie, here," said Devon.

"Anyone unaccounted for? Any pets inside?"

"No," Sophie said between sobs. "Just everything I cared about in the world. Everything except the rest of the plants."

"So you're sure no one is inside?" he asked.

"Absolutely. Wait—nobody that *should* be there."

"Where were you?"

"I was in my house back there," she pointed to her own bungalow. "I closed the office at six. Then these two big guys came to the house. Next thing I knew I was being awakened by Devon here. She's my realtor."

"Wait a minute, what two big guys?" the responder asked.

"They're gone now. Two big guys—"

"I saw them running down the field over there." Devon pointed towards the vineyard.

"So where were you when she was—were you attacked, Miss?"

"I don't know what they—" Sophie began.

"I arrived just a few minutes ago," Devon offered. "I found Sophie on the floor, unconscious. But before I walked in, I saw these two guys running away over there." She hoped the fireman would get back to his crew and stop asking so many questions. Devon had questions of her own, and she was afraid Sophie would start talking about guns and shooting people.

God, where is Nick when I need him? She thought about the SEAL, her boyf—was he her boyfriend? Yes, that's what he was. He'd know what to do. She really needed to call him.

"Okay, I'm going to have our paramedics look you over." He picked Sophie up and sat her down on one of her porch chairs. It had a perfect view of her burning nursery office. Upon realizing this, he immediately moved her inside the living room of Sophie's house, laying her down on the sofa. He stepped outside while speaking into his radio.

"Sophie, not a word about the getting even thing," Devon whispered.

Sophie was in and out of consciousness on the couch, her head lolling from side to side.

"Fuckin' asshole—" she repeated over and over.

"Team is on their way. Hang on just a minute longer," he said. Then two dark-uniformed medics ran past him. One was a woman, Devon noted.

Devon stepped back and watched as they checked Sophie's eyes with flashlights, lay her down on the couch and examined a large bruise bulging just under her right eye Devon hadn't noticed before.

"Holy cow. I didn't see that—" Devon said as she hovered over Sophie to get a better look.

"Excuse me, but you're gonna have to stand back," the woman said gruffly. "You the one who found her?"

"Y-yes. She was on the floor over there."

The male attendant had tried to turn on lights. "Something wrong with the electricity?"

"It was off when I arrived," Devon answered. "I don't know what happened. Maybe the guys did it."

"Guys?" The woman looked up at her, her face reflecting the red pulsations from the fire engine flashers. "What guys?"

"There were two men running away when I drove up. I think they did this to Sophie. She says they attacked her. Drugged her, it sounds like."

The two paramedics whispered amongst themselves. Devon heard a blood pressure cuff. They'd unbuttoned Sophie's shirt. With tiny lights held in their mouths, Devon got a view of Sophie's face, which had turned gray. Her eyes were lifeless.

"She's crashing," said the woman.

"Ma'am, I'm going to ask you to step outside," the man said.

Devon almost got hit with a gurney being brought in by two large male responders. She slipped outside, coughed in the smoke of the evening air, and walked to the back of the house where the air was clearer. She dialed Nick's cell phone. Thank God he picked it up on the first ring.

"Hey, baby." His voice was so reassuring. Loud music and background conversations made everything else difficult to hear. But she heard that and immediately her nerves relaxed from the warm timber of his tone.

"Nick, I hate to bother you, but—"

"No bother, sweetheart. What's up?"

Devon peered through the back porch window. The gurney with Sophie strapped to it flew out the front door. Oxygen had been placed over her nose and mouth as all four attendants ran alongside.

"It's Sophie." Devon found herself having trouble breathing. She began running around the side of the house to catch up to them.

"Oh no. Is she—"?

"It's different than that. There's been a fire. Nick, she was attacked by two men and the paramedics are taking her to the hospital, I think."

"What hospital? Find out what hospital, Devon."

Devon reached the ambulance just as they had slammed the rear doors and the two paramedics had taken their seats up front. She ran to the driver's side, banging on the closed window, trying to get the driver's attention. He rolled down the window and looked irritated.

"Where are you taking her?" she asked.

"Memorial."

"Is she going to be okay?" She asked the driver who had started the van. She held the phone out so Nick could hear their answer.

"Not sure, she's in shock, and something else is going on. She take drugs?"

"Absolutely not," Devon started, "But she said they gave her something."

"Who?" Both Nick and the paramedics asked her in unison.

"She told me her attackers gave her something that knocked her out. She was on chemotherapy until about a month ago. She's taking something for pain—"

"Look, we gotta go. Sorry. Who's her doctor?"

Devon's mind went blank and couldn't remember. "I'll find it in the house and call the hospital. Will that work?"

"She needs all the help she can get."

They drove off, almost sideswiping a third engine that had arrived.

"Oh Nick, did you hear all that?"

"I'm going to the car right now. I'll be on the next flight up there. I think I can catch the midnight flight. Pick me up at the Santa Rosa airport. I'll text you the details."

He hung up without saying goodbye.

CHAPTER 23

Nick's plane taxied a short distance and pulled up a few hundred feet from the portable structures of tiny Santa Rosa terminal. Except for the paved runway, it reminded him of a clean version of some of the no-name villages he'd been dropped into in the Middle East.

The welcoming committee in his stomach was jumping up and down with pointed hats stuffed with toothpicks. That part was the same. The crowd in the lobby was a whole lot different, though. No goats, no sand, no hardened faces of men and women who wanted him dead.

Last time he'd held Devon was nearly a month ago, and so the nightmares had started back in earnest. He'd resisted the mindless sex he usually used to relieve the problem. Funny how getting entangled with a woman got him disentangled from himself, and he needed to be with Devon. She distracted his worry, kept him from the nightmares and uncertainty of his past creeping in and spoiling his future. In her arms he knew he'd find himself, because she was now the keeper of the keys.

When he'd left, the escrow had just been opened, as well as their possible future together, without any specific promises made. After Sophie's property closed, Devon was to come down and perhaps live with him in Coronado, where he hoped their relationship would progress to the next level. He'd missed her even more than he'd thought he would. And he'd actually been feeling a bit shy about his feelings for her, wondering if the timing was too soon, hoping nothing had changed on her part, worrying his need would show too much.

But that was before this latest incident with Sophie and the fire. His sister was in danger, which meant Devon was as well. Being in harm's way was something he understood. He and his men had signed up for that. But Sophie and Devon were innocents. Nick was good at scouting out the enemy and extracting information, the snatch and grabs. But protecting those he loved—yes, he knew he loved Devon, too—protecting them from evil people here in the states, was entirely another thing. He knew evil existed here. He knew some of the craziness from over there had migrated here and was now inside his own country. But that wasn't the job he was being paid to do. It was difficult to stand aside and watch as things began to unravel, and people he loved were getting hurt.

A buxom young Hispanic woman was having trouble with her bag, which was stuffed into the tiny overhead bin above his head. Nick stood to help her get it down. Her beautiful dark eyes flirted with him a moment longer than they needed to. He found himself blushing in spite of himself. After he handed her the bag, she tore her eyes off his upper torso, turned, and began making her way down the center aisle towards the front of the plane. Nick watched the carpet as he followed silently behind, trying not to look at the lady's lovely ass.

Christ, would you get a grip? He was here to see his dying sister, and he'd been counting the days since he'd last seen Devon, too.

Twenty-two.

As if he'd marked every one on the calendar, Marky teased him relentlessly about his celibacy. It was certainly a record he'd not come close to for six years, ever since the two of them met.

As he deplaned, he spotted Devon behind the iron turnstile and fencing of the outdoor arrival gate. Her dark hair was worn long, just the way his fingers loved it. As he approached, her smile warmed him all the way to the soles of his feet. His small head rose to attention, ready for a long-needed up close and personal. He had a serious snake skin of doubts, worry and pain to rub off, and she was the only one who could do it.

"Hi," she whispered in his ear as he held her in his arms at last. His body found every surface her soft flesh that he could press against him. She smelled how he remembered; her orange spicy cologne almost made him lose it.

"Missed you, baby," he said as he bent down to kiss her. His hand migrated up to the back of her neck as he rubbed and squeezed wherever he could get purchase.

They parted. "I'm not sure we can see her, but let's try. Nick, she's in ICU."

"Yes. I've been in contact with her attending. She's pretty sick, and time will tell if she can bounce back. They're looking for signs of internal bleeding," he said as he swung his arm around her waist and hoisted his soft bag over his right shoulder. He directed them out the glass doors to the parking lot.

It began to drizzle again, but Nick thought the smell of wet pavement was pleasant. He never liked the odor of the dirty alleyways and sand-filled streets overseas, wet or dry. Tonight, rain protected him in a cool blanket of mist.

Devon pointed to her Lexus so he moved in that direction, still holding Devon tight against his side as they walked. "Have you talked with her yet?"

"No. They wouldn't let me. I was hoping maybe they would tonight, with you here. I'm not family."

"Like hell you're not." He gave her a squeeze and felt her melt into him even more.

She handed him the keys and they headed south on the freeway towards the hospital.

"So tell me what you know," he asked. He noticed her eyes were red from crying. "Hey, you okay?"

"Oh Nick, I feel so bad. I was supposed to be back at Sophie's hours before I got there, but I had some new clients who came in and kept me—" Devon looked up at him with huge eyes. "You don't think that was all arranged, do you?"

"You never met those people before tonight?"

"Never. They said they found me through the Internet. Nick, I don't really advertise on the Internet. The company does that for us."

"Okay." Nick didn't like the sounds of it, but wanted to eliminate the possibility of conspiracy if he could. "But they could have found you that way, right, maybe through one of your listings? Called the company and gotten your information?"

She nodded. "But they had my cell phone number. The secretaries will usually leave us a voicemail if they give out the number. Or an email. I got neither."

"So what makes you think someone would want to delay you?"

"Just all these little things that add up to one huge coincidence that Sophie was left all alone. Emma was supposed to be there, and I tried to text Sophie,

SHARON HAMILTON

but she never texted me back. Normally, Emma would have done it for her if she was asleep."

"Did Sophie have an explanation for why Emma wasn't there?"

"I don't think she knew. Nick, I can't remember if I asked her now. She did try to reach her."

"So Emma might have left Sophie a message, too. Maybe she got held up."

"Yes. But I didn't expect that. I left thinking she would show up at her usual time. It was my fault entirely Sophie was left alone. I should never have left until I saw Emma arrive."

"Don't beat yourself up about this. Maybe this *was* all orchestrated. But, let's not jump to conclusions, okay? Makes us all crazy."

Devon nodded but Nick could see her bottom lip quivering.

"You talk to Emma about this?"

"I will. Tomorrow morning first thing I'll call her. Sophie said she already left her a message."

They rode in silence for a few minutes. Devon took a deep breath and continued.

"And there's more, Nick."

Nick's stomach lurched. He squeezed the steering wheel and braced himself. Things were adding up to be anything but a coincidence. The fire put everything squarely in the criminal category.

"When I got there the office was in flames, but I saw two men running away from the back of the house, over the fence and into the vineyard. I told the police about them. If I hadn't come when I did, perhaps they would have torched Sophie's house, with her unconscious in there."

He reached for and clutched her left hand. "Just glad you came home when you did, Devon." He kissed her fingers. "And glad you weren't hurt as well."

The assault had all the look and feel of something orchestrated, but the perpetrators were long gone. His mind was strategizing and prioritizing what came first, what second. He began to develop a plan.

"First, we go check on Sophie. Then we go back to her house, unless you don't feel comfortable there."

Devon took a minute to answer as Nick pulled into the Memorial Hospital parking lot.

"I'm okay if you're there. But I refuse to stay there alone. I suspect this has to do with the sale of the property to that awful neighbor. That's all Sophie would talk about when she was conscious. She's convinced he's behind this."

Knowing his sister, she was probably right.

They could see Sophie through the glass doors. A large nurse came up to them, opened the doors and barred their way.

"My sister is Sophie Dunn. Can I see her?" Nick asked.

"Let me check. I think she's stable, but I have orders to check before visitors."

The nurse came back and gave Nick a hospital gown to put over his clothes, eyeing Devon suspiciously.

"She's her best friend. She'd want to see Devon," Nick said as he wrapped an arm around her and pulled her inside next to him. She was given a gown as well.

Sophie was hooked up to an oxygen mask with tubes and electric patches coming out from underneath her light blue flowered gown. Her face was indeed ashen and the shiner on her cheek and brow was going deep purple. Someone had struck her with a blunt object and Nick saw she was lucky not to have lost her eye.

He gripped her hand, which was also bruised, and immediately Sophie smiled.

"My big little brother. My hero." She opened her lids slowly and Nick saw the red blood clot invading all of the white of her left eye. Otherwise, she didn't appear to have sustained damage.

"Bet that hurts," he said as he touched his own eye.

"Not as much as the cancer. I'd let them bugger up my other eye if it would take away the cancer pain." She saw Devon. "Sweetie, thanks for coming."

Devon leaned over and gave Sophie a careful hug.

"I think they're moving me tomorrow to a regular room." She brushed her hand in the air, rattling several of the plastic tubes hooked up to her. "Got a screamer over here, but they gave him something to shut him up. I still can't fall asleep for very long."

"Probably the adrenaline pumping through you," Nick said as he observed the number of purple bruises on Sophie's other forearm. "Sophie, you put up a fight, I see," he said pointing to her bruising.

"I've had those for weeks now. They just never heal. I think it's the cancer, or the drugs they had given me. Should clear up now that I'm off all that stuff."

Nick observed some of the bruising looked to be fresh.

He brought a chair for Devon to sit while he sat on the bed next to her. "I think you have a good team. I've spoken to your doctor. He's Navy-trained. You got a good one."

"Thanks, Nick. He's also kinda cute, too."

"That didn't come up in the conversation," Nick answered, glad she could focus on something other than the pain. "But it does mean I won't be leaving Devon alone with you here." He winked at Devon who was shaking her head.

"No, you don't want to let her get away, Nick. She's a keeper," Sophie hoarsely whispered.

"I have no intention of letting her get away," he said as he grabbed Devon's hand and kissed it.

"Atta boy." Sophie winced as she tried to move, and began a series of hacking coughs.

"How can I help?" Nick asked.

"My legs are stiff, and my lower back. I must have landed wrong when I fell. Just bend my knees a bit, maybe get a pillow."

Nick found an extra pillow on top of a shelf above the headboard, placing it underneath her knees. "You don't get to elevate your legs above the level of your heart, not yet."

"Thanks. That's much better."

"You want something to eat?" Devon asked.

"Hell, no. Just the mere thought of food turns my toes yellow."

"So you must be the SEAL." A very handsome, tall African-American in a white lab coat entered the room and held out his hand.

"Dr. Harris? Nice to meet you," Nick replied and frowned at Sophie, who shrugged her shoulders in response.

"She couldn't stop talking about you. All the daring things you've done for this country," Dr. Harris continued.

Nick could feel embarrassment and a little anger creep into his demeanor. "Sophie, we talked about this. You're not supposed—"

"Oh, chill, Nick. Dr. Harris, show him your forearm. You know the one."

Harris rolled back his coat with a huge grin. As he did so, Nick saw the frog-tracks tat on his right arm extending from his wrist to inside his elbow.

"Son of a bitch. You didn't tell me you were a Frog. And Team 3, too? You knew my LPO, Kyle Lansdowne?"

"Hell no. He was waving flags and learning how to march in the color guard at Great Lakes when I left the teams. But I have to say, some days I still miss it."

"I understand." Nick couldn't envision leaving the teams, and up until meeting Devon, had nothing on the outside that could pull him away from it. "But there does come a day."

Harris slapped Nick on the shoulder. "And then you pass the torch. But I still got your back, brother." The doctor was easily three inches taller. "An honor to be able to care for your sister."

"Thanks, man. Honor to meet you, too. So when do we get to take Sophie home?" Nick asked.

Harris frowned, and looked at his feet.

"We all know the eventual outcome, sir," Nick added. "We have no illusions about a miraculous recovery. But she wants to be home, and that's what we'd like to do. Unless something else can be done for her."

"Just checking a couple of other tests that won't be back until tomorrow. She might get lucky tomorrow."

"Hell, I've given up on getting lucky. I just want to go home to die," Sophie said as she struggled to sit more upright. Nick helped her reposition the pillows while Devon and Dr. Harris were silent.

"Hey, Doc," Nick held Sophie's hand up. "I'm not liking those bruises on this hand and her forearms. I don't remember seeing them before, and she says she's had them for weeks. A couple of them look new."

"I told you, Nick, I got those from the treatments," Sophie blurted.

"One of the things we're checking. She's a little anemic," Dr. Harris said. "How's your appetite?" he asked Sophie.

"What appetite, do you see an appetite laying around here?" Sophie answered.

"I'll order some broth," Harris added softly, patting her knee.

"Don't bother. I'd like a Margarita, though. Maybe some chips."

"Sorry, dear. No can do. But if everything checks out later in the morning, we'll get you on some real food and get you somewhere with less drama."

"Thank you. Getting used to the buzzing, the running and the carts crashing into doors and walls, and I've only been here, what, two hours now?"

"Get some rest, and try to sleep in." Harris turned to Nick and Devon, "All of you. I'm going to do the same, but I'll be here, not far away, so relax and get your strength back up."

It gnawed on Nick like a shrapnel wound that wouldn't heal that Sophie appeared so matter-of-fact about staring death in the face. She wasn't nearly as strong as she pretended to be. He knew when the time came, even tough SEALs would cry out for their mamas. He'd witnessed it in the field a few times. Not often, but he'd told a man or two to just let go, "deploy upward, soldier. The man upstairs has new orders for you now." He wondered if Devon would be the one to be with her on her last day, and made a note to himself to prepare her for his sister's end, in case he wasn't there.

Dr. Harris assured them the staff had instructions were to wake him if anything important came up. He also told them the police were to be informed of any unwelcome visitors. Sophie had allowed detectives to interview her just before Devon and Nick arrived. Nick knew that was a good sign. He kissed her on the cheek, controlling the signs of worry, said his good-byes, and allowed himself to focus on his long-awaited reunion with Devon.

There was enough sexual energy in Devon's car on the ride back to Sophie's to power it if the thing hadn't been a gas model. He wouldn't let her drive. He preferred his Hummer, but if he'd had it they would have never made it home, since it had such a roomy second seat. The Lexis felt like a toy car from Disneyland.

He stole glances at her and found her smiling, and he didn't let on he knew she was doing the same to him. He needed to feel her soft flesh beneath him. He'd imagined it every night before he went to bed.

But his mood changed completely when they got to the end of Sophie's driveway and found one large red fire truck blocking the area where the office used to be, now reduced to a smoldering pile of ash with occasional plumes of smoke rising. In the distance, Sophie's house could be seen beyond the rubble.

"They said someone would check on the fire throughout the night," Devon said in answer to the question he never uttered.

Nick pulled around to the side and parked. After letting Devon out, he walked over to talk to a young fireman in jeans and a dark slicker who came up to check them out.

"I'm Nick Dunn, the owner's brother," he said as he showed his military ID. The fireman whistled and raised his eyebrows.

"Sweet. I'd say you're cleared. There will be an investigator back again tomorrow to try to determine the cause of the fire, so don't get freaked if you see someone poking around early tomorrow."

"I understand. So they haven't determined the cause of the blaze?" Nick asked.

"He's pretty sure it's arson, but we're not allowed to make that official. We should know in the morning, though."

"Any reason why we can't stay here tonight?" he asked. "In the house, of course."

"As long as you don't mess with the scene."

Devon spoke up, "There wasn't any power in the house when I got here."

"Luckily there were three meters, one for the office, one for the house, and one for the well. We found the house main breaker turned off. When we flipped it back on, we checked it out inside and everything looks good. Water's shut off to office, but house looks fine."

"Okay, good."

"We had to use some of the water tank contents, and still might have to use more if hot spots develop, so not sure how much reserve you'll have. I'd go light on usage until it can recover," the fireman said.

They heard the fire truck pull out of the driveway as they were closing the door behind them. It felt eerie inside the house, as if the ghost of something evil had invaded this once-happy home. Maybe it was because Sophie nearly lost her life here, but something was off. The hairs at the back of his neck began to stand up.

"Devon, I'm not getting a very good feeling about this place right now. I don't think we should be spending the night here."

"My place is feeling rather lonesome. And so am I."

He was grateful she agreed.

"Works for me."

Devon's condo was in the old part of town in a mixed-use rustic building that predated the 1906 earthquake. Fashionable lofts had been created over trendy restaurants and boutiques. Everything was closed except for a few bars that were sparsely populated. Nick hadn't realized this part of the city had cleaned up so nicely.

The parking garage was gated with a private elevator to her third floor unit. Her oversized door was made of beautiful, rich-grained mahogany. The spacious, open interior was starkly modern, which surprised Nick. The ceilings were over ten feet tall, since they were on the top floor. Her cherry cabinets matched the rich color of the mahogany front door, and light tan, tumbled marble countertops completed the contemporary look.

He followed her down a short hallway, past a guest bathroom on one side, an opened door to what looked like her home office across the hall, and to her bedroom door at the end. She touched a switch and simultaneously a fireplace lit up and low lighting dotted the room, including a faint spotlight on a painting over her bed. Nick walked up and examined the unusual painting, which was abstract, but in very warm colors.

"Nice," he said, turning around looking at the room. He felt a little like when he'd visited his grandmother's house as a child and his mother chided him about not touching anything. This was far from the bachelor apartment he and Marc shared in San Diego. Although it was clean, theirs was about as sparse as it could be. They'd even lived in it for nearly six months before they had any furniture, and the big screen TV, their first purchase, still stood on the cardboard box it came in. They used to eat on the floor against the opposite wall. Suddenly he was afraid Devon would never approve of his lifestyle, which meant he wasn't so sure she would approve of him.

Until he saw her leaning against the doorframe. She'd dropped her purse and jacket on the floor and was slipping off her shoes.

"I'm glad you like it," she whispered.

He perused her body, from ankles to the shadow below her chin, then met her eyes and smiled. "I like it a lot. Every part of it."

She shrugged her shoulders and gazed down to her feet, wiggling her toes. She was blushing. When her eyes found his again, there was no mistaking their smoldering heat, just like the fireplace switch she'd just turned on. He could almost hear her sizzling as well.

He'd missed her so much, it took all the control he had to hold himself back. They felt like a couple. She wasn't in any way distant to him, but he wanted to be careful with her.

"Are you going to make me wait?" she asked with heavy-lidded eyes.

"All good things come to those who wait." He said as he stepped to her. "I've missed you more than I ever could have imagined possible." He brushed her lips and cheek with the back of his fingers. He placed his forehead against hers. "I want to be—"

He saw her eyes watering.

"Honey, have I hurt you?" he asked.

"No, Nick. Honestly, I couldn't be happier."

With her head cupped between his two palms he bent down and kissed her, easing into her mouth, soaking up the sounds of her breathing. Devon was a whirlwind of sensations; the way she wrapped her arms around him tight, the way her taste and muskiness drove him crazy, her moans coming from her need of him. He descended into oblivion willingly.

She led him to her bed, pulling her little black dress over her head but still standing. He quickly removed his clothes, and walked naked to her lithe body, waiting for him.

He kissed her fingers. "This is so right, Devon."

Her eyes sparkled in the light of the fire. "Make love to me, Nick."

It was something he was very definitely going to do, and he was going to make it memorable. She was everything to him. She was his inspiration. He wanted to devour every inch of her body again and again.

CHAPTER 24

Next morning, lying next to Devon's sleeping form, Nick hoped Sophie would get stronger. Perhaps they'd find something they hadn't detected, something they could treat her for that would improve the quality of her life. He knew it was a long shot, but he was filled with hope this morning. When he was with Devon, everything seemed possible. Even Sophie living to a ripe old age was a possibility.

Nick placed two calls to Dr. Harris, but only got the Duty nurse. Devon listened while she explained Sophie had finally fallen asleep and Dr. Harris had left strict instructions to not let her be disturbed. They weren't going to attempt to move her until Dr. Harris arrived sometime after noon. She recommended they not visit until well after lunch.

Devon asked him to take her to the bistro on Fourth Street, and they arrived just in time for brunch. They got a table by the fireplace, the same one they'd had before. Instead of sitting across from her, he pulled up a chair and they sat side by side, staring into the flames. With their backs to the restaurant, it was almost as if they were totally alone. His firm thigh against hers was reassuring, but the sexual tension still caused her breathing to be labored.

What is this?

It wasn't nerves. It was energy. Pure energy, which she drew from him. Did she have that same effect on him, she wondered? Her spirit had been released. A dull rumble like kettle drums being played with woolen mittens vibrated her insides. She was excited to be alive as never before.

"I like how you dress up all professional for me after we've had sex. You look hotter than hell, sweetheart."

She loved hearing this. "I didn't dress up for you. Usually I'm *un*dressing for you."

"And that's a good thing too. A beautiful thing." He kissed her.

A cheesy scramble with buttered sourdough toast was placed between them. She'd been so hungry when she ordered. Now, as she stared at the food, she realized the butterflies in her stomach had taken away her appetite. She actually loved feeling hungry. Hungry for him most of all.

Nick wouldn't pick up his fork until she did. His thoughtfulness touched her and as she looked at his lips that quirked up at one corner, she saw he was begging for a kiss.

So she leaned into him and brushed his lips as she said, "I know it's eggs, but you might consider the oysters for dessert."

He completed the kiss against her. "I don't need anything but you, baby."

She picked at her food, but Nick tore into the breakfast with gusto. Flames from the fireplace in front of them warmed her cheeks, but the feel of the side of his muscled arm and thigh against her body as she rested her head on his shoulder was even hotter.

He offered a forkful on several occasions, and she accepted mostly because she liked the way he watched her mouth work. In between his feeding they would kiss.

She had been thinking it couldn't get any better than this. She could stay in the cocoon of this warm morning forever.

Out of the corner of her eye she saw movement. A group of men gathered on the sidewalk at the other side of the glass picture window, engrossed in discussion. One of them was the broker who had tried to force her to accept an offer on Sophie's property. She felt odd about seeing him here, and nervousness snaked up her spine.

"Nick, look. That's Mr. Silva, the broker who tried to show your sister's property."

Nick glanced outside with a slow but steady adjustment of his head. Devon thought perhaps it was his intense stare, but the men suddenly turned and regarded him. Mr. Silva faced Devon and gave her a slight bow and then adjusted so his back was to them, saying something to the other two men he probably didn't want understood.

"I don't trust him. I didn't like him then. Your sister doesn't like the neighbor, either."

"We've got to hope that the Fire Department gets some leads on the fire soon. Not much we can do about it, except protect Sophie." He wrapped an arm around Devon's shoulder and shook her. "It's going to be okay. Not much they can do since the property is already in escrow, right?"

"Well, the buyers so far don't know about all this. I have to call them this morning."

"Sophie has insurance, right?"

"I think so, Nick, but to be honest, she's not been thinking clearly, and things have been slipping."

Nick took a drink of water and crunched down some ice cubes. "Yeah. I was afraid of that."

"We have reports that are on their way. The buyers have to approve all that. Nothing is done until the escrow closes and she gets her check."

Nick took a quick peek at the group of men again. "Come on, Devon. I'd like to get you away from here."

Devon walked hand in hand with Nick until they reached her Lexus down the street. She watched him take a quick look around the vehicle, even managing to check out the undercarriage. His muscled forearms pushed against the sidewalk as he brought himself up to standing position easily with a snap. He dusted his palms.

"Just being extra careful. I guess I'll be looking for incendiary devices the rest of my life. Sorry."

He hung his head and rolled his shoulders, but his eyes told her he was not nearly as casual as he tried to look. Devon peered down the street in both directions, looking for Mr. Silva and the group of men, but saw nothing that caught her eye. She allowed Nick to open her door for her.

"Nick, I need to go to the office so I can give the buyers a call. Or should we try to see Sophie first?"

"No, let's get hold of the buyers. I'll wait in the car while you make that call."

"That's probably a good idea." She didn't really want to expose him to the attentions of the other women in the office. But then she thought about it.

Time to come out of my shell a bit. Trust him a little. And myself.

"On second thought, Nick, the ladies at the office might appreciate it if you sat in the waiting room." She watched for a reaction but didn't get the one she wanted.

"Oh really?" He squinted. She loved the mystery there. "You trying to get rid of me, sweetheart," he said in his best Bogart voice. "Or is it you want to show off your trophy boyfriend?"

She bit her lip at the sound of the word.

Boyfriend.

"Well, thought you SEALs like all the attention. We've got our share of hotties."

"Dance card's taken, baby," he said as he gave her that smoldering bedroom look. "I got it major bad."

"Glad to hear it. Me too."

They kissed. "Your wish is my command," he whispered. "I'll go anywhere you want me to."

"Well, I can share you with a few of the lovelies for just a few minutes, as long as I'm the one you go home with. I won't be very long, Nick."

"Some of them were at the big nursery liquidation sale, if I remember right."

"Yes," she chuckled, "And have never stopped talking about it, either. You guys left quite an impression on most the female population of Sonoma County."

She knew he was being modest, perhaps even a little shy. His head was turned to look out to his left so she couldn't see his expression. She'd always thought of him as being so egotistical…until she got to know him. Now she saw his calm demeanor and confidence as strength instead of bravado. Or was it that she was being more able to handle the bravado? It didn't matter. She just enjoyed being with the man, doing anything.

The realty office was a small bungalow with steep slate tile roof, bordered with rose bushes. She'd always liked the location, and the fact that the owner's wife had such a green thumb. Devon often brought big bouquets of fresh roses to sit on her desk.

Nick deposited himself on a Mission-style leather couch and picked up a decorating magazine, which made Devon smile.

"What?" he asked. His green eyes giving her the come-on that melted her bones. That damned little corner of his mouth twitching up to the right made her want to jump him right there. His huge veined hands were clutching a pale green magazine with a picture of a flower garden on the cover.

"You interested in decorating?" she finally asked.

"You should see my apartment. Since I'm hoping a certain female will come down and visit me," he paused, and then continued, "I was thinking I better start transforming it from a crash pad to something she might not want to run screaming away from."

"But then you'd catch me," she said, accepting the challenge.

"That I would, Miss Devon. I'd make you pay as well."

"Hmmm. I'm thinking we might have to role-play a bit on that one."

"I might have to restrain you to keep you from running away. But somehow I think you might like it."

She blushed just as a pair of high-heeled younger agents in tight skirts walked past and drank in the sight of Nick's large frame casually taking up the entire couch. They leveled cool glares at Devon.

"I was kinda hoping for the restraints, myself," she said within earshot of the girls. It embarrassed her and she felt her ears go red at the tips, but she enjoyed the risqué feeling of their sexual banter. One of the ladies turned around with her palm to her mouth. Devon wiggled her eyebrows up and down at Nick, surprised at her own bravado. "Back to work," she said as she went back into her office.

He stood and followed her in.

"Back outside." She pointed to the couch. "All good things come to those who wait, remember?"

"Within reason."

"Oh, so it's reasonable you want now. Well, I've got a house payment to make, and if I don't make some calls, I'll be borrowing from savings."

He'd stopped but he was still looking for encouragement.

She put her hands on her hips. "Back on the couch. I've got to have some privacy. Won't take long." Then she softened her voice and whispered, "I promise."

He went out, sat, adjusted his large frame, and picked up the magazine again, pretending to be interested in it. He was purposely ignoring her.

"I'll just be here, studying." Nick said to no one in particular with a sigh. He had that look that said everything. His warm smile and casual interest, just the right kind of interest without being a pest, allowing her to take the lead sometimes, appearing to enjoy just being around her. It was quickly becoming such a pleasant routine. The more she spent time with him, the harder it would be to say goodbye when he had to go back to San Diego.

At her desk, she dialed the number for the buyers.

"I suppose you've seen the papers this morning?" she asked the buyers.

"Yes. We were wondering what the bank was going to say about our loan now."

The loan had been approved, subject to the appraisal and approval of the property reports.

"I'm sure she had insurance. I'll be checking into that today. We might be able to just get a cash contribution instead of having them rebuild the structure. That way, you could do whatever you wanted there."

"They do that?"

"Well, we can ask. Can't say as I've had this experience before. A lady in our office burned a house down after an open house when she left some candles burning. In that case, the owner decided to stay when he saw what the remodel was going to look like. But with Sophie, she has no choice. She has to sell. So, we'll just have to see, as long as you're comfortable with it."

"Okay. We're kind of nervous about all this. Kinda like a sign from above, you know what I mean?"

"That's why I'm calling you. Once I have the reports, that's when we'll have to make up our minds what to do. I just didn't want you to think that everything was off just because of the fire."

"What caused it?"

Devon didn't want to give her suspicions. Besides, it was nothing she could prove. But her instincts told her she was right. "The fire investigator hasn't completed his report. You'll know it as soon as Sophie and I do, and not a day later."

"Thank you Miss Brandeburg."

"Not at all."

The next call she made was to the house inspector. She needed him to speed up getting the written report for the inspection done before the fire. She also wanted him to come back out to verify there was no permanent damage to the house, even though the office/showroom was a total loss. She also called the well inspector.

"Report's already in the mail to you," he said.

"I told you to email it to me."

"No problem. I'll get it to you later today."

"Everything okay with the report?"

"All within acceptable levels, except for the arsenic levels. But your client has a filter at the water tank to take care of that."

"Did you test the water there too?"

"We don't usually. The arsenic level is pretty low, almost acceptable levels. She's got an overkill system on the tank, so I didn't think there was a need."

Devon questioned this for a minute and then dismissed it as being overly worried. "But you'll note that in your report."

"I certainly will."

She left messages for the escrow officer and the lender. Satisfied there wasn't anything else she could do, she went to join Nick in the reception area.

She heard him talking to someone, and couldn't mistake the laughter of several young women in response. She found him in the center of a bevy of young staffers and newbie agents, all asking questions about the teams and wanting to know if he'd been part of the Bin Laden raid.

"Nope, I'm on a different team." He sneaked a smile in Devon's direction as she watched heads turn toward her. She knew her chest was splotchy red and her cheeks flushed. Nick saved the day and got the attention off her. "Well, ladies," the crowd shifted to regard him, "my *ride* is here," he said in that damned sexy way of his The girls uniformly sighed.

He opened the door for her and the real world came crashing in on them both. The heaviness lurking in the outer reaches of her mind came forward into full focus.

Sophie.

171

CHAPTER 25

Devon got a call from the well inspector on their way to visit Sophie at the hospital. The report had been sent to her computer and she'd print it out later.

She wasn't sure what she expected when they got to Sophie's new room, but it was obvious her best friend was fast becoming a mere shadow of herself. It worried her how rapidly Sophie was crashing.

Dr. Harris met them at Sophie's bedside in her private room. Her friend's eyes had become sunken, and when she searched their faces, there was something else there Devon had never seen before.

Fear.

Devon swallowed hard. The reality that her best friend's life was ebbing rapidly away hit her square in the stomach.

She felt Nick's hand grip hers harder. It was difficult for him, too. His huge chest was jerking with ragged sounds he was trying to hide. She realized suddenly that perhaps he needed her strength. It must have been new territory for him. Not the death part, but the part about losing Sophie.

And not being able to do anything about it.

Dr. Harris had finished checking Sophie over. His expression was grim. He shook his head to Nick very discreetly, but Sophie saw it.

"Don't hide this from me. Don't I got a right to know what's going on?"

"No one's hiding anything," Nick started. He knelt on the linoleum floor at her bedside, taking her emaciated hand in his huge paws. He kissed her like she was a queen. He placed her palm against his face, as if to say, *Come back, sis. Don't leave me.*

Devon reached out to rub Sophie's toes through the blanket, not knowing what else to do. Sophie pulled her eyes from her brother's bowed head, his face buried into her palm on the bed, and glanced up at Devon with that almost whimsical expression.

"Devon, I can't feel my toes. Come here so I can feel the warmth of your hands."

Devon lost it. She ran to Sophie's bedside. "God, Sophie," she sobbed. "You gotta hang on. It's too soon."

Sophie looked down on her with kindness as she stroked Devon's hair like a mother would pet a small child. "No, sweetheart. It's too late." Then she looked over at Nick, and she pulled their hands together across her lap. She placed both her hands on top of their entwined fingers. "But you have your whole life ahead of you. You were made for each other. Biggest mistake of my life was looking for Mr. Perfect instead of Mr. Right."

Devon's hot tears stained the white, loosely-woven hospital blanket. She wished she could trade places with Sophie. Through her tears, she saw Nick stare downward at the face of his sister. His jaw muscles were rippling, and she could see he was grinding his teeth. When he looked up at her, his hardness, his shell of composure was gone. His green eyes were vacant and the sparkle was missing. She rubbed her thumb over his fingers. Her own tears dried up as she gave him back what she had. She remembered what she'd said earlier, *I can only give you what I've got.*

She wondered if it would be enough.

"She's got to rest now. We'll call you in the morning," Dr. Harris said to the two of them. He smiled down on Sophie.

"No. Let them stay awhile. I don't want them to go," Sophie pleaded, her eyes wildly searching from face to face in front of her.

"Hon, you've got to build your strength. Tomorrow I have more tests ordered," the doctor said.

"Enough of the tests! If I was 90, you wouldn't be doing so much to try to keep me alive. I want to go home to my nursery, Doc. Let them take me home."

"Tomorrow. You can go home tomorrow."

"You want me to stay, Sophie?" Devon asked. She could see worry lines pop across Sophie's forehead and knew she was wrestling with the decision. Sophie was concerned she'd not see them again. It broke Devon's heart.

"Let's stay, Nick. Let's stay tonight with Sophie."

He nodded, trying to hold tears at bay. His bottom lip quivered as he leaned back. He stood and patted Sophie's hand, the one that held Devon's.

"I'll get another bed brought in here. It's going to be tight quarters," Dr. Harris said.

"I'll go help. Be right back," Nick said to the floor.

Sophie patted the bed for Devon to sit there. "Something about Nick. He has those places he goes. Very scary places. I saw it when he came back from his first tour. I'd seen it when our parents died, but I didn't recognize it. He will have a hard time with all this," she said as she opened her palms and drew her arms out to the side.

"You're not going anywhere, Sophie. Please don't talk that way."

"Oh, shut up and listen for once, Devon. I can't say these things in front of him. He has an unhealed wound from Mom and Dad's problems, and then their deaths. He wanted to save the house and couldn't. He was in high school and there wasn't anything he could have done, but he holds himself responsible for Dad's death. After our dad died, Mom just lost the will to live. And Nick has that same affliction. You're going to have to rescue him, Devon, because he won't ask for help."

Devon had never thought of Nick as needy in any way. He was always the teacher, always the one in charge. It didn't seem like the Nick she knew, to not be in control. She thought perhaps Sophie was delusional.

"Remember what I told you," Sophie said as they heard wheels rattling down the hospital corridor. "Rescue him. He needs to have someone to believe in. Someone to live for."

She nodded. "I understand."

"Devon, it's going to be rough. He's going to want to shut you out. You just don't let him do that. I don't worry about you, my friend." In a whisper she said, "I worry about him."

"I promise."

"Promise what?" Nick said as he wheeled the folded bed inside the room. Harris was on the other side and pushed as Nick guided it next to Sophie's.

"I wanted her to promise she'd keep me up to date on the fire investigation."

Devon watched as they placed the bed next to Sophie's and opened it up, carefully avoiding the equipment. A yellow blanket and two pillows were in the middle of the mattress. She looked up at her friend.

"So you, see, Sophie, we won't leave you tonight. We'll take turns," she said as she glanced up at Nick, who still avoided eye contact.

"Listen, I'm going to have a little chat with Nick and Devon, explain the house rules. You try to take a catnap, okay, Miss Dunn?"

Devon's heart lurched at the way he said "Miss." She followed the two men outside into the hallway as Dr. Harris closed the door behind him.

"She's very fragile. Honestly, she's going downhill very quickly, guys. I wish I had better news for you."

"How long will she be here?" Nick asked.

Dr. Harris looked down at his feet and then faced his Navy buddy. "I can't in good conscience release her."

The reality of what he said finally sunk into Devon. "You mean—?"

"I'm afraid so. She doesn't want anything heroic done. She's not fighting. I'm pretty sure she's not in pain. She has a tough outer skin, but inside she's caved. She's given up. Unless you can convince her. Prayer works. Not much else we can do, since her kidneys are failing, and there's nothing I can give her for that. Kind of out of our hands. Best get yourselves adjusted to what is coming."

Nick cleared his throat and spoke in a soft voice that cracked like a teenager's. "How soon, Doc?"

Harris shook his head. "No way to tell, really. Just enjoy every minute you can. But let her rest, too. She needs her rest. But one of those naps—" he swung his heavy-lidded eyes between the two of them, "will be permanent, if she's lucky."

Nick's chest heaved as he stood to attention. She saw the muscles in his throat constrict. She saw how deliberately he drew in his breath and let it out several times, calming himself, reaching for control. Her heart felt crammed between the grief of losing Sophie and the heartache of seeing the effect it was having on him. Sophie had been right.

What was coming next was going to be worse for Nick than for her.

He said little. He stood at the foot of the bed, his mouth a straight line, when he normally softened his full lips that would curl up at one corner or the other at the slightest provocation. He never looked Devon's way, but gazed down on the sleeping form of his sister.

Devon wanted to touch his hand, hug him, but she kept her distance, dimly aware that something was smoldering inside him, something dark and extremely dangerous.

She could handle the dark and dangerous part. She knew she could. What she found the most difficult was that he wasn't in the least bit interested in talking to her. It was as if she a stranger, like one of the nurses.

Should I try to intervene in that no-man's land? Should I tell him how sorry I am?

Unsure what else to do, she stepped next to him and held his hand. Nick flinched at her touch, as if he hadn't realized she'd been standing there. He squeezed, but it was that of a scared child, and not something reassuring, warm, not acknowledging anything other than the fact that she'd touched him. He was holding on to her. Maybe that was going to be all she could give him right now.

She leaned into his shoulder, hoping perhaps he'd raise his arm and hold her, but he stiffly watched his sister's breathing. She wanted to lay her head on his chest and hold him. Wanted to rub her hands over his shoulders. Tell him there was going to be a happy ending. Tell him it was okay to cry or show his feelings, but she knew that was a complete mistake. So she held his hand, felt the heat of this gentle giant, who was in pain, and there wasn't anything she could do to help.

"I'm going down the hall to use the restroom," she whispered.

He didn't look at her, but nodded his head and released her hand.

"Okay, then," she said as she pressed her hair back from her face and wiped the tracks of tears from her cheeks. "I'll be right back."

She turned at the door, "Nick, you want anything?"

He looked at her finally, and she saw the vacant eyes of a hollow soul. God, how she wanted to hold him, but there was something there that told her it wasn't safe, and she desperately didn't want to be sent away. If she was quiet enough, maybe eventually he'd talk to her.

She let herself out of the room, the door softly closing behind her. She found the public restroom down the hall, and before she could lock the door she was already sobbing. She sat on the closed toilet lid and put her face in her hands and let loose all the tears she'd been holding in. Her breath hitched, her ribs convulsing as wave after wave of pain washed over her.

She looked across the sink to the mirror on the wall. She was not only losing Sophie. She was losing Nick, too.

She thought about what Sophie had said. *Rescue him. He needs to have someone he can believe in, live for.*

She took a deep breath and finally focused on her red face in the mirror. Could she do this? Could she be strong enough for both of them? Or—and her eyes began to fill with tears again—could she survive the loss of both of them? Her life had opened up to some of the most wonderful, magical days she'd ever experienced, and she'd missed him when he went back to San Diego. What if he wanted to go back home and not see her again? Could she handle it, if that's what he wanted? If she couldn't convince him otherwise?

I honestly don't know.

She put cold water on her face and ran fingers through her hair, fluffing it out at the sides. She said a little silent prayer with her eyes closed. She had to go back and face them both, and she loved them with her whole heart.

Both of them.

When she got back to the room, Nick was lying down on the bed next to Sophie, holding her hand. He'd removed his shoes and curled in an S with his muscled arm lying down the length of his body. He barely looked up, but gave Devon a forced smile, at least.

She got out the yellow blanket and unfolded it over his beautiful warrior's body. "Why don't you rest while she is? Let me stand guard for a bit," she said to him. He nodded, rubbing Sophie's fingers with his thumb the same way he'd rubbed her fingers just hours before.

Sophie remained very pale for the next hour, and didn't stir. Devon suspected she'd been given a light sedative to keep her calm. She remembered how Sophie had slept fitfully in the past weeks, and this wasn't anything like that.

She picked up a magazine from the counter and sat back in the comfortable recliner, watching brother and sister napping. She imagined what they must have looked like as children. She suspected they'd been close even as youngsters. She could imagine them playing in the sand at one of the San Diego beaches, eating sandwiches barefoot in the summertime at a picnic table on a green lawn somewhere. She imagined what Nick's caramel-colored hair looked like with his deep green eyes. Or, maybe he was a towhead? Sophie's reddish-brown hair would have been unkempt and unruly, kept too long. She could see her insisting her mother leave it long. That would be so much like Sophie. And she'd keep brushing it out of her eyes but would never tie it up. She probably looked like a wild child growing up.

Sophie opened her eyes and stared back at her, smiling.

"Love you," she mouthed to Devon without waking Nick, who was snoring.

"Love you." Devon returned silently. She held her hand over her heart.

They stared at each other for several minutes, Sophie's peaceful smile like a bow on a happy package she might have wrapped at the store. She looked younger. A pink glow developed on her cheeks and Devon was gladdened to see the color return to her face.

Devon continued to hold her gaze, smiling, nodding. She almost woke Nick to show him how beautiful and healthy Sophie looked…until she realized that Sophie's eyes hadn't moved or blinked for the past few minutes. When Devon sat straighter and leaned forward, Sophie's eyes didn't follow her, but stared on, unseeing, as empty as the smile that remained on her lips.

No. This can't be. Sophie, not now. It's too soon.

She heard Sophie's voice replay in her mind, *'No, it's too late.'*

'I don't worry about you. I worry about him. Rescue him.'

She pressed the tears off her cheeks with her palms, licked her lips and took in a deep breath. *I can do this. I've lost her. I won't lose him.*

She stood up, folded herself behind Nick on the bed and kissed him on the ear, whispering, "She's gone, Nick. Sophie's gone."

Nick bolted to consciousness with a start. He sat up, squeezing Sophie's limp hand. He placed his palms on either side of her face, moving her open-eyed face back and forth. "Sophie, Sophie wake up. Please wake up."

At the moment he realized she was gone, he threw himself over her body and sobbed. Devon rubbed a palm down his back, keeping up a gentle rhythm, feeling the power and strength of him and the depth of his sorrow.

"Oh God, Sophie. I wasn't there," he sobbed.

Devon looked into the blank stare on her friend's face and suddenly realized that Sophie knew he couldn't handle her crossing over to the other side, but knew Devon could. So Sophie shared the reality of her own death with her best friend so she wouldn't be alone.

But now Devon was.

CHAPTER 26

Neither of them spoke on the trip back to Devon's condo. Drained from watching as Sophie's lifeless body was attended to, checked and certified, then covered, after her eyes had been gently closed by Dr. Harris, Nick wasn't sure what he was feeling. It certainly was a mixture of rage, disappointment or guilt—all the things he recognized as signs of PTSD, except this wasn't a battle somewhere in the middle of a scorched, dusty wasteland.

Devon was quiet, and he was thankful for that. He could tell she was a little afraid of him, and that instinct was good. He wasn't going to be very safe company. He really didn't want to expend the energy to reel himself in. He even wondered if he should be around her, since there was part of him that felt unpredictable and dangerous.

He didn't have a problem with death. He'd gotten very personal with Dr. Death over the years. He'd taken lives, seen buddies get wounded or killed next to him and had the calm patience to wait for the bad guy and get the retaliatory kill. Didn't bring his buddy back, but it had to be done. Just what he'd been trained to do. If his buddy was dead, it was time to calmly extract the price from the guy who made the mistake of thinking he'd get away with his kill shot . They never got away with it. Not when Nick was around. Not if they'd caused injury to someone on Nick's side of the ledger. Every single one of them would pay.

But with Sophie, there was no enemy. Might have been easier if there was. He could blame God, but he'd never been a believer. He'd wanted to grow up and grow up quick. He hadn't liked being a young, innocent teenager, vulnerable, with no bad-ass bigger brother or father to protect him. The Navy would and did do that.

Devon didn't turn on a ton of lights when they stepped inside her condo. He was halfway surprised they'd made it there, since he didn't remember the drive. Couldn't even remember if he drove, or she did.

I did. I just fuckin' put it on autopilot.

But this wasn't home. He needed to go back to the mindless activities and strong friendships of his buddies. He had no business being here. He wanted to bury all the memories with Sophie. Two painful days, maybe three, and then he'd be gone. Maybe never to return. He hoped he wouldn't have to.

He knew he should feel bad about Devon, but he couldn't find the space in his aching heart. There just wasn't any room. It was filled with blood and fury. Dr. Death sat on his throne and laughed at him. In time, he'd learn to laugh right back, and that's when the sucker would take a hiatus. Go pick on some other poor soldier.

But that could only happen in the group workouts, the trash talk with his teammates, the swims in the inlet and Bay, the runs on the beach where he'd go until he collapsed. Midnight runs. Maybe some skydiving where he'd wait a little too long to pull the cord, just to make sure he was alive enough to feel the fear. Five or six jumps in a row would give him the rush of life he needed. Yeah, he missed the sea and the freefalling. Sailing through the sky until the warmth of the earth greeted him, unthawed him, and welcomed him back to gravity.

And he'd have to get himself straightened out before the next workup. A few months of PT, then a couple special trainings, and he'd be rock hard and solid. Emotions in check, locked down. Covered in nylon, Velcro and Kevlar. A hundred pounds of equipment on his back, legs and shoulders, running full into the firefight or waiting on top of a building. Slow breathing, calculating the mission. One, two, three kills would settle his nerves. He might even think of doing it for Sophie. Now *that* thought scared him.

Devon had brewed tea. He didn't know how he got there, but he was sitting on a green leather chair when she handed him the warm mug. He took it without looking at her, aware that she wanted something from him, and he had nothing to give. Like he had numbed himself to anything on the outside of his boiling insides.

She put on some quiet music, came over to him as he held the mug on his thigh, staring at the floor.

"Nick, here, drink this. It will make you feel better," she whispered as her warm hands guided the mug to his lips. He sipped and burned himself, but didn't move a muscle.

He didn't care.

She left her palms on his knees, rubbing his thighs like she was rubbing a child who had gotten too cold at the pool. He remembered telling her he was a polar bear. He was certainly one today. Cold as hell. Except for the thumping of his heart, beating loud, vibrating his rib cage.

He took a deep breath and another burning sip, and winced at the pain he was beginning to feel.

"Is it too hot?" she asked, still kneeling in front of him like a supplicant, her eyes wide and dark as chocolate.

He glared down at her. *You really want to pick a fight with me?*

She didn't back down, which would have been safer. For him too. But she kept up the annoying rubbing of his legs, bringing to life the rage and anger, the *I-hate-everyone-including-you* feeling that suddenly gripped him.

He focused on her eyes while setting the mug down on the floor.

You really want part of me? Really?

He grabbed her hair at the nape of her neck and tugged, exposing her neck to him. He slid off the chair onto his knees in front of her as he kissed her neck, then sucked, running his teeth over the soft tissues. He could taste a little of her blood from the welt he created.

He detached her from his chest, unpeeling her arms from his shoulders, holding her off at a safe distance, his fist still in her hair. He studied her. She'd closed her eyes. He could see her tears overflowing her long lashes and streaking down her cheeks. He wanted to see her cry. He wasn't sure *he* could cry any more, but he wanted to see *her* cry, see her in pain.

"Open your eyes, dammit," he bellowed.

When she did, it was exactly what he wanted to see. Her fear. Her pain. He lived off that pain. It was his lifeline. The red blotch on her neck from the deep hicky he'd caused inflamed him, and made him rock hard. The sight of her blood made him want to fuck her senseless.

He ripped off her blouse, tearing the fabric. She tried to scramble away and he caught her by the ankle and tugged her to him.

"You want to play with me? You want something from me? *This* is what I need, baby. This is who I am."

She closed her eyes again and then, as if remembering his command, flashed them open again. She swallowed, waiting. He finished taking off the shredded blouse, jerking it loose from her arms without an ounce of tenderness. He removed her bra without tearing it apart but threw it across the room. With one hand he pulled at her pants and tugged them off her hips before he got her unzipped, while holding her upper arm roughly, squeezing her so hard he could feel her bone.

The scent of her panties was strong and she had sweat between her legs. She was breathing hard and he could feel her fear. It was a benediction to him.

Still holding her arm even as she wiggled and made little whimpering noises, he clutched at the triangle between her legs and ripped her panties from her flesh and sunk his head into her lap. He bit her labia, sucked at her cunt, making it a meal, devouring it, owning all of her.

But then she did something extraordinary. She arched back, falling into the carpeting, and moaned into him. With arms outstretched and fingers clutching the carpet, she lifted herself up and pressed herself into his mouth, forcing his teeth on her, forcing his tongue deep inside her.

He didn't want to see her pleasure. It actually inflamed him, made him mad. He grabbed the sash from the bathrobe lying over the chair and wound it around her wrists held high above her head, tightening them hard and making a knot.

She still writhed beneath him, moaning, which pissed him off further. He wanted to go down on her but his dick was crammed so tight in his pants it was causing him pain, which he welcomed. But he had to set it free.

He unzipped himself as she began to rise up, her bound arms coming to hook over his neck, but he shoved her back down into the floor roughly. Her eyes flashed at him and he smirked.

You want me, baby? You really want me? You see what kind of a man I am, and you want me?

He was rewarded when she shuddered and closed her eyes, more tears coming down her cheeks.

"I told you to open your eyes and see me. See me as I fuck you."

Her brave expression bore the shame he knew he would feel later on. It was lurking right there, but it didn't matter. He was on a kill mission. Nothing would get in the way of that satisfying fuck and debasement he needed.

His cock lobbed free and he stroked himself. He needed to sink into her deep. Her lips were tightened into an expression of pain as he plunged three of his fingers inside her. She arched her chest and her tits rose over her flat abs. She'd tried to put a leg up to his shoulder as he replaced his fingers with his stiff, aching cock. He pushed her leg aside roughly, aiming for fuller penetration.,

Devon's eyes grew huge as she began to grasp where he was going. That he wouldn't be able to stop.

His cock rammed inside her all the way to the hilt while his thumb kept up a steady pressure on her clit. He pushed as hard as he could, increased the pace until the sounds of the backs of her thighs slapping against his drowned out all sound.

His thumb pressed her nub harder as his cock began to spill.

Until he looked her in the eyes. He saw the cost of his fury looking back at him through tears of pain. Even some loathing.

His actions were sickening him, but he couldn't stop.

Devon took in a deep breath and screamed, "No."

Her voice echoed off the marble walls of the bathroom. Like he was hearing it from the television or some device, he looked up at the sound. He was acting in slow motion. His pumping action continued, until he felt her foot punch him in the chest, sending him backward.

She scrambled to her feet, covering her body up with her fallen dress. Her hands, still bound in the pink sash, clutched the black fabric as she backed up from him, the look of complete hatred coming straight at him, hitting him as hard as her foot had.

"Get out. Get out right now or I will call the police."

He knew it was the right thing, but his head was foggy. He wasn't sure if she had been talking him or to or someone else. Then, in a sudden wave of revulsion, he realized what he'd done.

And what he'd spoiled.

CHAPTER 27

Devon was used to being alone. She was not used to being violated, used as a pleasure doll, if that's what it could be called. The shame of it all was that her body had responded involuntarily at first, just as his had. She had met him in that wasteland she didn't know she had inside her.

Her instincts had told her to watch out, keep a safe distance from him, and she'd ignored those niggling voices with disastrous consequences. She didn't want to look at him. She tried to will herself to transport someplace else, any place else. Maybe she should join Sophie. Maybe Heaven would be a safer place than any reality that had Nick in it.

He reached forward, grabbing her bound wrists and untied her. She fought against him though it was useless.

"Don't touch me," she yelled, trying to kick him to knock him off balance. "Just get out," she mustered the bravado to shriek. Tears collected, threatening to wash over her, and her sobs would soon follow. She would not give him the satisfaction of seeing her cry.

Just a little while longer and he'll be gone. You can hold it together for just a little while longer.

She was going to carefully excise him from her heart with a rusty spoon, make it hurt, get a fever and perhaps die trying to heal. Or scab up so hard she'd never forget how life was not fair and people you thought you loved and trusted could hurt you in the worst possible way.

Devon would not look at him. She didn't want to remember what he looked like, if he was sorry or not. She didn't want to know. Didn't make any difference, anyway.

His fingers dropped the tie over the robe still lying against the chair where it had been left this morning, when the world had been a totally different universe.

His callused fingers reaching behind her head and pulled her forehead against his lips and kissed her there. And he whispered, "I'm sorry."

The man walked out her door and down the hallway while she stood naked in her living room . She heard the elevator doors open and then knew he was gone. Out of her life forever.

Why had she thought she could help him? What insanity had overcome her, that she would agree to Sophie's last dying prayer? And now she'd be grieving not only the loss of her best friend, but the end of the new, fresh love that she'd hoped would bring light and something miraculous to her life. And there was something else she'd discovered. Though her heart hurt, hanging parched and lifeless in her chest, her body craved him still.

She hated herself for that.

She walked to her shower, ready to rid herself of the stink of him, his mouth on her, any smell of his legs and arms, the musky scent under his chin and at the top of his chest, and—she heaved a sigh and turned on the shower. She poured shower gel all over her and scrubbed.

In the back of her mind Mitzi Gaynor was still young and alive, on a beach somewhere with a big blue sky background, washing her hair, and singing.

But unlike Mitzi, Devon wasn't going to be smiling at the camera anytime soon.

Or singing.

Nick walked with his hands in his pockets, still smelling her on him. His fingers were sticky with her juices.

Everyone he'd ever cared about was dead, and just because Devon had thought for some fucked-up reason she was going to be able to stand between him and his grief, he'd destroyed her innocence. Why had he even touched her in the first place? If he could only take back the last forty days. She deserved way more, and now it would never be the same because he'd been so angry he wanted to wipe out everything that was soft and beautiful and right in the world.

When he thought about it, he was angry with Sophie, and that was a fucked-up thought, for sure. He walked down the sidewalk in the trendy downtown neighborhood and headed into the first bar he could find.

He perched on a black leather stool and tried to focus on the basketball game blaring on a big screen TV in front of him. The heavily made up bartender with big tits smiled, and yeah, she knew that look. She'd been doing this for a long time. She didn't even try to talk to him, just let her fingers play an imaginary piano on the wooden bar while he made up his mind which kind of poison he'd ingest. Nothing she was going to say to him was going to make a shitpile of difference. She knew that. Well at least there was one person in the world who understood him. Some stranger who was paid to diagnose and deliver the dose of his own demise.

Then he remembered Marc. While Nick had been with Sophie and then caught up in his fire-breathing psychotic session with Devon, he'd neglected to tell Mark that Sophie had died. Marc had feelings for her. Right now that was the only thing that made him sad. So he dialed his roommate.

"I was beginning to worry about you, Dunn. But I figured you'd surface—"

"Sophie's dead, Marc."

The pause was difficult. Marc hung up.

Nick redialed him. The phone went right to voicemail. "Hey Marky, I'm sorry, I'm in a really dangerous place, man. But you need to know, she didn't suffer. And I was with her, sort of." He sighed into the receiver as he hailed for another beer. While on the phone, he nearly downed the whole thing. "Mark. Mark." He felt the tears coming on and couldn't finish. He disconnected, stood up, threw a twenty on the counter, slipped the handle of his bag over his right shoulder, and left the rest of his beer on the bar.

The coolness outside chilled him and somehow made him feel better. He knew where he could go, if he could get a cab.

The cabbie inquired several times along the steep road, probably trying to reassure himself Nick wasn't a freakin' serial killer.

"No, man. Look, I've just lost my sister. I want you to just drop me off at this special place."

The guy wouldn't stop checking his rear view mirror every ten seconds or so, scrunching in his seat several times as they came upon the field with the lights that glowed from Cloverdale to San Francisco. Even though it was cold, the crickets were still chirping. He heard a few frogs echoing from the little creeks and streams nearby.

He handed the cabbie twenty dollars and asked him if he had a blanket he could buy. The college kid got out, searched his dirty trunk and threw an old, stained, quilted bedspread at him. "Keep it, mister. But I'm not coming back."

"No problem," Nick said, but of course the cabbie didn't hear him because he was nearly ten feet away and speeding up as fast as he could to get out of Dodge.

Nick wrapped the smelly quilt around him, tossed the bag aside and sat down. The lights were the same, bright and full of hope and promise. The grasses that he could smell and the sounds of the crickets were just like the night he made love to Devon, when he was sure they had a love that would last forever, or a lust that would at least get him halfway there until fate would carry them the rest of the way. He hadn't dreaded the next day like he did tonight. He had never felt so alone in his life.

The last time he would ever touch her had been tonight, when he'd kissed her on the forehead. He should have said something else, something meaningful, something that might ease some of the pain, like she'd tried to do for him. But he'd been afraid of what would come out. Now that he knew what he was capable of, he was going to stay as far away from her as possible.

Marc rang Nick back about a half hour later.

"So when's the funeral, or did you leave me out of that one too, you fuckin' asshole?"

Yeah, he deserved that. "I'm going to work on it tomorrow. I have no idea what to do. I don't even know if she had any requests."

"Of course you didn't." Marc sucked in air on the other end of the line. "She gave them to me."

"You're kidding."

"You're fuckin' lucky I'm not up there. You need to get a couple of your teeth knocked out."

"So email it to me—or—or fax it to me?"

"You are a major prick, Nick. Think the whole fuckin' world revolves around your sorry ass."

Guilty as charged.

"I'm flying up there tomorrow. Already got my direct flight."

"'kay."

"Can Miss Devon put me up too?"

Nick's chest filled with cool night air and then he blew it out. " No, I'm not going to be at Devon's."

"You're kidding."

"It wasn't going to work. All the stress of Sophie. We broke it off, Marc."

"Sure you did. She's under your skin unlike anyone I've ever seen you around. You'll go to your grave regretting it if you let that one get away."

"Not going to happen, Marc. It's already done. Nothing I can do."

"Like hell. Well, I can tell you've been making some colossally great fuckin' decisions, as usual. There someone else?"

"No Marc, there is no one. I'm all alone and it's going to stay that way."

"Pick me up at ten at the airport. You got a car?"

"I will have."

"I got one ordered at the airport. You think you can find a cab to get you there?"

"Fuck you. I don't need a nursemaid," Nick said, getting angry.

"Yeah, fuck you, too. See you tomorrow at ten."

Until Marc's call, he hadn't had any focus and wasn't sure he wanted to do anything but join Sophie. But his friend needed to do this for Sophie. *He* needed to do this for Sophie. After that? Well, he'd just have to wait and see if life was worth living.

CHAPTER 28

Nick arrived at the terminal at Charles Schulz International Airport a good hour early. It wasn't because he thought the plane from San Diego would come in ahead of schedule. It was because he had nowhere else to go. And he didn't want to be alone.

Last night, he'd walked down the country lane until got to the bottom of the hill and found a decent motel nearby. The room smelled of cigarettes, but he wasn't choosy. It offered a good pancake breakfast and he suspected he'd need some carbs for the headache he was on track to earn. After he'd checked in, he walked across the street and purchased a six pack of long-necked local microbrew, frosty and with a heavy, hoppy head.

He hadn't turned on the TV, but sat propped up on his bed watching the black screen anyway. He'd thought about all the motels he'd stayed in and all the adult movies he'd devoured. He couldn't get the images of what he'd done to Devon out of his head, almost like it had been some other man in his personal video. As if she'd been unfaithful to him. Maybe it would be easier in time to blame her.

Not.

As numb and as vacant as he felt, he couldn't quite make himself go there.

He'd fallen asleep that way, nursing the last beer, and in the end spilling it on the bed.

The little prop jet made the windows rattle. He remembered being that guy, worried for his sister but so grateful he had Devon's fresh face greeting him. He'd never forget how she looked that day. A little shy, gazing into his eyes as if trying to reassure herself he was still there for her. Yeah, he'd been there for her *that* day. How had things changed so fast? If only he could do it all over again.

He'd make it through the preparations for Sophie's final farewell since he had Marc to help him. He told himself he'd just focus on repairing his relationship with his roommate. He'd certainly understand if Marc didn't want to remain friends. He had it coming.

Mark carried a suit bag slung over his shoulder. Nick realized he hadn't brought one with him. He rolled his shoulders and moved his head from side to side, his neck still stiff from falling asleep against the plastic bedframe.

"You look like hell, Nick."

"I'll bet. I feel worse."

"Let's do this," Marc said as he put on his sunglasses and they walked outside into the sunlight.

Devon had a visitor at the office. It was an investigator from the Santa Rosa Fire Department. He was an older man in his late fifties, with white hair, and looked like he had a fondness for fried food.

"Morning, Miss Brandeburg."

"Please," she said as she pointed to the comfortable leather swivel chair in front of her desk.

Her rear still smarted when she sat, and she closed her eyes, willing the sensation to go away...and it did. "This about Sophie Dunn's fire?" she asked.

"Yes, ma'am. We've run into a couple of things, and I need to ask you some questions."

"Go ahead."

"The police said you saw two men running into the field over the fence."

"That's right"

He read her the description of her interview with the detectives. "Anything more you'd like to add about that?"

Devon blinked twice without taking her eyes off him. "Like what?"

"Like were they lingering anywhere special beforehand?"

"No. I think they'd just came upon Sophie. Looked to me like they intended to do something to her house, or to her, although I didn't see them with her."

"Yes."

"I was paying more attention to Sophie, with the fire and all."

"I'll bet." He adjusted his legs. "Did you recognize them?"

"No, like I told the police, I'd never seen them before. They looked like young laborers. Grubby clothes and knitted caps over their heads."

"And looked to be young?"

"Yes, definitely young. I mean, anything from high school age to early twenties, I'd say."

He was making notes in his spiral notebook. After dotting a period somewhere, he squinted and glanced up at her. She could see he'd been a handsome man at one time, a nice man, she'd have to say. She was grateful for the protection and concern of someone who didn't have any designs on her.

"You want to tell me who you think did this?" he asked.

Devon had no hesitation in telling him. "The neighbor, owner of the BV Home Winery." She pulled a file from her desk drawer. "Mr. Enemorio Rodriguez. He has a broker named Ulysses Silva. I've only spoken with Silva."

"And why do you say this?"

"Sophie had a small land war going on with him over boundary issues, you know. Fences, and apparently the winery was running low on water. He'd drilled wells all around the northeast portion of the property line, wanting to tap into the aquifer Sophie's well came from. She had a very good commercial well."

"You ever see anyone but these two over at the property?" he asked.

"Just Mr. Silva, as I've told you. He claimed to have a buyer, a Chinese lady, but I don't think that was anything legit. I later found out from my manager that Silva has only one client, Mr. Rodriguez."

"I see. Have they contacted you since the fire?"

"No, why? You know, you should interview them."

"Oh, I intend to. Rather, the police are working on that now."

"And why is that?" she asked.

"Because we're fairly sure this is an intentional act."

Although it didn't surprise Devon, hearing the man say it coalesced her fear into one giant dark piece of sludge in her stomach. "Do you—" she stopped and looked at her hands folded on top of the manila file folder atop her desk. "Do you think I'm in any danger?"

The inspector frowned and checked his nails. She could see he was going to downplay his concern. She was beginning to be able to tell when a man was about to lie to her. Her allowed a brittle smile to escape her lips.

"I'd be careful. I wouldn't go over to the property without an escort. The police told me you have a boyfriend who I guess is a war hero, and he'd—"

"I'm sorry, but he's just Sophie's brother. He's not my boyfriend, and except for being the joint beneficiary of her will, has nothing to do with me."

"But I thought—"

She leaned back in her chair and put on her professional demeanor. "Things change." She sealed it with a smile she hoped gave him the message she didn't want to discuss it any further.

The receptionist brought in a faxed copy of the well report and laid it on Devon's desk. "This just came for you."

She flipped to the back page under conclusions and found the language she expected, "evidence of arsenic, slightly higher than acceptable Public Health standards. Recommend water treatment…" and they recommended a system she wasn't familiar with… "at water tank and annual monitoring for any increase."

She decided to have them inspect the water tank before it completely recovered, since they'd nearly emptied it from the fire, or so the Department said.

Devon met Williams Well Drilling at the property later that afternoon. The young technician had already collected water samples from outside the tank before she'd arrived.

"I'd like to check the house too, do a water quality test there as well, especially since there was a fire."

"Sure." She followed him inside Sophie's house. She looked at all the mementos, things her friend collected over the few short years she'd tried to carve out her own piece of Heaven. Pictures of her parents and of Nick growing up were in her bedroom. Devon had never noticed them before. Although she tried, she couldn't help staring down at the photographs of a tall, gangly kid with light brown hair, and a beach boy smile that must have flustered all the twelve-year-olds at Camp Wa Tam. He sat with a group of boys, felt hats on their heads, making them look like merry men of Nottingham for the camp photo. Sophie was at the back, one of the counselors. But Nick was the one her eye went right to. A shadow of the man she thought she knew.

"Miss Brandeburg?"

She heard the technician's voice coming from outside and realized she was now alone in the house. Chills traveled up her arms as the turned quickly and went outdoors to the sound of the man's voice.

He was standing on top of a ladder, overlooking the concrete water tank. He had a long rod with a jar of liquid hooked at the end of it. "There's something here I need you to look at."

"Yes?" she said as he carefully brought the rod and the glass jar down the ladder.

"Go on up there and tell me what you see," he said as he pointed to the ladder. Devon was grateful she'd worn her low-heeled pumps today to minimize the soreness in her thighs and calves, instead of the spiked heels she normally wore,. She climbed the ladder and peered down.

Nothing caught her eye. At first she was expecting a body or something sinister because her stomach had clenched up. "I don't know what you're talking about, here." She called out to the technician.

"You see those rocks at the bottom of the tank?"

She looked down and could see several large, amber-colored volcanic-looking rocks covered in nearly four feet of water. "I see them," she said as her voice echoed off the insides of the tank.

"They shouldn't be there."

"What are they?"

"Well, if I remember my geology correctly, those are some of the largest chunks of realgar I've ever seen."

"Realgar? I don't understand."

"It's arsenic sulfide. And very deadly." He stood with his clipboard to his chest, pushing his dark-rimmed glasses back on his nose. "Someone intentionally poisoned this water tank. And what's significant to me is that they poisoned the drinking water only, but not the well."

CHAPTER 29

The service was to take place in two days. The two SEALs worked together to set up arrangements at the church Sophie had occasionally attended as a youth. They turned down an offer for the women's auxiliary to cater a light lunch, since they didn't expect many people to show up.

Several of the team members were coming, though, and Nick was thankful for that.

Marc had been on the phone securing musicians for what Sophie had asked to have played at the service. Nick wrote up a biography of his sister, something he had never expected to do, taking it by the church office for the announcement, and for the benefit of the minister performing the service, who had never met Sophie. He'd always thought, because of the nature of his job and her occupation, that she'd be writing the bio for his funeral, not the other way around.

There happened to be a spot near his parents in the old rural cemetery where a couple of his team buddies were also buried. He paid for it, and declined to purchase the plot next to Sophie's for himself.

He considered that a good sign.

Devon was dreading the funeral. Mark had called her to let her know about it. Part of her was grateful Nick hadn't made the call. The smoldering ashes of her former self and feelings for him were cooling like the ashes at Sophie's now-decimated sales office.

The folded paper program, lying atop her crossed thigh, had Sophie's smiling picture. It had been taken on a sunny day. She could recognize the huge veined hand gripping Sophie's shoulder, but no other part of Nick's body was visible. His arms had protected Sophie, made her feel as safe as she could feel that day, her wide confident smile literally glowing in the photo. But those same arms had dished out something else just as powerful to Devon, and it was something she hoped that in time she could forget.

She knew the grieving process did strange things to people. Everyone had their own personal path until they either did or didn't find peace. She'd been initially so concerned about Nick's feelings, she'd ignored her own, until now the hurt and pain of it kept her awake at night and drove her back into her work as never before.

The new wrinkle in the investigation, the likelihood that Sophie was murdered, was just one more deadening burden she had to bear. She wondered if Nick knew, but dismissed it as being none of her business.

Focus on your own yard. Quit looking at other people's lawns.

The organist began a quiet fugue as Devon watched a tear fall on Sophie's picture, expanding into a small blot on the cream-colored paper. She heard the wooden bench seat groan as several large bodies filled it to capacity. Out of the corner of her eye, she saw Marc at the end of the row. When she turned her face their eyes met. She tried to smile.

Mark came to sit at her side and put an arm around her shoulder. She hadn't realized she was so starved for the touch of someone who cared. She leaned into him and quietly let herself slip into quiet sobs. He kissed the top of her head and shook her a bit, then whispered to her ear, "So sorry, Devon."

She knew he was meaning more than just Sophie, and she was grateful for his display of concern for her feelings. She felt comforted by the group of guys behind where she and Marc sat. Heroes who'd been to funerals many, many times. Who dealt with permanent separations on a daily basis. Men of steel. And men who were flawed as well.

Nick walked behind the minister when the music stopped, entering through a side door onto the dais. He stood with his arms crossed at the wrists, fists tight, his ribcage held high and his chin erect. He nodded to several of the guys behind her, acknowledging their presence, but didn't look at either her or Marc. It was better that way.

Several times Devon had to look back down at the program picture, now stained with several teardrops, to keep from losing it altogether. Nick's voice broke, and he had to clear his throat several times as he told Sophie's story, about some of the funny things they'd done as kids. She wanted to be disinterested, but she couldn't help listening.

A beautiful song was played about golden threads and a colorful tapestry of life events woven together,

"Sewer of dreams weave my destiny,"

The young singer's voice made her insides tremble.

What was her destiny now? Would she live to regret not falling in love, having a life with children and grandchildren? A comfortable place to share with the man of her dreams? Would she ever feel safe in someone's arms again, let her heart reach for something again and have the faith and willingness to take the chance she'd be hurt again?

At the end of the service, she allowed Marc to gently help her stand, not allowing her to walk on her own. She turned to address the dozen brave sailors who dressed in suits and ties and looked upon her, shifting from foot to foot, some biting their lower lips, some nodding to her, but none of them afraid to make eye contact. She drew strength from them. She wanted to thank them, and began to.

"Thank you so much—for everything you did for Sophie, for—" but she couldn't continue as the tears welled up.

She took a deep breath and accepted someone's handkerchief as she wiped her cheeks and knew that she probably looked horrible. Eyes puffy, red cheeks, makeup wiped off and lipstick gone.

Several of her friends from the office were waiting for her outside the circle. Devon suspected most of them were not there for her benefit. Glances were exchanged and acknowledgements made as a result of the weekend many of the SEALs had spent at the nursery during the liquidation sale.

Nick and the minister had taken up places at the rear door to the church, shaking hands with the few people who had attended. He got hugs from all the guys on the team, words expressed. Slaps on the back.

She could see the red circles around his lower lids and the way his breath hitched, his neck muscles tensing as he swallowed and tried to inhale again.

She and Marc were the last through the receiving line. She looked into Nick's green eyes and, although she was still afraid of him, knew that she couldn't hate him. Marc respectfully removed his arm from her shoulder, and that brought another flood of tears to her eyes. Extending her hand, she said the words she would have said to anyone in this situation, "Nick, I'm sorry for your loss."

He shook her hand and placed another on top of it, angling his head to the side. She could see the self-loathing in his face, but the firm resolve that he'd owned up to it, admitted it. "I'm sorry too, Devon."

She knew he was. He was having to work twice as hard to keep it together with her as he had with his buddies. His callused hand slipped away quickly and he diverted his gaze to address Marc. They hugged.

Drained and feeling unsteady, she continued to traverse the foyer alone, preparing to drive home and go to bed. Marc asked if he could take her for a sandwich or a bite to eat of some kind. She meekly agreed and they passed by several of the men clustered around groups of the younger girls from the office. The men were all handsome in their suits, with their straight backs and proud chests. They were all sizes and colors, but they were all there, even Kyle and his beautiful wife, Christy. She felt the burden of remembering happier times from her San Diego visit. Back when she could see herself living there, becoming part of their community.

She stopped and greeted Kyle's wife, who gave her a firm and comforting, wordless hug.

"Thanks for coming up, Christy. I wished it could have been under better circumstances."

"Not to worry, Devon. There's lots of time for that. Kyle and I will come up some time and you can show us around your beautiful county."

Devon appreciated her words. And now she didn't have to get jealous over Nick's attention.

Kyle stepped forward and placed a palm on Devon's shoulder, giving her a squeeze and shaking her gently. "You need anything, Devon, you just let us know, okay? We're here for you."

Devon nodded, but looked at the floor.

When will I have cried enough?

She lifted her gaze to the handsome team leader with the bright blue eyes.

"Thank you. I appreciate everything you and the boys have done. Sophie really—" Again she broke and this time she couldn't hold it in. She fell into Kyle's chest and grabbed him around the waist, clutching the fabric of his suit, and let the tears flow. Both he and Christy rubbed her back. Several of the other men came over and put a hand on one shoulder or another.

Words were whispered she couldn't understand, all intended for her ears, but her sobs completely drowned out their voices. Kyle let her cry. When she stopped shaking, she lifted herself off his chest and pulled her hair from her forehead and cheeks.

"Sorry." She dug a handkerchief from her pocket and wiped her eyes again.

"No. You take all the time you need," Kyle said as he tried to pull her back into him. But Devon straightened and stepped back, determined to hold herself up on her own.

She turned and addressed the team again. "Thank you. Thank you all for coming."

Marc led her gently out the front doors by the arm. As she glanced over her shoulder, she saw Nick standing against the hallway in the shadows, well behind the other members of his team, a dark and troubled look on his face.

He was staring right back at her.

"So, how're you holding up?" Marc said as he sat the cappuccino down in front of her.

"How are *you* doing, Marc?"

He looked to the side. "Not sure. Kind of numb. I miss her. Miss the humor, and her guts." He gave her a sad smile.

"Thank you for doing what you did for her in the end."

"Not in the end. I don't think she wanted me to witness that."

Devon sipped her cappuccino. "But you brought a rosy glow to her cheeks, something none of the rest of us could do. And for that, I thank you."

She remembered having coffee here with Nick, and the little heart-shaped design the barista had drawn in the foam. Today it was a feather of some kind. She shared Marc's nostalgia for days gone past.

The silence between them was exactly what she needed. As she sipped the warm liquid, closed her eyes and savored it, she realized she'd forgotten to eat this morning. "Hmmm. The first thing I've put into my stomach today."

"I'm starved too," he said. Her own pain mirrored his. They were both starved for the affection of someone who was no longer present in their lives.

The bistro was dark inside, which was just fine with Devon. She knew in the wrong kind of harsh light she'd look like a drug addict. Her frown after they'd ordered got Marc's attention.

"Talk to me, Devon. What's going on with the investigation?"

"They found large arsenic crystals at the bottom of Sophie's water tank. She'd been drinking a lethal dose for who knows how long, maybe years."

"How could that be?"

"It's odorless and tasteless."

Mark shook his head, a vacant stare crossing his face. She could tell he was really hurting. Devon found comfort in wanting to ease his pain, so she reached across the table and grabbed one of his hands and held it in both of hers.

"I wish you could have been with her at the end, Marc. My biggest regret is that we didn't call you. But we didn't know."

Marc's half smile tugged on her heartstrings. "That's okay, Devon. I think that's the way she would have wanted it."

"I'm not sure of that."

"Makes me not want to waste a day of my life. Wish I'd have met her some years earlier, before her sickness." He brought his other hand up on top. "You never know, do you? The right person comes along and God's sense of timing sucks."

Devon agreed.

"Look at you and Nick. At another time, with Sophie healthy—"

"Marc, I don't want to talk about that anymore. I'm trying to put that part of Sophie's last days out of my mind."

"He loves you, Devon, you do know that."

Devon removed her hands from the table. "No he doesn't. Someone else lives in there, and it isn't the man I thought I could love."

"He's still there."

She had to smile. Strength from the team and this gentle man's presence was boosting her spirits. "I appreciate what you're trying to do. I'm afraid Nick will be someone else's project, not mine."

They looked into each other's eyes. It was unspoken, but she could see how they could heal each other, and she rejected the idea. She was surprised to feel the strength of her own spirit beginning to come out from its cage, on fire, like a Phoenix. It was in that moment she knew she was going to be okay. She would bear the scars her vulnerable heart carried for the present, but there would be bright days ahead. She was sure of it.

"I hope he gets help, Marc. He needs more than what I could give him."

Marc nodded and gave a brave smile. "You're a strong woman, Devon."

"Oh, but not nearly as strong as I'm going to be." She watched as Marc reacted with a chuckle.

"That's going to be an awesome sight. Something I'd like to see."

"Marc, are you flirting with me?" she found the strength to say.

"Ma'am. I do believe I am."

It was Devon's turn to chuckle.

They were served while Devon told Marc about how the escrow was going. She talked about the police investigators she'd talked to several times.

"How are they going to prove it?" he asked.

"I have no idea. My job is to make sure the property sells. The young couple who made the offer are waffling a bit, but I believe your teammate made a payment to the power company, and I made the last mortgage payment—"

"*You* made the mortgage payment?" he asked.

"Yes, Marc. I make a lot of money, and I pay cash for everything." Her words almost got stuck in her throat as she said, "I live a simple life."

Marc changed the subject.

"Why would someone want to hurt Sophie? Can't be over the land."

"Yes, I think it's exactly over the land," Devon answered.

"Why?"

"Because she couldn't be bought out. She was too stubborn. It didn't matter how much the neighbor would pay for it. She wouldn't sell to him. I think he felt if Sophie was out of the way, the next owner could be more reasonable."

"Because of the water."

"Yup. Water-scarce area. Lack of water has made it impossible for him to plant on the land he's optioned all over the valley floor. Sophie was the stumbling block to his empire expansion. Now they have to just prove it."

"Does Nick know?" Marc asked.

Devon shrugged. "I have no idea. Haven't spoken to him in almost three days. You know that, Marc."

"So what happened, Devon?"

"I don't want to talk about it."

"He said he was ashamed of something he'd done." Marc sat back and pondered the floor. "Was it something he should go to jail for, Devon? 'Cause if it is, I've got to do something about it."

Devon was grateful she could answer truthfully. "No."

The sexual part had been consensual. What he did wasn't the problem. It was the way he did it that hurt. Like she was something he wanted to consume, not pleasure. Someone he didn't have any feelings for. The coldness and the intensity made her shiver.

But, as sad as it was, he had not violated the law. After all, she'd asked him to stop, and he did. She hadn't minded that he wanted something intense to ease his pain. She wanted the same thing. But the intensity without the strong connection, making it an anonymous hookup, a cheap biological act instead of sharing something beautiful in common—that scared her. She'd had to fight him off, and he very nearly didn't stop. And yet, her body had wanted him in spite of how he'd treated her.

But that wasn't the way lovers were supposed to treat one another. Nick had been her only, she had hoped would always be her only. But as inexperienced as she was, she knew that what he did wasn't about giving or receiving pleasure. It was what people did to exorcise demons.

Perhaps that was the scar that would take the longest to heal.

CHAPTER 30

Nick expected to feel better after the funeral and the burial. He walked with his brothers over to several other team guys he knew were laid to rest there. They paid their respects. Some of these fallen boys they'd known, some not. They watched an elderly gentleman being wheeled by a teenager to a spot in the back by the fountain.

Looking over the expanse of green lawn and colorful flowers, an occasional flag or balloon adorning the silent markers, the dirty fishpond with no fish, and the trees that needed trimming, he was struck by how ordinary it looked. Or maybe it was just the way he felt. Sophie would have an opinion about how they took care of the walkways, the shrubs and trees, and of course the lack of decent water for at least some feeder goldfish. He knew she didn't consider it normal to have a pond with nothing but scum living there.

Ordinary. Not special.

He had acted dishonorably with Devon. He didn't deserve to wear the Trident. He didn't deserve to represent his country doing anything, including pushing papers at a desk job somewhere. And there was nothing wrong with that, either. Took all kinds of service. But the training and the investment his government had made in him, the way the public honored the SEAL community—that he didn't deserve. He didn't feel like the hero everyone thought he was.

When it came down to it, he was not just a man, but someone who didn't trust himself. Today he would tell Kyle he was getting out. He'd move somewhere in the mountains, work on a few acres and try not to interfere with anyone else's life. He had enough savings to buy something cheap, far away from anything familiar, where he wouldn't run across anyone he knew.

Kyle had been watching him all during the internment. Maybe his LPO knew as they rolled Sophie's casket down into the ground he felt like climbing on top and just staying there. It was a blessing Devon chose not to attend. He preferred to remember her walking out of the church, the look of worry, and not an ounce of softness in her face. That was good. Good for her.

Kyle asked Nick to stay behind when the fellas started walking back to the van they'd rented.

"Nick, you okay?"

He drilled Kyle a look he knew the man would feel all the way down to his toes.

"So, how's it going to be, Nick? You gonna take care of it or will you make someone else do it?"

"Sir?"

"If you don't go see a shrink in the next twenty-four hours, I'm going to recommend you not come back to Coronado. Ever."

Nick winced and tilted his head, unsmiling, examining the lilies on Sophie's grave propped up by a thin wooden stand. He thought the flowers were too showy for her. The roses were drooping already. The team's money should have been spent somewhere else. But still, he was glad they sent it, or there wouldn't have been any, and that would have been a fuckin' shame.

"Nick. I'm taking you to the hospital right now." Kyle started to grab Nick's arm to haul him towards the van and Nick knocked him on his ass with a push Kyle wasn't expecting. He could hear swearing as Cooper, Fredo, Armando, Jones and Christy piled out of the van and came toward him like a herd.

The others dog-piled him and Nick hit his head on the brass marker of the grave next to Sophie's. He thought the metal was cold just before he felt the sharp prick of a needle in his neck, and then everything went black.

Cooper had administered a sedative, and with Nick out cold Kyle looked down on his specialist. He could take him in for a temporary civilian hold, or have the team escort him back to Coronado, in a career-ending move.

He saw his beautiful wife standing off to the side. She knew not to interfere, but he hated the fact that she'd just seen the dark underbelly of their profession and the effect it had on all the guys. A gross illustration of what could happen in an instant over in the killing fields if a guy took his concentration off the mission and onto something personal. Other guys got killed when that happened. When there was hesitation.

He knew it was risky, but he decided not to take Nick in. Perhaps a good sleep would help repair the injured parts of his psyche. Some would go out and get drunk, but he also knew alcohol was the last thing Nick needed. Anyone needed in these circumstances, really.

The Team members were waiting for a signal from him, each man having his own silent conversation. Kyle could hear their internal thoughts as clearly as if they'd been shouting. They weren't thinking about Nick so much as what they'd have done in Nick's place. How close they could come to unraveling over something that happened at home. And this had happened, luckily, at home. Maybe that was the worst part, he thought.

He had planned to send the team home today, but now he didn't dare. But he had to ask them.

"Okay, I'll give Timmons a call and tell him Nick's off his rocker, but that we think a day or two might straighten him out." He looked at his comrades. Heads either nodded or looked at the ground. No one objected.

"I want you to know that if you choose to, you can still go home today." He glanced over at Christy and saw a resolute shaking of her head, *no*.

That's my girl, Christy. He was grateful she was in it for the long haul. Just as tough as she was beautiful. And maybe she could help, but not until he had determined that Nick wouldn't be a danger to himself or anyone else. He knew part of his job would be to translate what had just happened so she could understand enough of it that she wasn't afraid for him. He knew she didn't feel fear for herself, but for him. He thought maybe she was stronger than he was in some respects. He so much wanted to be alone with her. He so much wanted to snuggle with his toddler son, Brandon.

But looking down at Nick, he reminded himself that part of their pact was never to leave a wounded soldier behind. This wasn't the real Nick. This was the wounded Nick lying before him. And he'd never give up on him. Ever. As he glanced around the circle of his team, he knew they all felt the same way.

Unlike on deployment, when they were carrying a hundred-plus pounds of gear and protected with armor, each of them stood in their suits and ties. And sunglasses. His men in black. Brothers forever.

They brought Nick back to the hotel they'd been staying in, and made a schedule for guarding him. Cooper wanted to sit by him at first to monitor how he was doing with the shitload of stuff he gave him to keep him sleeping. No one knew which Nick would show up when he finally did wake, and they talked a little about that and how to handle various scenarios. There would be no fighting, breaking of furniture or other public displays of his anger. And if he couldn't be contained, he'd get a cage at the psych ward, and Kyle said he'd look into that next.

They booked an extra room so the team had semi-privacy for the calls back home they needed to make. Kyle called Timmons first to make sure there wasn't anything else going on that required their immediate deployment.

"You think he's going to crawl back to life, Kyle, or is this mercy mission all in vain?" Timmons asked him.

"No way to know, sir. I'm hoping the sleep will help, but we don't know."

"Thank God he didn't punch you."

"No, sir, he didn't. I think that shows some restraint."

"And you keep him away from any kind of weapon, you hear? You've searched him, of course."

"Of course. And we've zip-tied his wrists."

"Good. He'll be pissed when he wakes up, but let's just hope his own body will do the job."

"He's going to need time off, sir. Not sure he could make the next rotation."

"Roger that. I'll do the paperwork. I'll put him on limited duty until your workup. Think of something. But if he does something public, I'm booting him. As much as I love the guy, he's got to walk part of this road himself. If he can't, then he's no use to us. You understand that, right?"

"Yes, sir. I do."

After he hung up the phone, Armando came over and placed a hand on his shoulder. "Hey, boss. We got this. You go be with your Christy."

Kyle slumped over, bracing his arms on his thighs and then stood slowly. He was sore, and he knew just what to do to work out some of the kinks, and just who to do it with.

CHAPTER 31

Devon looked at the estimated closing papers that had been drawn up before the ordeal of the fire and Sophie's death. There was going to be a decent sum left over after all the loan fees, back taxes and late fees were paid off. Nearly a hundred thousand dollars. And although Sophie had instructed them to share in the proceeds, Devon knew that she'd direct title to issue the full amount to Nick. She'd take her commission, something she didn't want to do, but figured it might appease Nick a little when he found out about the proceeds.

Two detectives knocked on her open door. She recognized them as the ones she had talked to previously. Twice.

"Come on in."

They sat before her desk like clients. "You have any contact with this Mr. Silva or Mr. Rodriguez?"

"Not a word. And I halfway expected they'd interfere with our escrow, too." She saw them glance at each other. "What aren't you telling me?"

"Mr. Rodriguez had a crew come over and board up the house."

"What? He can't do that." Devon was furious. "He doesn't own the property."

"Apparently—well, he says he bought it," the older detective said.

"That's impossible."

"Have you talked to the prospective purchasers recently?"

"I—I was just going to call them. We just came from Sophie's memorial service."

"I'd do it now."

Devon dialed the Hallbergs and got Donna Hallberg on the phone first.

"Devon, I was just going to call you."

The hair at the back of Devon's neck began to stand up. Her stomach tightened.

"We've decided not to purchase the property, with all the fire and the problem with the well."

"There's no problem with the well," Devon insisted. She knew where this was going, but she was trying to head it off before it caught too much momentum, if that was possible.

"Well, we don't want to argue with you, but apparently there is some arsenic contamination—"

"That can be rectified. The tank can be removed. The well is fine, so getting another tank is no problem."

"We just don't want to take that risk."

Devon felt there was more, and she knew she wasn't going to like it. The detectives sat passively, as if they knew more about her transaction than she did. "So, you're just going to cancel, just like that? Don't you want to see what we can get the insurance to do for you?"

"Well, let me have you speak to my husband."

That was always a bad sign when one spouse wanted to switch the phone to the other one. David Hallberg came on the line.

He began talking in a sheepish tone, and it was hard for Devon to follow what he was saying, but then she heard the phrase, "offered us two hundred thousand dollars to walk away, well, not walk away, but assign our contract to him."

"He can't do that."

"I'm sorry, but we went to see an attorney this morning, and yes, we can. And the money is already in our bank."

Devon closed her eyes.

"If—if you're comfortable, we'd like you to help us find another place to set up our nursery, that is, if you're not mad," he said. "We appreciate how hard you've worked for us."

"You do understand that the neighbor is the prime suspect in Sophie's murder?"

The detectives sat up in alarm.

"The attorney you went to see, would he defend you in a criminal case if the authorities question your benefitting from Sophie Dunn's demise?"

Devon heard the other end of the line go silent "You think that could happen?" David asked.

"You didn't call me first. You just entered into this arrangement, and I imagine you used the attorney Mr. Silva recommended, and without consulting me, correct?"

"Well, he said he would defend us without charge if there was a challenge to it."

"Or if you were arrested?"

Devon knew she was dashing her chances of ever having a successful relationship with the Hallbergs, but she was furious. And her fury was escalating. The detectives stood and were making motions for her to hang up.

"I'm afraid I have to go, David. But I think your next call should be to a criminal defense attorney. If you hold on a second, I'll get you three names and you can pick one for yourself."

The line went dead.

"Miss Brandeburg? We didn't ask you to do this. Half of what you told them wasn't even true."

Devon stood up too. "Then you tell me. Was Sophie murdered or not?"

"We don't have an autopsy."

"And why is that?"

"Because she was buried today, as you know, and we are attempting to get hold of her brother. Do you know where we can find Nicholas Dunn? It would be a lot faster if we got his approval, otherwise we have to get a court order."

Devon checked her cell phone and wrote the number down on her card for the police detective. "Does he know anything about this?"

"As far as we know, no."

"He's a Navy SEAL. You'd best tell him while he still has some of the other members of Team 3 around. I know they're here today, but not sure for how much longer."

"Thanks Miss Brandeburg."

After they left, Devon wondered how Nick would handle the news, and hoped to God they listened to her admonition. He'd be a dangerous combination of terror and skill if he got focused on revenge. As much as she disliked the cretins who poisoned dear Sophie, she was more worried now about the plot ensnaring Nick.

CHAPTER 32

Nick forced himself to wake up. His mind was in a fog. The images in his vivid dreams involved exploding IEDs and screams of the wounded. Then there would be the image of Devon's nude body at his feet.

Wake up! Wake up! He squeezed his fists and was relieved to find he'd been restrained. No weapon in his hand. He watched as the vision of her body floated away from him. He began to hear sounds of the TV next door. He was warm. He was fully clothed. He was lying on a bed in a hotel room.

He opened his eyes. He felt the tears streaming down the sides of his face, and dampness on the pillow under his neck. The heaviness in his chest felt like someone with a boot was standing on him. And the pressure came from the inside too. His hands were shaking. He had a headache.

He flexed and squeezed his fingers, moved his arms up and down, then rested them above his head on the pillow. Something familiar about this made him close his eyes, and that's when he saw her again, her arms above her head, her body turned on her belly, hair covering her face. Her creamy arms stretched out in front of her, tied tightly with the pink sash. He heard her moans, her sobs.

He inhaled and opened his eyes. It didn't erase the images and sounds.

He heard talking in the next room as several males discussed something. He heard his sister's name. "We'd like to get permission to exhume her body," the man was saying.

He heard shuffling motions as someone approached the bedroom door. He closed his eyes and pretended to still be asleep. Through tiny slits in his eyes he saw Cooper's worried face. Heard as Cooper shook his head and told them to come back in an hour. Said he'd revive him in an hour. Cooper said he wanted to let him sleep a little longer. Hell, *he* wanted to sleep.

Exhume her body? That meant they suspected she'd met with foul play, which also meant someone was responsible. That they were questioning the cause of death. There was only one person who could be responsible. He thought about what he should do as he wiggled the zip tie back and forth until it nearly melted in his hands and he was freed.

Someone had tucked his shoes halfway under the bed. Laid his sport coat on the chair. His tie had been removed and he found it on the dresser. He tested the strength of it and decided it would do. It wouldn't be pretty, he'd have to jerk it tight and quick. Pull until all the air was forced from the neck, until he heard the crack of the windpipe cartilage. But he was a trained killer. He could dish out death like some ate their granola. That was the one part of him that wasn't damaged. Everything else was a throwaway.

There wasn't anyone to live for. Not even for himself.

Cooper checked his cell and swore there was no message from Kyle, Fredo or Armani. Marc had returned and was resting in the room across the hall. Cooper knew he'd promised the police he'd revive Nick if he didn't wake up on his own in an hour. He had nearly fifteen minutes to go, but decided he'd go check on his patient.

Carefully turning down the lever door handle, holding it down so there would be no squeak of the hinges, he opened the door a crack.

Holy crap!

Nick was gone.

Devon knew she was the only one now who had the authority to find out about Sophie's things. If they were boarding up the house, what were they doing with all the contents? Sophie wouldn't want her things thrown away, her place treated with such disrespect.

It hadn't been Devon's choice to sell to the young couple. She'd told Sophie she could make more money, and perhaps it would have been easier on her to sell to the neighbor, but no. Sophie had to be the beautiful, stubborn woman she was.

Just like her brother.

She wondered if he was at the house. Or what he would do if he found them violating Sophie's space. It was still Sophie's space. It didn't belong to Mr. Rodriguez, not if Devon had anything to say about it.

The drive over was quick with, very little traffic. She turned down the gravel driveway off Bennett Valley Road, spotting the nursery sign in the ditch, as if flung there by someone who didn't care. There were two pickup trucks with an anthill of men unloading sheets of plywood and nailing them over the windows.

She pulled up to block one truck, and got out of the car.

"Who's in charge here?" she asked a dark-haired youth with a baseball cap worn backwards.

The youngster pointed to a man helping to lift a stack of plywood off one of the trucks.

She waited until the plywood was unloaded and then handed the man her card. "Excuse me, sir, I'm the listing agent on this property and the owner didn't give permission for any work to be done here."

"I understand the owner is dead, ma'am." He took a handkerchief from his back pocket and wiped his forehead. "Maybe you just didn't get the memo?"

"I'm well aware of the fact that she's dead. We have a contract to sell this property. No escrow has closed. "

"Look, you'll have to take it up with the new owner."

"I'm telling you there is no new owner. Whoever told you to do this didn't have the authority to do so. He's lied to you and you're going to get in trouble."

The man shrugged.

"There has been no change in ownership. No escrow has closed."

He shrugged again and continued to work.

"Can you at least call him and verify that what I have said is true?" She saw one of the men take a box from inside Sophie's house and start to load it into one of the trucks. "Excuse me!" she shouted across the yard. "That's stealing now. Now you're stealing!"

The worker looked at the foreman who nodded back at the house and the worker disappeared inside, coming out empty handed.

"Call him," Devon demanded.

"I don't have a phone, Miss."

She practically slammed her phone in the man's face. "Call him right now."

"No ma'am. I don't have his number. So sorry. I'd like to help, but I've been hired—"

"Hired by Mr. Rodriguez, right?"

"Yes."

"And can you tell me where I can find him?"

The man pointed across the vineyard. "I spoke to him about two hours ago. That's when he instructed us to get the wood and start securing the property."

"What about the contents?" Devon was furious.

"Beats me. Maybe he made some other arrangement you don't know about. I don't make up the rules, I just work here."

Devon put a call into her broker, who she could not reach. She called the Sonoma County Sheriff's Department and asked for one of the investigators and got their voicemail. She called 9-1-1.

The dispatcher wanted to know the nature of the emergency.

"I am a realtor and some strangers are boarding up a house I have listed."

"Ma'am, what is the emergency?"

"These people are trespassing. They have no authorization to damage the owner's property."

"Ma'am. This is an emergency line. You must hang up immediately and call the local law enforcement agencies. Unless there is someone hurt?"

There's going to be.

Sweat streamed down her back, her armpits and her chest. She couldn't get in touch with anyone who could help her. She even tried dialing Nick's number, uncertain if it was the right thing to do, but she was desperate to get someone to assist her. But no one answered.

She called the Sonoma County Sheriff's office again and told them about the emergency she was having. The dispatcher said that there wasn't anyone available to come out to the site, that personnel were responding to "real emergencies." Devon cursed and hung up. She wished she had Marc's number, and tried Nick's number again, which went right into voicemail. Wherever he'd holed up, he'd either turned off his phone or it lay in some ditch he was sleeping in.

She walked over to the heavyset foreman, inhaled and in a booming voice shouted, "You *all* are trespassing on private property. I am going to have you all *arrested* and sued. If you'd like to wait around for the *police*, go ahead. But trust me, you are all going to go to jail. I'd hate to find out a couple of you don't have papers to stay in the United States legally."

The foreman tried to shut her up, running at her, trying to grab her arm. Devon kept yelling over the top of his head as he attempted to get his hand over her mouth.

"The *po-leeeece* are on their way and you will be arrested for breaking and entering!"

Breaking and entering? Can a person be arrested for boarding up a house?

But it got the desired effect. A whole truckload of day laborers hopped into one of the two trucks and took off, sending sheets of plywood sailing in all directions as they tore down the driveway. The foreman yelled something to two other men standing by and they ran to retrieve the wood.

Devon remembered the baseball bat Sophie had by the side of her bed. The one she had intended to hit Mr. Silva with that first day she met him. She ran inside, looking at the complete disarray of the house, the papers everywhere, broken dishes, trees and plants overturned and picture frames lying broken on the floor. She rescued the picture of Sophie with Nick in happier times, cutting her fingers on the glass as she extricated the photo from the broken frame. She quickly slipped it into her pocket.

The baseball bat was right where Sophie had left it. Her bed was littered with debris. Crunching over broken things, Devon grabbed the bat and ran outside. She started her destruction of the pickup's windshield, bringing it down with a satisfying *whop,* which brought yells from the other side of the yard. She swung and took off the driver's side mirror, then hit the tail lights. As the men approached she swung and attempted to catch one in the gut, but discovered too late her aim was off and she'd hit him too low. He collapsed where he stood, doubling over on his groin.

The end of the bat was slippery, red from her own cut fingers. She pushed the hair out of her face and took a stance like she had on the varsity softball team and got ready to swing again. She was going for a fucking home run this time.

The two remaining men backed away. "Look, we don't want any trouble."

"Too late. If you get your asses off this property *right fucking now,* you might get away." She heard a distant siren and saw the remaining two workers exchange panicked glances. "I'd say you just fucking ran out of time." She ran up to them.

"Okay, okay, hey. Lady, we're going." They held their palms out in front of them in a defensive gesture.

She watched them pick up their buddy, dump him in the back of the truck and start up the engine. Loud mariachi music blared to a blue, cloudless sky, and then trailed after the truck down its dusty path.

She thought the sirens were getting louder. Throwing the bat into the front seat of her Lexus, she darted out onto Bennett Valley Road, almost getting hit by a Mercedes coming the opposite direction. She checked her rear view mirror and although the Mercedes had wound up on the soft shoulder of the roadway, in a spray of gravel, they had come to a controlled stop in the opposite direction.

She tore as fast as she could down the half-mile stretch to the Rodriguez estate around the corner.

The gate had been crashed open. She had a very, very bad feeling in the pit of her stomach. A twelve-passenger rental van had rammed into a ten foot water feature, knocking the statuary of a large fish onto the ground in pieces. Water sprayed everywhere.

Glancing toward the front door, she noticed it yawning open. She turned off the car, grabbed her baseball bat and ran inside. Halfway there, she tossed her heels as being completely useless, and ran in her stocking feet.

The inside of the house was cool and dark. She could hear groaning and the muffled moan of someone trying to say, "No."

She followed the noise. Nick was standing over a man she figured was Mr. Rodriguez, his back to her. He had him in a chokehold and was attempting to get a tie out of his pocket. Rodriguez's shirt was covered in blood, apparently from a broken nose. Both men were covered in dirt from what she'd assumed was a scuffle on the floor littered with the remains of a potted plant.

She took a deep breath and screamed at him. "Nick!"

The blood curdling scream initially made him jump as he checked over his shoulder and squinted.

"Devon?" He said.

"You let him go, or so help me I'll knock your fuckin' head off."

Nick tightened his grip on Rodriguez.

"Oh, so you want to play, you son of a bitch? You want a piece of me, huh? You want this? You wanna play rough, now that I'm going to bash your head in? Come on, Nick, come and get it. Let's see how a big, tough Navy SEAL can get it on with a varsity softball player."

She was breathing like she'd just run a marathon. She was so into it, she hoped he'd challenge her. Devon wanted to smack him so hard she'd wipe out all his teeth, his jaw and maybe an eye. She was dying for that satisfying crunch of bone and the spurt of blood.

Nick dropped Rodriguez into a heap on the floor. He was looking at her, up and down. He didn't smile. He was completely taken aback, and even took one step away from her.

This emboldened Devon, who took two steps in his direction, raising the bat above her head. "I had no idea I wanted to smack you so hard. You goddamned son of a bitch. You total freakin' asshole turd—" she stopped for a minute to find the word, "You—you—you stinkin' warted green toad."

Was he laughing at her?

"You think this is funny, Nick?"

Rodriguez had slithered behind a desk and was on the phone. But just in time, as she was standing three feet in front of Nick, with her chest heaving and her bat ready to plunge into his skull she heard the click of weapons being readied behind her, and the bellowed command,

"Drop it, lady!"

At first she didn't think it applied to her. The cops only went after bad guys. Nick had a smirk she wanted to wipe off his face, so she squinted, pursed her lips and lifted the bat higher over her head, readying her aim.

"Drop it or we'll shoot!" That's when it registered they were talking to her.

She didn't take her gaze off Nick but blinked two times in succession. She wasn't sure where she was, but she obeyed the command and dropped the bat to the floor. Someone behind her retrieved it. Someone else grabbed her wrists and handcuffed her behind her back. That brought her back to reality.

Nick stayed where he was, and accepted the handcuffs at his back too.

Perfect, just fucking perfect. An officer lead her away backwards, tugging on her cuffs. She didn't lose sight of Nick until they turned her around, protected her head and placed her in the back seat of the squad car.

CHAPTER 33

Nick wasn't sure he could believe his eyes. He couldn't shake off the vision of Devon standing in front of him, blood on her cheek and forehead, her shredded stockings and her black suit skirt covered in dust, her hair worse than when she'd gotten soaking wet that first day he'd seen her. The half-untied bow on the cream-colored blouse was ridiculous.

He was as shocked as he would have been if she'd managed to hit him between the eyes. Sitting in the back seat of the Sheriff's car, behind a screen, handcuffed, he watched in slow motion as the vineyards passed him by, as the driveway to Sophie's place came and went. There was a fire truck there and he wondered what had happened, and then remembered Devon's appearance and knew, just knew, she'd had something to do with it.

He stopped straining to look at the beehive of activity there and sat back, examining the dirty squad car ceiling. And he started to smile.

He was going to be arrested for assault, no doubt ending his career. Maybe he'd even get jail time. He'd managed to do something he was never supposed to do: cause a public display. Draw attention to himself or his SEAL community. Interfere with local law enforcement.

And he discovered he was happy again. Really freakin' jump-for-joy happy.

He started to laugh. The deputies watched him with a mixture of disdain and sorrow. Yeah, he was mental, all right. The sight of Devon with that baseball bat raised high. Her hair all mussed up like he'd just fucked her for two hours straight, not all prissy and well groomed. Hard jaw and eyes full of intent. No matter what happened to him, just seeing her that way had been worth it. *So* worth it.

A Navy SEAL and a varsity softball player. He chuckled again to himself. That should be a book someone should write. True love. Covered in blood, ready to kill each other. It might have been worth it to let her do it, just to see what she'd do next.

He hadn't had any idea she liked sports. They'd never talked about it. Never knew she played softball. God, she must have been a great player, too. Get her mad, go for revenge. She'd be hell on wheels, all right. Still, he should have known. Why hadn't she told him?

Oh, yeah. That would be because he wasn't letting her do much of the talking, he'd been such a selfish prick, wallowing around in his own mental bullshit, he couldn't see the diamond right in front of him. And before that, well, he was pretty consumed in the little sounds she made when he pumped her. Those little whimpers. The way her forehead creased as she bit her lower lip and accepted him. If she'd told him anything at all, he probably wouldn't have paid attention, he'd have been too busy fantasizing about that sweet little mouth and the noises it made.

Like oxygen suddenly flooded him after being deprived, he started to feel warm. So nice to get out of the fuckin' cave he'd been living in. The blue-grey place of despair and self-pity. Even if he sat in a cell for the next ten years, he could remember what Devon had done today and would have to say he'd do it all over again.

He was so absolutely proud of her. Fearless didn't even begin to describe what she was. She was a throwback to some warrior princess girls were always reading about when they were teenagers. The ones who save the world and then go home and cook dinner.

She wasn't going to let Sophie's property fall into the wrong hands. She didn't care what it looked like, whether or not anyone came to her aid, whether or not she got hurt. She was just like him. She just wouldn't quit. And when he'd just about quit the whole world, Devon still hadn't.

She's stronger than I am.

Who would ever be able to walk away from a woman like that? Talk about crazy. *That* was crazy!

For once, although it was totally inappropriate, his big head and his little head were in perfect agreement

Devon was helped out of the car by two female attendants who were clearly disturbed by what they saw. She avoided eye contact with anyone. The guys in the car were trying to catch her eye. Kept asking her questions about real estate. She tried answering them professionally, after first brushing the hair from her face with her bloody hands. She could only guess what she looked like. She felt like asking them if they'd ever consider buying a house from someone who looked like her?

So maybe she could go with it. Use her mug shot on her stupid plastic signs? She started to chuckle at that one. Wait until the ladies in the office and her broker found out about what she'd done. Oh yes, and the paper, that liked to print stories about the multiple deals she did, the one time she did a twelve-sided transaction with five title companies, ten realtors and fifteen buyers and sellers, including a guy in prison and a family in France. Who cared now?

So much for being the top producer and having your picture plastered on bus benches and shopping carts where they put baby bottoms. So much for the awards news releases. The 1099 with the upper six-figure income. None of it mattered. In fact, it got in the way.

She'd probably lose her license. So be it. Maybe she could take some of her savings and work Sophie's nursery. Maybe she needed to get her fingers dirty. She knew how to promo, she knew half the town.

And she knew how to defend her turf with a baseball bat. She hoped she could get that bat back. It had a satisfying weight to it and she liked the noises made by the things it came in contact with, human or otherwise.

The matrons gave her a onesie prison jumpsuit in light blue. She asked for a shower and was granted the opportunity to wash her hair, though she had to buy the shampoo and they didn't have cream rinse. She used a little shampoo as a face cleanser rather than the soap that smelled it was partially made of lye.

The reality of her situation came home when she sat on the cot in her cell. That's when she started to shiver. She got cold.

And, God in Heaven, she missed Nick.

Timmons repeated everything Kyle had told him. The rest of the team guys wanted to hear what he had to say in response. They'd not stopped talking about the chemistry between Nick and Devon. The whole team, all two hundred men, minus one, would know all about it soon.

But Kyle explained she managed to do what they had messed up doing. She had rescued Nick, as Sophie requested, and if it wasn't for Devon, Nick would be looking at thirty years. And she'd saved him in the only way it was possible to save him. She matched him.

Kyle knew Timmons's marriage was loveless. But he loved his daughter, so he put up with the pink bedroom and the doll collection his wife "invested" in.

"I'm having a hard time picturing all of this, Kyle," Timmons said.

"Believe me, sir, I would have given anything to see those two in action. The stories are pretty incredible."

"I can't say that's much of a love story, son."

"Believe me, it is, sir. Those two were made for each other."

"And you think Nick is right as rain?"

Kyle hesitated. "I think he'll need some time off. But, believe me, if we can get everything straight, which should not be a problem since they've arrested Rodriguez for murder, he'll have someone who's got his back better than we could ever do."

"Well, shit. Damned if I know anything about it. I haven't been in love for over twenty five years."

"Sorry about that, sir. You try counseling?"

"No. We're as close as we're going to be. She gave me my daughter, and beyond that, she didn't have anything else to give, I guess."

Devon and Nick were arraigned in the same courtroom the next day. Nick felt some of his helpless anger creep back when he found out Devon made bail for both of them, if they needed it, and paid the attorney to appear. They sat five chairs apart in the offender box.

"You look good in blue," he finally said out of the side of his mouth without looking at her.

"Orange isn't your color."

He laughed. "I still can't forget that look on your face when you—"

"Bailiff, please instruct the prisoners to be silent in the courtroom," the judge barked.

They had to wait nearly forty-five minutes for their turn. There wasn't much opposition to dismissal of Nick's case. The attorney Devon hired had a copy of the police report, citing the arrest of Sophie's neighbor. The Assistant District Attorney almost apologized to him for the inconvenience he'd suffered, especially after the loss of his sister.

But with Devon's case, there were actual damages to the pickup truck owned by Mr. Rodriguez, even though Rodriguez probably wouldn't be pressing charges and would have his own set of legal issues to deal with. The DA knew he'd kind of botched the case initially, something the sharp defense attorney argued. In the end, the ADA didn't put up much of a fight, and allowed the dismissal.

Nick and Devon were escorted from the courtroom back to the holding cell to change into street clothes. Just before he ducked into the entrance to the cell, he turned to her and whispered, "Don't wear panties."

She wiggled her eyebrows up and down and said, "I'm bringing my baseball bat, too."

Nick was the first to exit the building. Kyle held out the keys to a red mustang convertible the team had rented for him.

"Sweet ride. Thanks, guys," he said as he walked around it, admiring the shiny candy-apple color and the tan leather interior. They'd delivered it to him with the top down. The warm September night was perfect for a ride out to the coast. Or a little back seat action. Nick's mind was flooded with possibilities, and he honestly didn't know which scenario to pick.

And then he saw Devon coming out with a Victoria's Secret bag slung over her arm. Christy gave Nick a knowing wink. He intended to slide over and give her a thank-you kiss on the cheek, but he couldn't take his eyes off Devon.

Nick was mesmerized by how her beautiful her long hair was clipped up and hanging down in soft curls everywhere, covering the back of her neck and shoulders. She wore a red dress with a large brass zipper down the front, with a hemline that came well above her knees. If he was right, even though she carried the Victoria's Secret bag, Devon didn't have a stitch on underneath.

The brass zipper was pulled down a dangerous eight inches or so, and he didn't see anything but flesh underneath where the zipper mated on top of her chest.

Her confident walk and sparkly eyes as she speared him with a look kindled something more than lust. He saw a woman who had come into her own, faced her fears, and could look him straight in the eye as an equal in every way. She had grown up, bloomed in front of him. Even when he rejected her, she'd stood by him. And he could see she always would.

She stopped a foot away from him. Several of the team guys behind him were whistling and shouting rowdy words of encouragement.

"Well, sailor, you look pretty good in blue." She stepped up to him and he wrapped her in his arms, pulling her in to press along the full length of his body. His hands traveled over her rear and he smiled knowingly.

"You feel real good in red," he said.

"I follow instructions."

"Do you? That's interesting."

"Well, within reason." She turned and raised her eyebrows at Christy, who handed her the baseball bat. "Just in case."

CHAPTER 34

Devon loved the feel of Nick's arm on her shoulder as he drove down the Valley of the Moon. The vineyards were awash in color, green leaves turning golden or deep burgundy. The tourists were gone since the harvesting were crush was over for the year. There would be specialized barrel-tasting here and there, but most the wineries were shifting gears for the fall and winter holidays.

The Waterwheel Inn was a welcome sight. The first time she'd walked down the crushed granite walkways lush with overgrown blooming lilies, her nerves had made it impossible to enjoy the ambiance fully. That evening she had entered the suite a girl, ready to have her first experience with a man she thought she knew. She emerged a woman, but still an innocent. Nick had been patient with her. He had helped her bloom with attention to her smallest detail and walked her through that doorway to womanhood like a gentleman. He'd been so careful to make sure her first experience was a good one. Who wouldn't love a man like that?

Now she walked beside him as a woman who not only felt passion and lust for this rare breed of warrior, but as someone who could match him stride for stride. She was more than an innocent he needed to protect. She had taken on the role of protecting her man as well.

She could still remember the butterflies in her stomach, the way his fingers slipped over her skin. She'd always wondered what it felt like to have a man touch her in those intimate places. To watch her flame up and meet him halfway. She found herself shivering with anticipation, and need.

"You cold?" he asked as he drew her to his side.

"More like excited, actually."

The rumble in his chest sent tiny fingers dancing down the back of her neck. "Can hardly wait," he whispered and kissed the top of her head. His smooth, athletic gait excited her as he led her up a set of brick steps to a special stand-alone suite covered in grapevines. With its own patio, it had a private view of the azure pool below and felt like a cottage in the trees. Lush plants lined the edges of the wet areas, sending their fragrances into the warm night sky filled with stars.

Accompanied by the soothing sound of water spilling into wooden troughs of the giant wheel, they stepped under the rose-colored canvas awning covering the patio, in front of one large hand-hewn door. Nick held her face between his massive palms and whispered to her lips, "No more secrets."

She spoke between his soft kisses, "No. No more secrets."

He ran his fingers through the curls at the back of her head and squeezed. His kisses traveled down her neck to the tops of her shoulders, under her ears.

"Devon," he whispered as he smoothed his lips over her neck, triggering that familiar and enticing dull ache between her legs.

She loved the sound of her name on his tongue, the vibration in his chest. When she opened to him, a soft growl vibrated as he sank his tongue in deep. She felt the rock wall of his torso and the growing need in his pants and pressed herself against him. She would be the softness to his hard. Sweet balance she hoped this man would need forever. She wanted him to depend on her, worship her as much as she worshiped him.

At last, their bodies parted, until only their lips touched.

"Thank you, Nick."

He nibbled on her bottom lip, with a whispered groan. "Tell me what you are thanking me for."

"Thank you for coming back, baby. For coming back from the edge of the world."

"I was lost without you, sweetheart. You found me."

She laid her cheek against Nick's chest and listened to his heartbeat as he caressed her shoulders and back, working his hands down lower to trace the curve along her rear, squeezing her ass and pulling her into him again.

Her fingers followed the line under his jaw, over his lips as she touched him, let him lick her fingers, then she kissed him back, kissed her own fingers and pressed them back to his lips. The warmth of his hold on her waist and ass were sweet intimacies she never wanted to be without.

"Tell me all your secrets, Devon.," he breathed into her ear, tracing the arc with the tip of his tongue. "Tell me what you want me to do to you, sweetheart."

She smiled, let her hands slide over the front of his pants, and squeezed.

Her breasts began to hurt, seeking attention. Squeezing her elbows together she pressed herself against him again. She rubbed the bone of her sex against his thigh, and felt the dull ache for him intensify.

The sky was getting darker as lights glowed in the bushes and along narrow pathways that snaked all over the property. She loved the flowers, the sounds of the leaves when the breeze rippled across their tips, the steady pulse of the cascading water. She was drunk with the scent of him, the taste of him, the sounds of his voice and his breathing.

"You want to go inside?" he asked as he traced a finger down from her chin to the top of her breasts. The backs of his fingers slid inside as she looked up into his eyes.

"Your skin is—"

"Made for you to touch. Made for you to kiss," she finished.

He hooked a finger in the brass ring of the front zipper of her dress, and pulled slowly, running his tongue over her lower lip. "Yes," he said in a sigh. Angling his head down he peeled back one part of the dress and saw her exposed breast with the stubborn nipple peaking.

She stood before him with her shoulders bare, offering her body to him under the moonlight, waiting for him to taste her.

"Oh, my. Miss Devon, you have been a wicked little girl," he said as he appreciated the view, then leaned forward to suckle and savor her pert nipples. She felt how they puckered and knotted from the stimulation of his tongue. His warm breath on her chest made her sex ache. He held her at the waist and slid up her ribcage, until his thumbs dove into the zippered opening just above her navel.

"These are spectacular," he said to her as he squeezed her breasts. The dress dropped to the floor. She hooked her thigh around his slightly bent leg, rubbing her need in long strokes until she began to come.

"Tell me."

"What?" she said as she leaned in and kissed him back.

"I want to know all about you. All your secrets. All your secret fantasies, the things you've never told anyone else. I want to know about them. I want to do them to you, honey."

Devon could feel the moisture pooling between her legs. She crossed her ankles and squeezed, sending the pleasure radiating from her core up into her belly, ending in her nipples, which knotted..

"Does it ache, Devon?" he asked.

"Bad. I got it bad, Nick."

"Yes, I feel you, baby. Let me take you inside."

"I want to be outside, under the stars."

He pulled away and examined her face in the reflected light of the pool.

"Please," she said as she leaned in to squeeze his groin.

"Baby, anything you want. How could I possibly refuse?"

"I want your hands on me."

"Where? Show me, baby."

She held one of his hands by threading her fingers along the back of his palm, and slid it up her thigh.

"You like that?"

She nodded. She moved him closer to her center.

"Use my hand, baby."

Devon loved the feel of his warm fingers burrowing in the soft tissues between her legs. She pressed his forefinger around her nub in circular fashion, making her jump. She rubbed with firm pressure against his hand, until his hand found her parts all on its own.

She could smell her need and hoped he could too. She went up on tiptoes and said as softly as she could, "taste me."

He led her over to a padded outdoor chaise and gently guided her down. With her back propped against the back of the lounge chair, he parted her knees, beginning to kiss down the insides of her thighs. She loved the look of his head buried in her crotch, hearing the lapping sounds, feeling his hot breath on her flesh, the way he sucked and licked and sucked the sensitive divot at the top of her thigh just outside the lips of her labia. That place was so sensitive she began to vibrate.

He licked her slick opening, sucking up her juices, stroking over her clit and running his canines over, coaxing the little nub, making it throb. She laced her fingers in his hair, softly stroking his ears, pressing her thumbs against his forehead and drawing them down to his temples. He rose slightly and penetrated her belly button with his tongue, which sent her in a long guttural groan he matched with one of his own.

"You like that baby?"

"Yes, Oh Nick—" she started to slide off into oblivion.

"Give me what you've got, baby. Let me taste it." He kissed her peach, then slid two fingers over her pubic bone and pushed deep inside her.

Devon arched back, raising her pelvis to him.

God, she needed his mouth and tongue on her. As if she'd commanded it, he went lower and plunged his tongue in deeper, curling it, rubbing it against the insides of her channel and sending her skyward. He looked at her above her flat abdomen. His eyes were dazed as he drank from her. He added his forefinger, and then sucked and pressed into her again.

"You like that, baby?" he asked as he pressed her clit with his thumb, massaging it back and forth.

"Yes." She could hardly breathe. She felt her moisture coat his fingers as he inserted them, then his tongue and then his fingers again.

"God, I've missed you," she sighed.

"God you're beautiful."

She rolled her pelvis back and forth as he tenderly stimulated her sex, sending her into a throbbing state of early orgasm. "Come for me, sweetheart," he said.

She rocked back and forth on his hand, then arched her way back up to sitting position and pressed her wet peach into his hand, onto his fingers, moving back and forth on him until the little vibration told her she was so close. With just a few more loving strokes she was writhing home, looking into his eyes, watching as the top of his head bent down and her orgasm quivered in his mouth.

"Take me, Nick. Take all of me."

"Hmmm. Baby, you taste so good. I could just do this all night long, but I desperately want to fuck you. Fuck you hard, honey."

Devon's smile glowed under the dark sky. "Yes."

He helped her up off the chaise, gathering their clothes with his other hand. He unlocked the heavy door and showed her into the special suite. A welcoming fire burned opposite the king four-poster bed, shadows dancing on the black heavy timbers in the ceiling. Nick dropped their clothes where they stood and grabbed her.

"Never wanted anyone, anything in my life as much as I want you. And I never will."

She blushed, looking down at their toes, which were touching on the hardwood floor.

He raised her chin. "You saved my life, baby."

"You healed mine, Nick," she said. She led him to the bed, which sent Nick's eyebrows up in a tent.

She turned, pulling back the sheets. He reached from behind and brought her back solidly against his chest, kissing her neck under her ear. She felt his hands on her breasts, how the calluses felt delicious as he squeezed. From deep inside him she felt the low rumble of his voice, whispering her name groaning as he explored her body, as he tasted her. She had never felt so loved, so cherished.

Climbing onto the bed, he followed, hands smoothing over her cheeks. Folding her knees under, she sat against the headboard of the bed. Nick joined her there, their thighs entwined, his hands moving down over her chest to reach the space between her legs desperately needing his touch.

He slid down the bed as she pressed against the pillows at her back with her legs parted. He lifted her knees up, slipping her legs over his shoulders, licking her labia, watching her spread before him like a banquet.

"As far as beds go, honey, I think this one sucks too," he whispered as he kissed her nub.

"Oh, I hope so," she sighed. "The pillows smell nicer, though."

She watched the laugh lines at the sides of his eyes emerge, as he rimmed her opening with the tip of his tongue and then sank in to feast. She arched up, giving herself to him. He slid his knees beneath her butt, holding her off the bed.

He sucked her clit, running his teeth gently across the tiny stiff organ.

He kissed his way up her belly, taking care with her belly button then focusing on each of her nipples until they puckered into deep pink knots of pulsating flesh. He kissed the insides of her forearms, the valley between her breasts, the top of her breastbone and up over her chin. He claimed her mouth and demanded entry. She felt herself become pliable and liquid, melting into him and his delicious kisses.

"Hope you weren't planning on getting any sleep tonight, baby," he growled in her ear.

"I think I can handle what you dish out. You sure you won't fall asleep on me?" she asked him.

He was serious at that last statement. "Devon, I'm never going to do anything to you ever again you won't like. I will never, ever hurt you, baby."

"I believe you, Nick. But just in case, my baseball bat is in the trunk of my car."

"You're lucky they haven't outlawed them here in California like they do everything else."

"They should outlaw your kisses," she whispered to the top of his head. He nipped her right nipple and she jumped.

His fingers found her opening and again she arched to his touch. He was the perfect combination of patient and ardent lover.

At last his cock was there, waiting for her direction.

She whispered in his ear, "I have a surprise for you."

Nick frowned, his eyes still sparkling.

She climbed off the bed, finding the red dress. Inside the pocket she'd put something very special, something she'd asked Christy to get for her. Nick was waiting in rapt anticipation.

She opened the foil packet and brought out a purple condom with ridges on it and funny little plastic nubs near the tip. She stretched it over his engorged cock watched as he bobbed it up and down to show off.

"Come here, Devon. Enough with all this play. I had plans."

"You're not the only one with plans," she winked. Inside her purse she pulled out the pink tie from her robe.

Nick's smile evaporated.

"Not what you think, lover." She sat on top of him, holding his arms above his head. Weaving the pink tie in a figure eight around his wrists, she secured them to the rail of the headboard. She tied it tight.

Mounting him, she rubbed the latex against her sex. He was pushing up into her before she could be firmly seated on him.

"I'm not used to being unable to use my hands," he said as he thrust deep inside her.

She closed her eyes, loving his urgency. Her muscles began to convulse. The little nubs were doing their job. She slowed him down, then ground down on him, feeling the delicious friction. "Oh," she said as she squeezed her breasts together, "Nick if you only knew how this feels."

She discovered she really liked controlling his rhythm, even though she knew she was holding him back. He moved his hips, thrusting sometimes deep, when she let him, sometimes to the feel of her moving up and off him. She rocked her hips back and forth, the little nubs rubbing against her channel.

She didn't have to open her eyes to tell Nick was frustrated as hell. His groans when he'd missed a full deep penetration were mournful. And when they came together, she knew he wanted to pull her onto him deep and hold her there.

"Devon, you're killing me."

"Not really."

"Untie me." He whispered. She smiled down on him and he returned her smile and winked at her, just like he'd winked at her that day five years ago when he'd walked into her life and stolen her heart.

"You're a little hellcat, you know that? Here I've been dreaming about fucking you all day, and this is what you're up to?"

"Just a little bit of frustration, that's all. Makes the pleasure all that much better, baby."

He was fidgeting with the sash, but she'd secured it well.

Carefully, Devon changed positions on him, without removing him from her sex, arching back towards him. His thrusts sent new ripples of pleasure through her as the device tickled new places. Her orgasm was just about to…

Nick had somehow slipped from the bondage. He picked her up by the waist and threw her onto her back. Extricating his hands and wrists from the sash, he then pulled the condom off his cock and threw it aside.

This was unexpected. "You don't—"

He had covered her mouth with his. "No talking. I'm fucking you, Devon, just like I thought about doing a hundred and ten times today."

He sunk in just at the point of her orgasm. She arched, barely holding on to her sanity as he stroked in and out, each time deeper and deeper. A slow fire flew up her spine, lodging at the back of her neck. It was where he held her with one hand, the other lifting her butt cheek for a better angle.

He adjusted her to the side and rammed into her at a forty-five degree angle, filling her with all new sensations as her relentless orgasm drove her to new heights. Lights exploded behind her eyelids. He was sucking her nipples, pressing his thumbs up her spine giving her shivers of pleasure.

Sweat beaded on her upper lip and forehead as her insides flexed and released against him. Nick locked her into an intense gaze as he seated himself deep, pressing against her ultra-sensitive cervix. She felt him stiffen, then arch backward as he began to spill inside her.

She realized she'd been holding her breath when he collapsed on top of her. She felt the heat from his cheeks and forehead and his heavy breathing against her chest. She felt the pulsing of his heartbeat, his arms curled around her body as he clung to her.

"Baby, baby, baby," he whispered to her chest. "You surprised me."

It was exactly what she wanted to hear.

Devon woke several times in the night and needed him urgently again. They were hot and fast and they were slow and sensual, and none of it mattered as long as it was her body he played, her mouth that he whispered into, her soul that he fed. She'd take him asleep, or awake. She'd wait for him when he went overseas, and make his welcome homes more memorable each time. Try to think up things she could do to surprise him.

She'd miss him terribly, she thought as she watched him sleep with his chin on her breast, his muscled body draped over hers, as possessive in sleep as he was awake. She felt inspired to work at his side, to build a dynasty, a legacy of love, not for the world, but for their intimate, personal spaces as they explored each other.

It was that partnership that thrilled her. Sex would always be great with Nick, she knew that. But though he'd had many sexual liaisons, she was certain she knew him better than any of the rest of them, just in the short time since he'd come back into her life at Sophie's request. She knew that there was a place in him that only she could fill. And, matching her lack of experience with loving a real man, no other woman had ever been to that secret place he'd saved without realizing it for her alone.

She didn't worry about how long it would take to explore all of him. Her life with him would be savored, enjoyed, and renewed every day they had together.

A pink blush was beginning to warm the insides of their room. He thought about what they'd done, how full his heart felt on this glorious new day.

When they'd retired to the big bed inside by the fireplace last night, the lovemaking had been arduous. The showers more than showers. Nick watched the rose-colored sunrise paint highlights against her soft skin as she slept. He could watch her forever, didn't want to sleep. Didn't want to ever be more than a breath away from her.

He didn't know what he'd do if they cleared him to go overseas, but he had five months of limited duty to explore every inch of her body before he had to decide. She'd had the idea to build a new home on the place where Sophie's dream had first been born. He had just enough time to design something she'd love, a tribute to the piece of Heaven Sophie had sought.

The home he'd build them would be filled with light, with views of the vineyards and Bennett Peak, blending his past with her as his future. He'd do all that before the Navy decided about him. He'd just have to check in regularly. Maybe they'd visit San Diego a few more times together to get her acquainted with some of the SEAL families. Christy and Kyle loved her. But then, what wasn't to love about Devon?

In the end, being a SEAL was important to him, and it was his job to show her that, and help her understand what it was like to be part of that life. In the meantime, she'd have a beautiful house to live in that would remind her of the magical, golden love they shared, and would always share.

He enjoyed watching her, playing with her. She'd learned about experimentation, keeping the sex thrilling, trying new things. She had clocked his rhythm from those sessions last night, and learned how to prolong the pleasure of her body. Learned when to slow down and when to speed up, when to push him over the edge and then slide down the rivers of ecstasy with him. He loved her brazen, loved her shy. He loved all the parts she played, the fire along with the cool, strong waterwheel of her soul. He'd be there for her for the rest of his life.

He planned to ask her this morning to marry him. And he knew she'd say yes. But he'd make it a secret she'd have to figure out, with consequences for wrong answers. He loved the consequences sometimes more than the satisfaction of her discovering all his answers. He'd try to string it out, make her squeal with delight, and then he'd ask her.

He could spend his whole life being her lover right here in this very room. If God granted him one wish, that's what he'd ask for. An eternity at her side, inside her, and wrapped around her. The perfect marriage of love and need and honor. He felt whole, refreshed in body and soul. He'd make it his life's mission to bring joy to her every single day, worshiping her, his student, who had saved the teacher in every way possible.

The End

OTHER BOOKS IN THE
SEAL BROTHERHOOD SERIES:

PREQUEL TO BOOK 1

BOOK 1

PURCHASE ON
amazon.COM

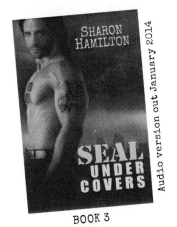

Audio version out January 2014

BOOK 3

PREQUEL TO BOOK 2

Audio version out December 2013

BOOK 2

Connect with Author Sharon Hamilton!

sharonhamiltonauthor.blogspot.com

sharonhamiltonauthor.com

facebook.com/AuthorSharonHamilton

@sharonlhamilton

http://sharonhamiltonauthor.com/contact.html#newsletter

OTHER BOOKS BY SHARON HAMILTON:

The Guardians Series

(Guardian Angels, Dark Angels)

PURCHASE ON
amazon.COM

BOOK 1

BOOK 2

The Golden Vampires of Tuscany Series:

PURCHASE ON
amazon.COM

BOOK 1

BOOK 2